The Dragons

Robert Reed

GREATSHIP STORIES

A Guide's Less Than Gentle Nudge

I feel as if I should warn you. This is a book for the committed.

Perhaps you have never read anything by Robert Reed -- not a novel or even one slender short story -- and happy in your innocence, you have picked up **DRAGONS** with the full intention of tearing through it in short order. Well, good for you. I hope you love every word and you can't wait to find out what happens in the later, still unwritten titles. But would-be readers should be aware that this is actually the fourth novel in a planned series. Prime Books published the first three novels, all wrapped inside one cover. **THE MEMORY OF SKY** came out several years ago. There were reasons to pack the books that way. Mostly it was because Barnes and Noble, that warehouse for every good idea from 1997, didn't want to touch the project if modest sales were followed by diminished sales. The book earned very good reviews, and copies were sold, but the sales didn't match any participant's dreams. And because of that experience, I am trying something different.

Also a few years ago, I self-published a giant book filled with Great Ship stories. Unfortunately I wasn't quite finished with the project. The collection definitely needed another pass or two by an editor's eye, even if it was only my own lazy eye. But my agent had an agreement with the epub publishers, and there was a window when manuscripts were punched out in all of the proper languages. For free. That's why I moved before the volume was ready. That's why it remains full of typos, and in addition, I've seen the print-on-demand version and hated the layout. But still, **THE GREATSHIP** has been a huge seller for me. A warhorse by my standards. So this is why I've decided to publish **THE DRAGONS OF MARROW** on Kindle and in their beta print-on-demand program. If everything works, this effort will drop my work into thirteen nations, in English, and a fat portion of the modest profits will come my way.

At the very least, I would hope that you would want to read **THE MEMORY OF SKY** before **THE DRAGONS OF MARROW.** Another good primer would be **THE GREATSHIP.** But the Marrow/Greatship universe has many stories. There are 23 short stories and novelettes and novellas in the series, all now available on Kindle. I have ironed out the worst of the problems with the dozen from **THE GREATSHIP**, and I've added more recent tales, including "Eater-of-bone," which is almost a novel in length. Obviously, I want my audience to read everything connected to this project. But being a rational sort, I realize that won't happen. So if I might make a suggestion for a reading list:

"Alone"
"Mere"
"Rococo"
"Camouflage"
"Marrow Redux"

"Marrow Redux" is a special project. I took the
original "Marrow" novella, which was nominated for
the Hugo Award back when Barnes and Noble was
great, and then I rewrote all the details. For
instance, my immortal captains have gotten tougher
and quite a bit smarter, and one character is rather
more handsome now. And the ending is quite a bit
different too. So different that it couldn't have been
sold that way originally, and that might make
"Redux" worth a close reading.

Two older novels drift in the Greatship universe.
MARROW and **THE WELL OF STARS** have done
very well for me and for Tor Books, and that's why
they're still in print. And that is why I can't find any
route back into their text. When I wrote them, I
hadn't yet dreamed up the story that I'm telling now.
So for the purpose of this future history, let's just
agree that those two novels are close to the actual
events, but only that. Close.

If you aren't familiar with Diamond and his world,
and if you refuse to read the earlier Greatship
stories first, I will give you this much: **THE
MEMORY OF SKY** ends where **THE DRAGONS
OF MARROW** begins. There is some overlap in

action, and quite a lot happens after that, and this story will be followed by three more novels. Which, by the way, I will mention in this work's AFTERWORD.

By the end of this journey, I should nearly 70 years-old.

Oh, and here's another warning, and a promise.

Perhaps you have read everything written in the Greatship universe. Congratulations. Maybe you feel well-versed in that subject and its characters, and you come into **DRAGONS** with a rugged confidence about what you know. Well, you are not ready. Not truly. Because much time has passed and much has changed in the universe. Except for all of those critical conundrums that will never change, that is.

And the promise?

In the first section of this new novel, I spell out in clear detail what Marrow is. What it has always been. An obvious answer that I figured out only a few years ago, in a fever.

Every beginning is small.

     The universe?

     A dab of incandescence and possibility.

     My voice?

     One whisper suffocated by terror.

     Life?

     Stubborn little eddies infesting the keen cold dark.

     And death?

     Always near and always listening. Which is why I whisper, and whisper back to me now, if you can …

Imagine a room.

     The room is a perfect sphere drawn from some gray substance, slick and half-lovely. The room has no windows or doors, vents or seams. There is no writing or artwork, much less any trace of whatever lies Beyond. But this simple gray wall holds at least one genuine miracle. Inside a very young universe, no other material is half as strong or a tenth as enduring.

A material this impressive surely deserves a wonderful name. Yet the gray marvel has no name, compelling or banal, and the room itself lacks any designation. There are no praenomens here. Whatever whispers first knew this place are spent, and the hands that built the flawless wall are dead, and what remains is the terrible, inevitable logic of a realm that has no equal anywhere anywhere anywhere else.

Emptiness fills most of the room, and brilliant light, but a single dense ball is locked at the center, held securely by overlapping, incorporeal buttresses. The ball's surface is iron infused with water and ammonia, plus traces of every rare element. Iron is the envelope wrapped around a core built from abstract configurations and wild oddities -- a passionate ensemble ending somewhere beyond this universe's accepted laws. The iron pretends to be a sphere, but roundness is a lie. The crust never stops quivering, torn by quakes and superheated pulses of electricity that press against the buttresses. The black skin splits, fires surging while molten metal spreads across the injured surface, and whenever the buttresses weaken, the crust rises, pushing a little closer to the nameless gray wall.

Something else exists inside this lost room.

Besides the filthy, lying iron, and the failing buttresses, and the light.

Wherever the ground is cool, between fire and flowing iron, steam relaxes into a hot liquid. This is a complicated, intensely busy water. Fat forms tiny lipid sacks, each carrying dissolved salts and proteins, and carrying knowledge too. What the sacks know can be chemical, intricate helixes woven around small, changeable meanings, guiding the production of more sacks and more busy water. But there are other types of knowing, simpler than memory and infinitely more robust, and those lessons thrive inside each of those trillion scattered drops.

The iron constantly shatters and flows, but all of that vibrant energy feeds the living water, allowing it to make busy daughters and inert spores. Ten trillion cells boil, but the lucky and the best escape by drifting high above the molten surface or swimming into the rare puddles, clinging to any refuge on a body that isn't close to being a true world.

Gravity is minimal.

Distances are quite small.

A wise presence, knowing quite a lot about the universe beyond, might believe that the room and iron ball are nothing but a peculiar experiment set in motion and then misplaced.

And the life?

Contamination. A sloppy breath must have delivered wild spores just viable enough to germinate. Bacterial mats and the lone cells are the residue. Surely nothing more than that. Life is a curiosity, insignificant and unlovely, and if the iron ever found the urge, it would quickly incinerate all of this watery business.

Except life is not a multitude.

Every cell belongs to the One.

The One knows its own nature. Each sack of water recognizes every other sack as being another essential piece of itself. Life might exist elsewhere, and maybe the aliens conduct themselves differently. But here, in this tiny place, cooperation is as inevitable as metabolism. No cell eats another unless the meal is dead or dying. Each existence makes ready for unborn generations. The iron never stops slaughtering what lives, but a few spores always escape, lifted high by the funeral steam.

If this was just a battle between fire and water, then the stalemate would hold. Except a larger war is at work here. The iron bleeds and swells, and by small measures, the buttresses weaken and the radiant light fades. According to a schedule already ancient, the iron and its passengers finally reach a nearly perfect night. Tasting darkness, life builds its best spores and sleeps deeply, and then the iron spreads a little too far, triggering a blinding, scorching flash.

The buttresses suddenly regenerate.

Instead of growing, the dirty iron slowly shrinks, wounded and perhaps scared, shriveling to a point not seen in a very long while.

The One bear this abuse quite well.

Life is always a gambler's pleasure. Whether you are One or Many, good luck will often outrace wise planning. And the One have been exceptionally fortunate -- a soulless beast armed with flailing tails and no mouths, ruled by urges as simple as can be, yet enduring every catastrophe.

Harder and harder, the buttresses push and the iron recoils under the pressure, and then the buttresses reach their limits and another flash arrives. From here, the buttresses can only weaken, allowing the iron another long fiery expansion.

No conscious witness stands over any of this.

No eye of a normal sort, no voice that makes itself heard.

Yet what happens inside the nameless room is important. What happens and does not happen matters more than any genuine world matters. Or a star. Or the swirling majesty of a million galaxies.

The iron swells.

Flash, and the iron shrinks.

Then the flash comes again, and the buttresses loosen their grip.

The gray wall has no windows, but the room is not perfectly isolated. The powerful buttresses are fed from invisible realms, their energies fighting to contain what will never stop trying to escape. Inside the iron is a realm --a tiny fierce deeply chilled realm -- where normal laws have no grip. Where the abnormal leaks its own power as well as an unstaunched trickle of new matter. Every cycle makes the iron ball grow larger that before and a little more massive, with visible and inescapable consequences.

If the One had a voice and the wherewithal, it would ask:

"What happens when the room is full?"

This is what must happen. A spherical space of fixed dimensions can no longer contain its furniture. Or its cargo. Or whatever the imperfect ball happens to be. Hot iron and those cold living places have no choice but to press against the nameless gray material. Yes, that wall is exceptionally strong. Certainly strong enough to hold against normal pressures. Because the iron must be contained. Nothing else matters. What is here and much of what exists beyond here were built for a simple function, to subsume what cannot be allowed to slip loose.

Inevitable, merciless Death. That's what waits inside the iron, while the grayness hides the tender, unfinished universe.

The room might resemble a prison cell. That is the easy explanation, incomplete and dangerous, yet not particularly untrue. A monster lurks below, and the monster must forever stay where it is, and the conundrum leads to a blunt, half-perfect solution.

The room has filled. There is no emptiness anymore. No light and no escape. Iron presses furiously against the grayness, and the trapped bacteria are squeezed and heated, cell walls failing, genetics shattering, even the hardiest spore unable to escape.

Think of a trigger.

Imagine a hidden cord or calm button or some very simple chant that will trip the trigger whenever the buried monster pushes past an inevitable point.

The carnage is nearly finished now. A little smear of simple-celled nothings survives inside the last nugget of frozen iron. But their hiding place is crushed, and they are lost, and a device built to last forever recognizes that the One is dead and moves to the inevitable next stage.

The grayness shifts its nature.

That spherical wall instantly surrenders its latent energies.

The explosion is asymmetric and surgical. Imploding stars cannot muster this kind of magnificent display. Yes, the iron burns white-hot, but most of the onslaught passes through the molten body. The core is the enemy. Punishing the enemy means converting mass into energy, devouring a portion of that gray wall while giving the room a little more space, making it ready to again defend not only its own perfection, but everything that hides beyond.

The One is dead, but Death has its own boundaries. Mechanisms older than every language won't fail now. Buttresses are reborn. White iron turns red and then black again. Water reforms, carbon compounds boil out of the faults, while oxygen and nitrogen weave a new atmosphere so that a fresh dew may glitter in the buttress' light. This is a universe built from simple ingredients and quantum practicalities that will never stop moving with one another. Every possibility occurs and occurs simultaneously, and inside that infinite mayhem, within this one exceptional place, life always exists in multiple realms. Between this iron ball and this gray wall, the One is constantly dying, but the same One escapes that anvil somewhere else, and always at the perfect moment. That is why the iron will never shake this infection of life, and what began as a very small room is huge, and a ball of fundamental metal has grown into a genuine world, and the One has managed to become considerably more interesting than little dabs of busy, thoughtless water.

Rain and soil gather inside sharp valleys and protected cavities, and black forests rise from that organic feast. Under that canopy, many-legged beasts march from one meal to the next. Different beasts dance in the sky, hanging on brilliant wings, while giants swim the hot lakes and the short, impermanent rivers. And inside this parade of invention and splendor and pragmatism and lust, the ancestral bacteria continue to thrive.

Once more the room fills, killing the One, and a fresh slice of the gray sky turns into a focused, purging blaze.

The nameless world always shrivels, feigning defeat.

And the next cycle always emerges. When the iron cools enough, spores and tiny eggs punch back into existence. This is an event peculiar to this place, nowhere else. The new One doesn't have to be the same One. Infinity has no need for perfection. But proven shapes always return, instinct and passion riding inside each of these organisms. The dense and blasted but increasingly fertile world is quickly reconquered. Black vegetation and legged beasts serve as the eternal trigger. Except the One isn't simple anymore. The old unity has been diluted. Reaching the next moment with a full mouth and a nest of happy eggs -- that seems to be all that matters now.

And worse still, the gray wall above them has never been so thin.

That wall obscures quite a lot. Oceans of stone are braced with more grayness, and there are rooms inside the rock, often tiny but sometimes vast. Some rooms are filled with sterile ice or sterile air, chaotic hallways weaving between them, and that enormous and thoroughly contrived realm lies buried inside another gray sphere that wanders dead through a dirty vacuum, which itself is a remarkable room populated with horrors and ignorance.

I am those nested spheres, and I am falling.

Like the wingless spore, I am both inevitable and doomed.

Every event is inescapable.

And this is what must happen: Ignorant eyes gaze across the vacuum. A vast gray ball is seen drifting outside the galaxy, and new kinds of living water come to walk across the outer shell. The shallow rooms below are easily discovered. What looks like a giant machine deserves a name, and the Greatship is born and claimed and quickly infested. A multitude of species fly here from the nearest suns. These beasts demand study, and I study my reactions to each of them. Certain individuals deserve my whispers, my warnings, hints of my endless fear. But few notice, and none of them care. Not like they should care, no. And what is most inevitable comes true. One of these beasts, foolish as can be, digs a hole until the hole ends, its head poking into the secret room and into the fierce light, discovering a violent, tightly balanced stalemate that needs to last Forever.

That strange face looks down at the iron world.

What follows the face descends and enjoys a brief walk.

More time is crossed and some little piece of space, and the face and its tiny mind come to appreciate some of this hidden room.

Does the visitor see everything?

Impossible.

But does it understand enough?

I know this: Hope always walks ahead of what is known.

Full of hope, I call out to the visitor. As loudly as I dare. But the other voice is here too. Death is near. Death is a flaw in this universe. Death is the Bleak, and the Bleak shouts as I shout, and the visitor seems to notice some important noise. Or perhaps it hears nothing, but a critical insight offers itself now. Either way, the visitor decides to retreat now. Using plasma fires, it rips open the crust, erasing every footprint and lost body cell while killing its own alien microbes. Then while molten iron wipes away the final traces of its presence, the visitor returns to the sky and wipes that hole from existence. But I keep watch just the same. The visitor climbs back inside those far rooms, and then it walks, and I watch its motions and listen to its various sounds. And then it moves nowhere and says nothing, yet vanishes from view. Which is remarkable and terrifying. Where has the beast gone?

More time is crossed, and quite a lot more space.

Nothing changes, and no other face manages to find the hidden world.

My endless hope keeps reassuring me that one small invasion by one small creature will be the end.

But the inevitable must arrive.

One day, a new hole opens in the sky.

For the iron and the One, solitude ends.

The humans fall as a fierce, ignorant rain.

ONE

The room was small and dark until Diamond ran inside, then it was brilliantly lit and felt even smaller. The circular floor ended with a tall wall, windowless and capped by a domed ceiling. There were no furnishings or second doorways or any trace of former inhabitants. Electrical fixtures didn't emit the blue-white light. No, the ceiling glowed, or maybe it was the bright fresh and exceptionally dry air. A single hole was carved into the floor's center, resembling a fire pit waiting for logs and tinder and sparks. The pit and wall and every other surface was the same perfect gray. This material was familiar, and not just because the world where Diamond lived was one enormous room, its floor made from the same gray mystery. No, he was suddenly recalling a long braid of dreams about odd places and lost times where this grayness found its way into a boy's sleep.

Kneeling, Diamond dragged three fingertips across the slick chill face, and the mystery seemed to surrender its name. For the briefest moment, tongue and lips were ready to say one old word. To shout the new word. But then his normally infallible memory turned shy and the substance was an orphan again, devoid of parents and every history.

Standing, Diamond ran to the room's far side, hunting for passageways that didn't exist.

Grayness and doors. The Creation was built on nothing else.

An adolescent with cropped brown hair and pale eyes, Diamond was human only in the broadest sense. No body resembled his body. Nobody had his long legs and arched feet, the forgettable tiny toes and those anemic arms that didn't look capable of climbing any tree. Yet despite the apparent weaknesses, Diamond was unusually strong, and more impressively, that silly body could endure horrific injuries. Wounds were inconveniences. Death was just a delay, full recovery waiting on the other side. This ugly, odd body patched every wound, and his brain was a lump of magic sitting inside his human-shaped skull, and as far as anyone knew, only three other creatures were as durable as him.

The Corona's children.

Diamond was dragging every finger along the rounded wall when his brother arrived. King was a biped but not at all human -- a giant alien who should be and deserved to be even larger than he was now. But the violent day had stolen away portions of his mass. Dressed in breeches and silver scales and bright silver spikes, King stood with armored feet set apart, ready for the floor to jump beneath him. Two mouths were stacked beneath green inhuman eyes. The speaking mouth asked some question that Diamond didn't hear, and the eating mouth leaked a sorry wet noise. King's scaled hands made a bowl that carried a ball, and the ball was also made of the gray wonder, one of the its faces sporting fourteen little pegs that might or might not prove their worth as a key.

King repeated his question.

"Where do we belong?"

"Here," said Diamond, certain that he was right. Except once said, the word felt too bold by a long stretch.

Three genuine humans arrived next: Elata with Seldom, and then Seldom's older brother, Karlan. The same as Diamond and King, their clothes stank of burnt wood and incinerated flesh. All were gasping from chasing after Diamond, and they were exhausted by a day of war and slaughter and the utter collapse of everything. Like all tree-walkers, they had pretty yellow teeth and broad shoulders and toes that loved to climb and proud, substantial nostrils. The only world they knew was behind them, and that world was suffocating. Unless of course everything that they knew was already dead.

Diamond's sister scuttled in after them. Quest could pull her flesh into any shape, but what she was now might be her truest form. Tiny and low-built, she resembled a gigantic insect that would be happiest hiding behind a fat tree limb. A wingless bug with dome-shaped eyes that saw everything at once. Jointed legs carried her to the fire pit, and rearing up, she said nothing, ready to remake her body, perhaps, but at a loss for how she wanted to look.

The Eight appeared last. Miseries had shriveled them too, but the shared body was still gigantic, even beside King. White parachute cloth was tied around their waist. This body could alter its shape, but not with Quest's ease or genius. Eight souls were buried inside that massive, almost naked collaboration. Raised by the Creation's other humans, the papio, they grew up to look like their caretakers. Walking on arms as well as legs, the Eight sported one spectacular face with powerful long jaws and golden canines beneath yellow eyes that took in the room with a piercing glance. Those eyes seemed male just now, and what might be a young man's voice said, "This feels right. But we can't decide why."

Uncertain what to do, everybody watched everybody else.

Except for Karlan.

"Hey, have a look," the big soldier called out.

The fire pit was no longer smooth. While nobody was watching, a tidy bowl had appeared in pit's center, and the bowl wasn't just of a certain size, it was decorated with fourteen tidy holes arranged in an unmistakable pattern.

"Say something," King said, nudging his brother with the key.

"Like what?"

"This a great moment, a historic moment. Give us some important words."

But nothing momentous wanted to be said. Looking at the room and the pit and the fourteen holes, the boy admitted, "I was waiting for something stranger."

King handed him the key.

Diamond climbed inside the pit, aligning and then inserting the ball and its fourteen pins. Falling back to ordinary thoughts, he expected a fresh door. He hoped for a swift return to some familiar life. But he was wrong again. It seemed that he could never stop being wrong. Time passed without passing, leaving the seven of them naked, and everyone was weak, lying together on some new gray floor. A smooth gray ceiling was overhead, that ceiling falling away on all sides, vanishing behind ground that also dropped away with the distance. They seemed to have been set on the top of a hill, and this patch of gray ground was round like the room before, except there was more of it now, and the surrounding country was black glass dotted with pools of water and pools of molten red rock. Strange creatures were flying, all of them screaming nonsense, and single trees and little woods stood strong beneath a great room that had no sun yet couldn't be brighter.

Climbing the hill, apparently walking straight towards them, were too many children to count.

Diamond closed his eyes and opened them again.

The strangers wore clothes made from leather and hair and bone, and each carried some little machine that produced colorful light as well as noise. Those noises were words. The machines were talking, and the new world was full of wind and animal voices. But the children were silent. Maybe they were cautious, but they seemed very curious, marching barefoot across the sharp volcanic rock, every foot being cut and every cut healing instantly and perfectly.

For such a long while, every day had been a little horrible but ordinary. The awful war kept gnawing at the world, but at least Seldom knew where he was and what the rules were. The great forest still grew down from the world's ceiling, and he trusted each morning to begin with the familiar rain rising into a boy's face. The sun he knew and loved was one simple fire burning far beneath everyone's feet, and that's where the coronas lived, inside a next-door world full of steam and airborne jungle. Every previous day had brought the swift growth, those thickening banks of alien vegetation steadily obscuring the sun, and when tired minds needed sleep, darkness slipped out of its hiding places, night blanketing the horrible, commonplace human world.

This day would have been exactly like the others, but then the rain or some idiot happenstance shoved a dying corona to the human realm. Coronas were flying monsters hunted for their metal-rich flesh. The difference was that today's corona was enormous and plainly ancient, looking very much like another giant killed and cut apart thousands of days earlier. That first creature's gut held four invincible babies: Diamond and King, Quest and the Eight were the "corona's children." And how long were Diamond and the others trapped inside that pressure cooker? There was no good guess, except that it must have been close to forever, and there was no answers for where they came from or why. But with four children known, it was reasonable to believe in other enchanted babies hiding inside other ancient coronas. What if those new children could be raised as yours and turned against the enemy? That's why the tree-walkers chased after the old monster, and that's why their enemies, the papio, did the same. Fleets were launched. A battle raged in the open air. Desperate for any advantage, and in the brilliant light of a fresh morning, both species were infected with the worst kinds of hope.

Seldom's brother fought the papio and helped win the corona, and being the day's hero, Karlan was allowed the honor of slashing open the carcass and stepping inside. But there weren't any god-babies waiting to be found. Hundreds had died for nothing besides a peculiar gray orb, as simple and as inert as an old jar. People touched the artifact and nothing happened. Diamond and King put their wondrous hands on it, and nothing changed. But then Quest touched one of the fourteen pegs, and she did it in the proper way or the wrong way, and that was the exact moment when the trusted beautiful bright sun died.

Quest killed the world. Or she did nothing and what followed was a mess of fantastic coincidences. Either way, the coronas' world was shattered along with the sun. The wall between the two realms vanished, and the air inside both worlds began to drain away. Panicked, the coronas flew up into the trees where they killed thousands of innocent people. People panicked too, leading to more idiotic battles in the darkness. And in the midst of those horrors, Quest managed to claim the giant corona's corpse, remaking that carcass until it was her body, meat reshaped and fat distilled into a kind of rocket fuel.

That impossible body was what Seldom and the others climbed inside. Then Quest fell towards the bottom of Creation, riding on a column of fire. The sun was dead, but the gray orb would reignite it. That was the hope. The corona's children were convinced that they carried a key, and Seldom certainly wanted to believe them. The boy wished hard to find a fancy machine waiting for them. Maybe the sun was a fabulous electrical light. Maybe it was a rocket engine like Quest, but larger and pointed at the trees. Except no, what they discovered was a silly little hole waiting for sticks to be burned. Could anything be so simple? Diamond set the orb inside the fire pit, and Seldom imagined an explosion of light and heat. His body would be incinerated. Maybe even Diamond would be killed. But what they were doing was brave and right, repairing the source of life to a world that was far too fragile.

Except none of Seldom expectations would ever come true. No new sun was born. Certainly no light that was seen or heard or felt. What the key did was yank them out of the gutted, dark-and-losing-its-air Creation. Seldom found himself kneeling and panting on another gray floor, a fabulous glare nearly blinding him, and squinting, he turned his head to discover another gray ceiling.

The Creation was full of rooms. That had always been a rich possibility, something Seldom had told himself many times. Yet seeing the truth didn't blunt the shock. This new world was larger than any other room, but the gray floor under them was small and surrounded by glassy black ground. And there were children inside this room. Even from a distance, those new people enjoyed a striking resemblance to Diamond. They had his long legs and little noses, and they walked like him, and what's more, they were walking together, bringing a sense of purpose. These strangers intended to welcome the newcomers, or kill them. Or maybe, hopefully, send them back where they came from.

Seldom stood up.

This day was full of the unreasonable and unexpected, but the boy discovered an utterly ordinary terror.

He wasn't wearing clothes.

With both hands, he covered himself.

Which felt useless and silly, and Seldom didn't like feeling useless or silly. He hated any circumstance where he didn't have control, particularly when he couldn't be smart. Yet there he stood, a naked and very skinny fellow bombarded by the brightest light imaginable, a hundred strange eyes watching him, and the only hopeful idea inside his overwhelmed head was to believe that this was a dream and every dream passed as soon as he remembered how to wake up.

Eyes closed, Seldom smacked his forehead with the very best fist that he could make.

Nothing changed.

Eyes open, he realized that Elata was standing beside him. She was naked too, and Seldom stared at her exposed body. Which should have helped his spirit. But no, he felt more ridiculous by the moment. And even worse, the girl stood with hands on hips, looking unembarrassed and unashamed.

Elata didn't have a shadow.

Under the brilliant light, nobody created shade.

The Eight stood behind Seldom. Naked like the others, they rose up on legs and arms, yellow eyes studying the approaching children.

"What should we do?" Seldom shouted.

He didn't care who offered a plan. But good questions didn't have simple answers, and judging by the painful silence, this was an excellent question.

Shaking his arms, Seldom tried to force the nervousness out of his fingers. But that didn't work, and he covered himself all over again.

Karlan didn't worry about his appearance. Big strides carried him across the gray ground, and he stopped where the reef-like rock began, casually scratching his bare rump. Strong in so many ways, Seldom's brother was immune to shame, and he didn't suffer from doubt or anyone else's pain. Watching those approaching children, he rubbed his knuckles as if getting ready for a fistfight. Then glancing down at the hands, he smiled.

Seldom mimicked his brother. Staring at the back of his right hand, marking the veins riding inside that young brown skin, he wondered if it was the same hand that he woke with this morning.

Which was such a stupid thought, right up until Karlan shouted, "My scars. Some asshole stole my best scars."

With that, the soldier broke into a cackling laugh.

These nervous arms still felt like Seldom's arms. He shook them harder and looked at the others.

Standing on toes and fingers, the Eight turning their body in one slow, watchful circle.

Wearing nothing and needed nothing, King's scales had lifted away from his frame, making him even more fearsome than usual. But a quiet, nearly scared voice said, "This is bad, this is wrong, whatever this is."

Which was when Quest leaped off the ground. She had grown two pairs of transparent insect-like wings, and they sang as they beat, and then she was above them and the singing stopped and Seldom lost her in the glare.

The naked boy needed to pee.

He fought that embarrassing urge.

Then something else became obvious. Diamond. He would know everyone's hands. Seldom's friend had a genius for detail, for seeing the past that was never really past for him, and it would be nice if his friend offered insights. But where was Diamond? Not standing among them, Seldom realized. Didn't Diamond come with them? Was he still trapped inside the doomed Creation?

Seldom called his friend's name.

Which was when the naked girl finally glanced at naked Seldom.

Something here deserved a special smile. And a wink. Then Elata turned, pointing across the rocky black ground.

"There he goes," she said. "Diamond's running off to see his friends."

No conscious decision was made. There was zero contemplation to grand strategies and likely outcomes. One moment, Diamond was standing as tall as he could on those long legs, a mesmerized spectator absorbing this unexpected vista. There were people below and busy noises everywhere, this sudden, unsuspected realm full of wild energies. Not one thought was worth the trouble, much less coherent plan, and that's why instinct took charge. Or reflexes. Or something else that was simple and inside the boy's odd nature.

Diamond stood like a statue, then he was sprinting. Five long strides and off the gray floor, bare feet vaulting across what felt like shattered glass. Debilitating misery didn't exist for him, but there were ugly sensations as razors sliced into meat and found blood. Every sharp edge was trying to steal away his toes. Running with eyes down helped, and shortening his stride helped more, but best of all was a fast pace that put him in the air longer. Leaping instead of running, each foot had its chance to stop bleeding. Each foot had time to aim. Ten strides into the run, Diamond realized that he felt heavy. Because this was a different world and every object weighed more? Or because this body was taller and broader than before?

Those strange children should know. Walking together, still approaching, they were silent, always silent. But the machines they carried were chattering. Some were rectangular, some round, and quite a few were changing shape. Each device was carried in a hand or worn like a glove.

Not single sound was familiar, yet Diamond was convinced that the machines were talking to one another, words more like song than speech. Then that moment passed into the next, and every last machine fell silent. The song was finished. In the middle of a very long stride, the world became quieter, and when that happened and for no other apparent reason, every last child quit walking.

Diamond did what they did. He was maybe eight leaps short of the nearest person, a girl with her gaze directed past Diamond. The girl's bare feet were balancing on a dusty rib of smooth glass. It was easy to assume that she had just noticed the aliens standing with those strange-looking people. Her eyes were clearly fixed on some point beyond Diamond's left shoulder, and her face betrayed astonishment, and in the same moment, worry. Except what if these faces and eyes carried different meanings? One mysterious moment became another, and she took a rich breath, as if gathering strength or maybe courage, and those eyes dropped, focusing on the square machine riding on her opened left hand.

Diamond flexed his feet, the cuts half-healed.

Tilting her head, the girl acted as if she just heard a question. She carried a face rather like Diamond's face, except for countless differences that made it hers. The nose was even smaller than his nose, and she had his tiny teeth, white as bone, plus high cheeks and impossibly blue skin, dark and glossy. Or maybe her skin was another color and she wore blue paint. Bright hair, yellow and thick, was tied into a braided rope. A whiter, brighter blue danced inside the eyes. She wore a drab brown backpack and a blue vest that looked like leather, five white buttons down the front, and she had blue leather shorts and a yellow belt that resembled her woven hair, and the bare legs were blue and the tops of her feet were the same, and her familiar, unique face looked a little younger than Diamond's face, except that everything else about her felt tens of thousands of days older.

Diamond wanted to stand beside that girl.

Was this why he ran down here?

His motives were another mystery and he regretted being so rash, leaving the others without so much as a crisp, "Good-bye."

The blue girl turned her head to the right, then left, and the other children watched her, as if awaiting instructions.

She said nothing.

Except something was heard. All at once, galvanized by secret commands, people at the edges turned and broke into hard sprints. These were powerful bodies dancing across shattered glass, immune to their own weight as well as the packs strapped to backs and waists. What looked like pistols were carried inside holsters, and knives were tucked into belts. Before this, these might have been ordinary children out for a serious march, and Diamond just happened to be in their path. But now they were soldiers trying to surround his people. "My people," he whispered. And there it was, the simple reason he ran: To meet these strangers first, to help his people who he left standing lost on the hilltop.

The blue girl's gaze was shifting. Something overhead mattered, and Diamond followed her gaze. The ceiling was smooth gray and perfect and utterly unreachable. He knew this but had no idea why he felt certain. That brilliant sunless air was full of flying creatures, and maybe one of them mattered and maybe not. And when Diamond gave up watching, he discovered that the blue girl had done the same.

Three children remained close to their leader. Two boys and a girl wore the same long braided hair, and like her, they hid their voices. But it was an intense, very busy silence, faces staring along random lines while the mouths hung open, trading words nobody else could hear.

Thoughts. These youngsters could read each other's minds. And embracing that frightening new belief, Diamond used his mind to offer up his name.

No one seemed to notice.

So his mouth repeated his thoughts. "Diamond. My name is Diamond."

The two boys glanced at him, but barely. The top of the hill was much more important. And the second girl never gave Diamond so much as a glance. She was taller than the others, covered with milk-white skin and beautiful soft leather clothes and bright bits of stone, and her hair and belt were the color of spun copper. The milk girl was staring at Diamond's people, and then something changed. News or some odd thought surprised her enough to make her jump. That's what Diamond assumed. Long legs flinched, launching her into the air, and lifting one of the silent machines overhead, she shouted a single word that meant nothing, yet couldn't have sounded more terrible.

Every machine began to sing that word. The unexpected melody was captivating and gorgeous, and it was simple: Two notes repeated and repeated because they were so exceptionally important. The word had to matter, because every child was suddenly running hard, pressing towards the highest ground.

Once again, the blue girl glanced at Diamond, seemingly by accident, and then she ran past him, proving again that he wasn't an object of fascination.

The milk girl and one boy stayed close to their leader. But the final boy took a few strides before stopping. He was short and very strong, thick black hair set against steel-colored skin. Standing on a knife-like ridge, bloodied arches lifted him just enough to make his eyes level with Diamond's eyes, and that's when he sang the vital, two-note word.

"I don't understand," Diamond confessed.

The steel boy's machine was flat and square, and he waved it at Diamond's face, as if the newcomer was hot and needed a good fanning.

With mind and mouth, Diamond repeated his own name.

But the machine offered a discouraging sound, and the remaining boy grunted and ran past him. Except he wasn't as fast as the others. His pack was huge and badly overstuffed, and worse still, someone had taken the trouble to tie more cargo to the outside of the pack. Diamond counted seven objects bouncing and flopping. He stared for an amazingly long while -- a full heartbeat, perhaps. Then he finally deciphered what his eyes were seeing, which was simple and obvious and sad.

Heads.

Tied by their braided hair, seven human heads were bouncing.

Diamond managed a half-breath, and he looked up.

On top of that nameless hill, King was watching everything. But not the Eight. Where were the Eight? And if Quest was there, she wasn't letting herself be seen. Seldom and Elata and Karlan were staring at Diamond and at the blue girl. Even Karlan had to be worried, and Seldom was crying, he was so frightened. Except nobody was scared enough. Not yet. Diamond felt his willpower and courage collapsing, but before panic took hold, he reacted. Doing what was essential, he charged the steel boy, striking him in the shoulder, and when the boy stopped and turned, Diamond struck him hard in the nose.

The damage was tiny, two dabs of blood and some instantaneous healing.

Then the boy said one fresh word.

A curse, maybe.

"Diamond," Diamond repeated, pointing at himself.

Like flowing water, the boy's singing machine covered his right hand, and when that hand closed, what wasn't water turned into a glassy fist. Diamond stared at the marvel, bracing for the first swing. But it was the left hand that was dangerous. While Diamond leaned back, the steel boy lifted a knife made from sharp white and very powerful bone. Slicing into the soft tissues beneath Diamond's ribs, the razored blade carved the human heart in half, and that inconvenience was followed by a blue jolt of electricity.

Food and sleep and slabs of new purple flesh beneath the scales. King wanted each of those blessings. Reviving his body and his cherished poise would demand one long night flanked by feasts. But the evil day had no intentions of being done, and that's why King stood motionless in the bright air, wishing for very little. Ten nourishing breaths without fear, the chance to close his eyes briefly, and maybe, please maybe, a little piece of fat to chew on.

Babies made wishes. Babbling fountains of emotion and hope, and King had become an incompetent child once again.

"Quit," he muttered with his breathing mouth.

While his eating mouth shouted, "Pssshhh."

This miserable day began with a voice, and a lie. When King was still inside the bloodwood forest, at home and standing beside Diamond, a secret mouth spoke to both of them.

"This is the Great Day," the voice promised.

Both brothers heard those words and listened for more, except nothing else was said. No explanations or elaborations or any sense of the invisible speaker. King tried to make ready for whatever greatness came next, but morning brought the same awful war, and then the sun was extinguished and the coronas flew out of their dying realm. King had to fight an entire army, and he lost. But that gave their sister time to become a monstrous marvel, and she won the battle before carrying them down to save the Creation. They had nothing but the one plan. "The Great Day" meant that Diamond would be a wondrous hero, along with King and Quest. The sun was going to be rekindled, and even the hated Eight would benefit from standing beside those who hurt so many to achieve one spectacular good.

Too bad those were nothing but baby-wishes. In the end, there was no salvation. The dying Creation was abandoned. The corona's children and three monkeys had been thrown into a wilderness, their little group was surrounded by noise and odd, overpowering stinks. And because that madness wasn't awful enough, a fresh army of monkeys was marching against them.

King felt weak and small, but at least he still trusted his fear. Vibrant, magnificent terror gave him the spine to defend this ground against whatever dared challenge him.

But would the others stand beside him?

Not Diamond. His little brother was rushing towards the new monkeys. And the Eight? That treacherous sack of confused souls was galloping in the opposite direction, trying to escape. And where was Quest? A glance upwards found hundreds of wings, but nothing resembling his alien sister. Which left King with no one but naked tree climbers as allies.

Two of those monkeys were cackling about Diamond, trying to decipher the boy's mysterious plans. King watched Seldom reach for Elata's bare shoulder, but his hand lost its courage and dropped. Then the girl moaned, "No," and Seldom let out a wild shriek, and the girl stepped forwards, arms raised high as she cried, "No, shit, no. No."

What King saw next was more odd than alarming. A skin-clad monkey and Diamond were embracing. That's what the first glance told him, and what followed refused to be terrible. Diamond pitched forwards. Diamond was tired like his mighty brother was tired, and the strange monkey was only being helpful, rolling the newcomer over before setting him on the sharp ground. Only then did King notice the heads dangling off the monkey's pack, and he saw the long white hilt jutting from the wounded chest, and now the skin-clad monkey was working hard, shoving his knife upwards, cutting through the sternum and ribs, exposing the shredded pink organs inside.

King set his feet farther apart.

With a quiet dry voice, Karlan cursed.

Turning to the largest monkey, King said, "We need weapons."

Shrewd eyes looked at him. Shoulders lifting, Karlan said, "Smarter to retreat."

Just the idea weakened King's legs.

"Fly off like your buggy sister," said the soldier. "Or chase after the Eight monsters. Those are the geniuses. As long as you can, stay free."

Elata cursed.

"But that won't kill Diamond," said Seldom.

"How do we know?" she asked. "Don't be sure our rules are theirs."

An obvious idea, important and simple and chilling. Perhaps none of them were invulnerable in this world. Now King was more embarrassed than frightened. Walking to the edge of the gray ground, one hand grabbed a knob of glass and broke it loose. Then he tossed it and caught it, gauging its weight, which was considerable, and he imagined how the knob might fly.

Skin-clad monkeys were climbing towards them. There was zero time to count targets, but a blue female was close, watching King as she ran.

King whipped the rock at her eyes.

Stepping sideways would have been simple, yet the girl stayed loyal to her gait. No caution, no cowardice. The spinning glass came for her face and then dipped, striking her bare leg. A brief surge of red monkey blood was ignored. Of course it was. Those bare feet suffered worse walking across the razored ground. It was the boy running beside the blue girl who reacted. Angry enough to bare his teeth, he shouted quick words as he pulled a gun from its leather holster. That was a very silly weapon with a preposterously wide, oval-mouthed barrel, yet the girl stopped climbing and pointed at the gun while many words burst out of her mouth. This was a musical voice, a beautiful monkey voice, not one sensible lyric to the tune, yet lovely to hear.

King stole a heavier stone from the world and threw it as hard as he could, aiming for her mouth.

The blue girl and her boyfriend didn't notice. The boy had bright white hair and purple flesh decorated with vertical black stripes. His face was monkey-furious, but the voice was fearful, terrified. Then the rock slashed the girl across the top of her head, and both of them winced. A streak of blood dirtied that yellow hair, but the wound was ignored. The boy sang while the gun-hand trembled, and the girl just kept shaking her head, like a monkey saying, "No." And then she shoved her empty hand close to his eyes, enforcing his focus. Nothing mattered but this brief conversation.

The purple boy fell silent, listening while that pretty voice moved into softer, slower sounds.

King had exceptional ears, and this world was full of voices. He couldn't stop hearing animals buzzing and rasping, and all of the monkey's machines were singing the same two-note song, and the children were prone to muttering unconscious words to themselves. King even heard a single wavering note leaking out of the purple boy's gun. That gun was talking. Instinct or buried memory warned King that the pistol had its own mind, and that mind was declaring, "I am ready to kill."

King stopped tossing pebbles.

And then the purple boy put the gun to sleep and back to bed.

He and the bloodied blue girl were joined by a tall white girl. All the young monkeys were built from colors, and each sported what looked like ordinary weapons: Metal pistols and white-bladed knives. Every child wore or carried one of the singing machines, and maybe nobody was paying attention to these machines. But the song sped up and every child ran faster than before. The blue girl and her two companions were first to the hilltop. Their focus was absolute. Nothing mattered but their target, and King held no assumption but that he was the great animal of interest. Meeting them properly was what mattered. Standing at the edge of the gray ground, he kept his knees locked, scales raised high, every spine ready to stab. King would break these little soldiers while they shot him to shreds, and that imaginary battle turned real inside the head. Which was why King was shocked and then appalled when the idiot monkeys ran past him, flowing like rain around an inconvenient tree.

Quest was born inside a world of trees and humans, and she had survived despite every obstacle, including ignorance. Including hatred. Including the sense that this Creation nothing but an enormous prison. Yet didn't she always try to do what was right, or at least what was clever? In those little moments of guarded sleep, she told herself that she was good. And she certainly felt smart and sure when one of her fingers touched that gray ball -- the only treasure found inside the dead corona. But her touch killed the sun. Murdered it and doomed everyone, and after an life spent hating the world, she instantly and forever fell in love with the humans. With the trees. Even the chittering little bugs too small to deserve names.

But she would redeem her crime. That's why she carried everyone to the world's floor. Diamond was about to fit that gray key into the gray lock, and such a deep, ungovernable hope swept over her. Wasn't this the obvious, perfect ending? A simple act, and her tragic accident would be repaired. What was dying was certain to be saved. She imagined the fabulous brilliance that would flood the great wastes, light nourishing life, and that wonder included each of them. The corona's children wouldn't be charred to ash. She and her siblings would somehow return to the world of trees and shattered people. Even the little humans beside them would survive. In the end, Quest would earn redemption, and no reasonable survivor would consider her as anything less than a heroic deity -- the champion and marvel who deserved feasts and the kindest words, and if she wished, solitude among the trees and beasts that she completely adored.

But imagination had already failed her once today, and now it shattered again, tumbling all of them into a place of fire and black glass.

Quest's tiny, badly weakened body panicked, claiming her soul.

Growing the quickest possible wings, she flew.

Moments later, beating against her unexpected weight, she found the poise to ask why she was fleeing. Where did this terror come from? Memory. Some ancient memory gave her good reasons, spectacular reasons, only she couldn't tug free exactly what that recollection might be.

This was an awful, awful world, and those strangers had to be treacherous. That's why the fierce need to escape was reasonable. Quest threw her remaining power into stout wings and better muscles, and then she built a reasonable mouth, inhaling a few of the bug-beasts sharing the air with her. The little creatures were familiar in shape but only that. Two wings, four wings, sometimes six wings. They tasted nothing like the forest bugs she'd eaten since she was a baby. Sloppy catabolism gave her sugars and combustible fats. She flew and bolstered her wings and the black, fire-wrenched world was a little more distant, and then half-fed, she let her fallible imagination try to envision any destination worth so much effort.

Wings were carrying her towards the gray ceiling, and the grayness meant safety.

A lovely, beckoning ceiling.

Quest ate everything that could be caught, and she grew larger while she flew. Then something inorganic ended up inside her mouth. Unsweet and drier than stone, it flapped its own sharp wings, and she bit in reflex, and sparks bit her. Spitting the meal free, she and the mechanical beast gave each other some hard consideration before the smaller one jetted off on little gasps of fire.

Quest flapped, following a chaotic path into higher places. But even as the air grew cooler and a little thinner, the ceiling had no interest in coming close.

This exhausted body needed to glide.

Quest looked down. That round dab of gray ground was surrounded by black stone and wicked children. The Eight were missing, and Diamond was a pale naked shape lying motionless and alone, and King stood on the little hilltop with the three tree-walkers, waiting for the new enemies.

"We are doomed," Quest thought.

Yet her reflexes held a very different opinion, and that's when panic dissolved, yielding to another attack of fabulous, treacherous hope.

"Every day has its end."

Elata's mother loved to unsheath that salted proverb. Madam Taff was a grand believer in words that would make even awful days bearable. But what was true for bad times was true for the good, and inside any happiness, Elata couldn't stop thinking about how wonderful days always ended and the next mornings might want to eat her soul.

And here was another tooth inside familiar words: What if the worst days refused to end? What if they came one after the next, swallowing you with miseries beyond the uncomfortable ordinary? That's why a person found herself ready to be gone. Inside her head, the girl was constantly leaping from every high place, cheating one endlessness with another. Yet despite all the urges and opportunities, the girl didn't jump. No, she lived until the sun died, and what did she feel then? Weirdly, supremely glad. Not because of any pleasure, no. Simple fear was what cured her. A dying corona had failed to tear her apart, and bullets and rage did their best to shred her. Yet nothing succeeded. Then she finally made the jump, but inside the belly of a god-alien. Nothing could kill this girl. Not coronas or war or the spectacular fall: Death simply was not allowed. Her destiny was to stand at the bottom of the Creation. That was where Elata had to outwit the vengeful papio and their big guns. If she had been alone, she would have let the papio accomplish what monsters couldn't, what her own hands wouldn't. But the papio were threatening Diamond and Seldom, both of whom she loved, and she cared about the others too. More than she ever suspected. So she told one ingenious lie: A blunt, oversized fiction that saved everyone, including her ridiculous self. Diamond and his siblings were gods. That's what Elata explained to the papio. The corona's children were brought to this world to render justice on stupid humanity, and despite mistakes and a lot of unfair shit, these gods were now trying to save both species. So maybe it would be smart to help the gods, not murder them.

Of course that story might not be a lie. That's what Elata realized while listening to her own voice. Four remarkable souls, or eleven, depending on how the census was made. Maybe she sounded a little too certain about their majesty, and her details were nothing but hopeful noise. Yet the lie succeeded. The lie allowed her and the others to reach the end. The most useless room in existence was waiting for gods: A drab space fashioned by hands comfortable with nothing but the simplest gray. There was no time to debate what should happen next. Diamond used the key and then Elata was inside a different room and another world, and this brutal day was still chewing on the girl that should have died a thousand times already.

Bizarre wonders. That's what surrounded Elata. She wasn't thinking about proverbs or her private, suffocating gloom. There wasn't time. This new realm was full of light without any sun, heat without shadows, and the ground was infested with strange creatures who were a little or a lot like Diamond. A mortal girl didn't belong here. Sure,

Elata might sound buoyant when she spoke to Seldom, but that was only because everything was so crazy. Watching Diamond run off to meet those wild, skin-clad people … well, she had no choice but laugh. Novelty and fear made it easy to giggle. Then the wild boy stuck a knife into Diamond's chest, which on any normal day would be rude. Nothing worse than that. Except maybe the knife was more than a knife, or maybe different laws ruled this different world. Her friend was dead dead dead, and the wild children were savages ready to murder the rest of them just as easily as they had dispatched their bravest and best.

Quest. Suddenly nobody else was inside Elata's head. Quest could defend them. Diamond's sister would eat the first dozen bodies, making their meat into a fine new weapon, and with rocket fire and poisons, she would protect them from every one of these mad hazards.

But where was Quest?

Vanished. Along with the Eight, she realized. The only god left was King, and that boy couldn't think of anything better than hurling rocks.

Talking to Karlan was never fun, but Elata made herself stare at that round and hard and always indifferent face. And when Karlan felt her eyes and glanced at her, she asked, "What do we do?"

The big man answered with a laugh.

Seldom said, "We surrender."

The laugh darkened. "Surrender's when you lose the battle," Karlan said. "We can't pretend that much."

The strangers. They were wonderfully colorful, each different in the details of flesh and faces and the bodies too. But all of them wore skin clothes and bone buttons, and they carried or wore machines on their hands. They also carried backpacks and pistols and white-bladed knives, and the colored hair was braided like rope, and they shared the same intense expressions, which weren't child-like at all. These creatures didn't talk, but every machine kept singing, two shared notes ripping through the air, and the onslaught was close enough that Elata saw the stitching in the leather and the sweat on the kaleidoscope faces and guns bouncing with their holsters and more guns clenched inside sweaty, brightly-painted hands.

Each child was built a little like Diamond, long-legged and swift.

And they were nothing like Elata's gutted friend. They terrified her to where she forgot to breathe, and time had dried into a slow awful syrup.

The feral kids wanted King.

That was the only reasonable guess, and King made the same mistake. He stood like a trap filled with wound-up springs, ready to slash everything that came close. Except the first children sprinted past the giant. He wasn't worth a glance, he meant so little to them. Did they want clever Seldom? No, that boy didn't matter either. And the murderous, utterly docile Karlan was no prize either.

The swarm closed ranks, shoulder to shoulder, until Elata found herself standing in the middle. Nobody spoke, and for a few moments, nobody moved. Then the blue girl with yellow hair took a half-step closer while the machine in her hand became thin and clear. As if weightless, the marvel began to float. Like glass cleaned until invisible, its flat self managed to vanish. But the machine still sang those double notes, and the blue girl began to sing as well, giving what sounded like sharp orders to a squad of trained soldiers.

Pistols and knives were stuffed into holsters, into sheaths.

The floating machine fell over the empty blue hand again.

Every gaze was hard and fixed on Elata. Nothing in this amazing world was as fascinating as her little face. The girl had always relished attention, but this was too much. Too strange and too unwelcome, and this eternal day had discovered a fresh way to torture her.

Closing her eyes accomplished nothing. Elata felt the strangers staring. So she tilted her head and opened those eyes again, gazing at the glare and the remote gray ceiling. And inside that tiny moment, a familiar, very much trusted revelation offered its advice.

Of course this day could end.

Easily.

Elata didn't let herself think. It was the blue girl's duty to step as close as possible, a firm voice following its very tidy rhythm. Every word resembled song, and she was working to smile. A holster and gun rode her waist and her blue hands were empty, and opening both hands, she slowly presented the palms in a gesture that might mean peace or might mean nothing at all.

With a moan, Elata dropped to her knees.

The blue girl lowered herself, wanting their faces close.

Grabbing her own head, Elata unleashed a pitiful wail that shook every last one of her brood.

Then the blue girl reached for her.

A kind gesture, by all appearance.

And Elata grabbed the pistol and yanked it free. The weapon felt like metal shaped inside a hot forge, heavy and dangerous, and the handle was smooth between the fingers and not too hard to control.

Her audience was too startled to react, or they didn't care.

Either way, the girl turned the barrel, aiming quickly and badly.

A half-moment too late, the blue girl reacted.

The blast was small, the pain slow to come.

Blood.

Human blood had the same wondrous color here as in the trees of home. The flow was red and thick, spilling from the punctured belly, and thinking about her dead mother and the dying, left-behind home, Elata closed her eyes once again, convinced this would be the last time.

TWO

Draw the universe with one color and there was no color.

Blue had zero meaning inside the all-blue existence.

The same was true for incompetence and indifference. Those evils didn't exist until the good woman stood against them. There weren't any lies until there was truth, and weakness didn't exist until there was strength. Weakness happened to be what Pallas feared most: Softness, frailty, the failure of any will, but particularly the will inside her own good and not-good soul.

Birth and death followed by another birth. Righteous people often came into the world by that route. During her first life, Pallas was taught about enemies and about self-survival, and while most of those details were lost, a residue of instinct was certain to remain. Aptitudes and reflexes. That's what had to be etched into the bioceramic mind. And once the soul was declared ready, a skilled and happily forgotten hand would kill the child, her body swaddled in shadow-weave and packed inside a ready vault with the rest of her murdered siblings.

Vaults didn't usually wear construction dates, and nobody believed the rare exceptions. That's why there was no way to know precisely when Pallas went under the ground. But someone wanted the girl to wake innocent, and innocent in the best ways. Because the world that found her would be different from what she knew. A little different or profoundly so, and either way, nobody mastered change better than the empty, well-honed youngster.

Even after the aeons, certain memories were timeless. Her name, for example. She knew what she was called, just as she recalled that the first Pallas was a tiny world from the oldest place of all. Her adoptive mother often named babies while thinking about her own extraordinary past. Yet a gift should be generous, shouldn't it? And nothing was generous about that particular name.

"It marks you," the little woman warned. "Every 'Pallas' belonged to her, and the woman isn't trusted, and she's hated too, which is almost as bad. Plus anyone with a thread of sanity fears her. And that's why you're going to generate suspicion. Some of us wouldn't hesitate to kill you all over again. And just to be safe, kill you forever."

The two of them were speaking. Nobody else was present. Ten sleeps past her second birth, Pallas was still living beside the tall gray wedge that had kept her hidden for unknown aeons.

"You're lucky to be in my camp," said the little woman.

"I am lucky," Pallas said, clinging to optimism.

"And you're exceptionally unlucky," her benefactor added. "My babies are forced into long interesting lives full of deprivation. Plus there's endless work to be done. And a lot of creatures can't find the fun in my endless chaos."

"I like chaos," Pallas said.

A reflexive response, or truth? Unless it was reflexive and true. Pallas was suspicious of her own motives, but at least she sounded convinced. Didn't she? Too bad it was impossible to be sure. She had just learned this new language, and a lot more days would pass before she felt comfortable inside its notes.

"And I adore work," the girl added. "That's why you should make me prove myself."

"You say I should be your mother?"

"Yes, madam, please."

"And do we change the name?"

"If I'm tainted, I'm tainted. The name means nothing."

"Maybe you're right."

"But test me hard," the newborn insisted.

"I have and will. And others are going to evaluate you too."

There was no one else to see. The two of them sat with their backs to the soaring hyperfiber vault, and the volcanic crater fell away before them, the young land sprinkled with blue-gray foliage, oily and alien, sweet-scented and growing fast. These weren't the pure black plants that Pallas remembered from before. But she didn't mention that. Likewise, the horizon appeared remarkably distant, which was another unmentioned surprise. Ten long sleeps since the second birth, and most of this new life had been spent inside a shelter made of glass and feeding tubes and surgical hands that stuffed new knowledge into the cubby holes inside her bioceramic mind. Pallas looked at the horizon, looked at one bluish tree. Then staring up the vault, she recalled her first mother: Tall like the steel buildings that had stood over them. Except her first mother was stronger than steel. A beautiful creature in a hundred ways, but not pleasant or pretty or anything else that felt soft. That grim narrow face kept every weakness at bay, and Pallas smiled in secret, glad to have this memory outlast so many others.

Her new mother was tiny, and she smiled often. Yet she was just as strong as the tall mother.

"My brothers and sisters," Pallas began. "Where are they?"

The smile faded.

"You didn't trust them," Pallas guessed.

"I never knew them."

The vault was tall but slender, and inside, quite small. There was space for only five thousand carefully stacked children. But it was an exceptional vault just the same. Pallas' first mother had strict tolerances about people and everything else. Woven from a superior grade of hyperfiber, the wedge was shaped like a hatchet blade, and it was designed to float effortlessly within the liquid iron, its sharp end riding up, ready to escape the neutrino pulses that would come again and again. And that armored skin was thicker than it had to be, while the interior was chilled by redundant banks of lasers and kinetic traps and demon doors. Ten layers of vacuum kept the corpses perched on the brink of absolute zero. The outside world might die five times or five hundred and five times, but the vault would float patiently inside the liquid iron ocean. Suspended in that kind of deep cold, not even the most ambitious atom would vibrate. That's how the vaults were explained to the girl during her first life, and her birth name was Pallas, and her first mother was a great dragon who understood how to care for her eggs.

"How many of us survived?"

That's what Pallas asked her new mother.

The woman held up one hand, bony fingers folding until nothing remained but the little thumb touching the tip of this child's nose.

Pallas sighed, and she measured her own sadness.

"Why do you think she named you Pallas?"

"You told me. As a warning to others."

"But that particular name. Out of the thousands of possibilities, why not call you Vesta or Amalthea?"

"I don't know and you should tell me," was the girl's opinion.

"The color of your flesh," the little mother guessed. "Pallas was a terraformed asteroid. The Belters dressed that little world inside a deep ocean, lit from within and stained the most lovely blue."

The complement was absorbed, along with more grief. Pallas' siblings were dead. She didn't remember any them well but this was a loss just the same, and good empathetic people had to feel sorry for quite a lot, including their own survival.

Smiling, the new mother said, "Trust."

Pallas looked down at the smile. "I'll prove myself, and you will trust me."

"Promises and assurances. Never wrong to offer, and never convincing."

Pallas nodded.

"And you need to be warned about something else."

"My first mother?"

"Miocene. She is here, and she's already garnered power and quite a few enemies."

"There are other dragons?" Pallas asked.

"Several of note."

Pallas studied the woman's smile and the tiny hands with that one thumb still extended. Focusing on the smile, she said, "Mere."

"Yes?"

"That's your name."

"Yes."

"You are my dragon," Pallas promised. "Now and to the end of my days."

A world that could never die was born once again. The original inhabitants were inevitable; black brush and glittering insects, the worms and bacteria, resurrected themselves without fail. That piece of the cycle might be as old as light and gravity. But there was luck beyond luck inside this story. The good fortune began when several worthy dragons emerged from the nearby Infinity, yanking open vaults programmed to punch through the newborn crust, each vault jammed with machines and frozen people eager to build the new old-world. These were the first-generation creatures, vault-born and smart-born and prepared for everything. Except "everything" didn't mean that anything was easy. First-generations had to walk on the hot baby ground, enduring years of routine labor and starvation and too many burns for hungry flesh to heal properly. For those early ranks, every machine that wasn't rescued from a vault had to be built from the rawest materials, or it was stolen. And not only were these youngsters scarce, but they had to fight little wars with every other little nation, including the same dragons who would be loyal allies somewhere in the remote Tomorrow.

Second-generations could be vault-born too, though plenty were created here and now. Along with the surviving firsts, the seconds felt fortunate to enjoy just enough sleep and the freedom to sit down while eating. But having pillows and chairs didn't mean that anyone could stop working. Resources were chronically scarce. Great civilizations had to be built, and territory was every nation's priority, and territory was won through battles with traditional weapons. Ritual combat. That's how you forged an identity. Fight hard because it matters, and try to accept the permanent deaths. Only with borders and wealth could treaties be trusted. And only then did the dragons start to build cities -- comfortable extravagances inhabited by two generations, plus empty buildings and new streets ready to be conquered by everyone who came next.

It was the third-generation that always enjoyed the greatest luck.

Everyone knew it and accepted that blessing, and Three Wings was one of the finest examples of that inarguable fact.

The boy wasn't vault-born.Three Wings didn't exist and then he did, and this would be his only life, which made every day sweeter. It also helped that his father was first-generation, pulled from the earliest vault and famous for his battles and one very heroic death. The worst of the worst had killed Three Wings' father. The Waywards. Waywards were the bug-fed, bug-shitting people who controlled half of this amazing world -- the perfect enemy for a hero's son who was full of pride and grace and the need to prove his endless worth.

Every creature carried its passion. AIs craved data points and the lines drawn between those points. Animals ate and lusted. Fire, the greatest beast, dreamed of consuming the world again. And Three Wings' passion? To punish the Waywards on any occasion, with any tool. Yes, life was often wonderful, and life was beautiful, but his favorite moments involved standing over one of his victims, defining his hatred in stark, compelling terms.

Reputations didn't grow because someone rather liked doing this or doing that. No, the legend rose from total commitment, and when it came to blood, few humans were as enthusiastic as this violent boy.

Three Wings' nation was subdivided into clans, and most of the clans were small groups, platoon-level and intimate with one another. This boy's clan was led by a old girl who might be confused for one of those this-or-that kind of souls. Pallas. She was second-generation and vault-born, and coming from the distant past, she was filled with silly instincts. Cooperation first, kindness before thought. Fine ideas in that other age, but what age was that? Nobody knew. Pallas' vault was an ancient design done exceptionally well. Physical evidence claimed that it had drifted in the iron ocean for two moments less than forever. Then the vault forgot how to float, and it finally came to the surface, trapped inside a volcano's throat, waiting for Mere to find it. Nobody but that one girl had survived the aeons, and sadder still, she was buried with the wrong name. Pallas. A favorite daughter of the infamous Miocene.

Here was the conundrum: Should anyone trust the blue girl?

Doubts had been voiced. Even the softest people talked about precautions dressed to look like accidents. Precautions followed by a neat funeral for an ancient girl who died too soon. There used to be days when everyone wanted to hear Three Wing's input. After all, he was the fighter and the enforcer who refused to cringe before hard decisions. And sure, he could have said, "We need to be safe and kill her." That's what those outside the clan expected. Except they didn't know Pallas, and they sure as hell didn't know Three Wings. Those idiot strangers. Whispering the most awful words, yet wearing the most reasonable expressions. Smiles and common sense were proposing murder. To Pallas' lieutenant. And in response, Three Wings gave them painfully long pauses while staring at their idiot eyes.

To each outsider, he said simply, "If you kill Pallas, I will kill you."

"But we've done nothing," they might protest.

"And you'll keep doing nothing," the boy said.

His reputation had true power.

"Of course we won't," the cowards would swear.

But that wasn't good enough. Not by a long reach. "And if my Pallas happens to fall over her own feet, by accident, and if she's unfortunate enough to tumble into a river of quick white iron … "

"Yes?"

"You'll swim the iron too," he promised. "And don't think innocence matters. Because it does not."

"What are you saying?" they asked.

"I'm saying that from this moment and until the world ends, you need to keep that woman safe."

They were never anything but friends, Three Wings and Pallas.

And why?

Because different as they were, they shared one fundamental, irresistible idea. They lived in a wonderland, a world reborn and re energized, and only the blessed few could stand at the beginning. Beyond a few broad principles and some blunt, obvious rules, their lives were as free as any lives had ever been. Three Wings and Pallas could sit on any of a thousand volcanic hilltops, relishing the beautiful and rich, ever-changing wilderness, envisioning all of the wondrous futures that would last and last and last.

And how long would they be here?

One ancient measurement of time had persisted. Every four-hundred-sleep span was dubbed "the year." In a busy life, even a single year felt substantial, and Three Wings had thirty-one years invested into his extended, delicious childhood. Life was already a wondrous adventure. But if the colossal gray past was any guide, Three Wings and the blue girl could live magnificently for another million years. That was how long it would take the world to reach too far, triggering its rebirth.

This grand body.

This paradise.

The absolute, enduring heart of the universe.

Marrow.

Pallas was killed and then laid inside the frigid vault before the sky turned to fire, and the world burned and burned and burned again in her absence. But calculating the cycles was barely possible. The past was more legend than history, conjecture filling the looming gaps. And worse still, even the most authoritative accounts were poisoned with lies. Lucid counts of days and centuries were scarce. Pallas knew only that Marrow was growing. That was the single pure certainty about this place. The world underfoot would eventually fill this enormous chamber, pushing against the sky and crushing all life. Which was when the sky would erupt. Fire and light were nothing compared to the neutrino storm. Marrow would become a cinder, sterile on its surface, impure in its belly. Pallas did her best to understand the magic. But who could? Dragons were gods of flame, and dragons always emerged from the quantum froth. But no explanation felt complete. Some entity or willful genius must have built this realm, and simple, inescapable principles clung to that power. The original Marrow always rose again -- oily forests and jointed legs ruled by a few tireless instincts. Marrow itself was the greatest dragon, but this incarnation came with several more examples, each nearly as inevitable as the bugs. In total, perhaps several hundred dragons existed, ranging from the occasional to the spectacularly rare. And there was always the wicked chance that an unlikely universe would throw a new dragon into their midst. Outliers who didn't have to care about peers or eternal rules. Harbingers of chaos, they might not even appreciate their importance, and any grave mistake on any player's part would burn Marrow too soon, leaving the sky thinner than it needed to be.

But that dangerous period had passed. Was done. No need to worry about the unlikely today. This was a golden rebirth. Everyone agreed. The original Marrow was sharing its iron with a healthy mixture of familiar, well-proven dragons. The ritual wars had led to stable alliances that would persevere from here on. These dragons had been polished bright by Eternity, each an expert at being godly, and surprise was the least likely event, and a world too often brought down by war and even worse treacheries could sleep easy.

"Every dragon shapes her children."

A truth back when Pallas died, and then she was alive again, ready to turn her nature wherever her next dragon required.

Mere.

"The mistress of the artful vanishing."

One of Mere's nicknames, and deserved. When she wished, this godly creature was indistinguishable from the most ordinary lady. Tiny in stature, starved by endless life, she looked like a Wayward child fed nothing but sour worms and pain. Mere was the sketch of a skeleton wearing human flesh, those brilliant black-iron eyes staring at the world with undiluted wonder. But where would she find wonder? As ancient as she was … an entity that must have witnessed everything and probably ten thousand times … what could possibly be so spellbinding … ?

"Pallas."

"Yes, madam."

"Approach, darling. Come to me."

Pallas was always nervous in the woman's presence, and always happy. Jangled but joyful. "You wanted to speak to my face."

"To offer you a mission, yes."

The nexus sunk inside Pallas' neck had beckoned her to visit her dragon. Which was deeply atypical. Field assignments were delivered by invisible whispers, highly-encrypted and instantly erased. Millions of third-generation people shared Mere's nation, with the fourth generation beginning to fill the nurseries. And giving those black eyes to a single clan leader was a conspicuous waste of time.

"A mission. Yes, madam."

Long silver hair framed the face, and every motion from the little body was quick. This was no day to be an ordinary woman; Mere's fabulous age had never been more obvious. She carried a sense of Forever in her shadow, and the aeons lived in her dry dark voice. The girl standing before the desk kept remembering and remembering that this creature was older than great portions of the universe.

"Guess your mission," said Mere.

The dragon had a warm teasing smile.

"Scouting Wayward ground," said Pallas.

The obvious assumption. Supply lists were already being fed to Pallas' nexuses, including shielded vehicles and Wayward disguises. She was also being briefed, classified streams as well as higher fringes too secret to have names.

"You're sending us into the Blisters," Pallas added.

"You believe so?"

The Blisters was young volcanic ground on what might be considered the Waywards' side of the border. "We're going out to add to our maps."

"A twenty-sleep mission, yes. That's the official plan."

"'Official,'" Pallas repeated.

"You never know what might be found out there." That from a creature who had been everywhere else in the universe.

"We're on a hunt for old vaults," Pallas guessed.

Mere's eyes narrowed.

"Where in the Blisters?"

"Any ground you like. You have full discretion, my dear. And if you meet our neighbors, I expect you to treat them with all the fairness they deserve."

Dragon and girl were sharing a sealed office, in the midst of the freshly constructed capital city. Every conceivable tool was ensuring their secrecy. Yet Mere was obscuring critical details, leaving Pallas concerned, and thrilled.

"I'll do as you say," she promised.

"This is a very routine mission," her dragon lied.

A doubtful nod was given.

Reading her child's mood, Mere reached for the desk. A fully-charged juggernaut rested in plain view, its trigger able to accept only Mere's spidery finger. A tray of sweetened candies lay next to the murderous weapon, and the dragon offered the tray to her guest. Every candy but one was red. The outlier was black and shaped like a human heart, and that treat went into Pallas' mouth, delicious sugars wrapped around strings of complex proteins. An encrypted language set to work, educating her stomach lining and then her mind, and within moments, Pallas became the reigning expert about certain odd data that nobody should have noticed. An anomaly. That's what was waiting in the Blisters, buried and of undetermined size. The anomaly had been pushed near the surface recently, or it was still deep but huge. So it had to be a camouflaged vault, unless it was something else entirely. The AIs who noticed the anomaly? They had been wiped, as a precaution. Only two souls knew about the mystery's existence. Yet even still, the very reasonable explanation was that nothing would be found. Tainted data and a misplaced decimal point. That's what Pallas assured herself. Because the object's hypothetical size was a little too considerable, while Mere's finest sensors had barely noticed some very odd energy plays.

"Sorry for the routine and boring," Mere lied again.

"No mission's routine," Pallas answered, by reflex.

"And you deserve bigger prizes," Mere added. "But keep your clan busy and happy, and I'll see you again when you return."

"In twenty sleeps."

"Yes."

With that, Mere turned away. A simple gown had been woven from her own silver hair. Stretched tight, the fabric revealed the failsafe machinery that had been carefully stitched into that narrow back. Powerful tools and interwoven AIs were united to serve one function, and the apparatus was left visible for the best reasons. If anyone moved against Mere -- if any foe tried to capture or disable her -- she would unleash the failsafe. And when any dragon died, the hyperfiber sky ignited. That was the eternal rule. This current cycle would burn and collapse, and once again Marrow would be rendered as a fresh cinder. Which was how these immortal dragons could rule for hundreds of thousands of placid years:

Even the smallest, sweetest god held the means to annihilate every bad deed.

A routine map-on-the-sly mission. That's what Pallas claimed. A fountain of rising iron had transformed a hundred thousand square klicks of landscape, the freshly shattered country dubbed "The Blisters." That name came because it was twisted and split like human skin painted with molten metal, and because humans were lazy when it came to naming temporary features. The work promised to be half-dangerous, what with the Waywards believing they were the rightful owners. But Pallas' clan knew how to blend into landscapes, and they knew how to map and then retreat before anyone took offense. The only question was why work so wickedly hard at being invisible. That's what Three Wings noticed with the first briefing. Every transmission had to be wrapped in full Wayward signatures and encryptions that nobody could punch through, but that also added milliseconds to every conversation. And while looking like your enemy was reasonable, that usually meant the right clothes and standard Wayward field gloves. But changing your own flesh? Making yourself smell as if you'd been raised on bugs and wild water? This was a new level of camouflage, hard to achieve and far from pleasant.

So this wasn't just mapping-on-the-sly. Nobody asked, but that's only because soldiers knew better. There was a plan. Maybe an important plan, but more likely this was the dry run for something big and real. Either way, answers didn't matter. Soldiers weren't designed to know big, beautiful reasons. Wandering across a universe buffeted by invisible forces: That's how every warrior lived. And besides, there shouldn't be any fool walking this glorious world who believed every word that his bosses told him.

Pallas kept her clan busy, leaping from ridge to valley like a dance troop carried by simple inspiration. Yet despite all the posing, they were always near the Blisters' central portion, and in particular, the clan leader insisted on overlapping scans of a certain low hilltop. That was a detail that Three Wings couldn't ignore. Standing together, the two of them staring at the shared map, he jabbed two fingers into the little hill, squishing out odd bits of data that meant nothing to him. Then with his tongue still and his breath held, he stared at Pallas.

That cool blue lady looked at him and looked away. Talking to the breeze, she said, "Get a sleep and we'll talk tomorrow."

So Three Wings laughed and dropped the matter.

For one sleep.

The seventeenth mission day began, and bless her, Pallas made good on her promise. She offered her orders, at least to admit that the little hill was interesting to high, name-free authorities. She predicted a day of bland disappointment, and with that, the various stealth craft woke their engines, ready to fly. Camouflage was set high but not high-high. Today, anyone watching for enemies would notice the aircraft, and others definitely were watching. A big Wayward patrol was working its way across a freshly cooled lava field. By and large, the Waywards were a nation only in the most glancing fashion. Perpetually splitting into cliques and tribes and odd little sects, no group knew where every other group was, much less what their neighbors were doing. That particular gang of Waywards was studying a flock of half-shielded vehicles, watching them make a big pivot overhead before heading towards a distant rift valley. And the Waywards were still staring at the sky when Pallas and her people slipped in behind them.

It was a fine moment. Several dozen wild children shared the surprise, faces big-eyed, squared shoulders trying to hide the embarrassment. These youngsters were passionate believers in nonsense, and their dragon was the oddest, most dangerous beast ever thrown up by reality. But Three Wings knew how to play the role, utterly believable when he shouted at the kids, "Bless Till, from here to the end of the days."

"Till gives favor," said the boy in charge of those amateurs.

"To those who earn it," Three Wings cautioned.

"Well then, let's all earn it."

Nothing was more real than the masterful illusion, and the best way to fool others was to feed them something true. With that in mind, Pallas announced that her group was on a secret mission blessed by the highest and the best. They were here to investigate one simple hilltop. Odd signatures had been noticed. Gravimetrics implied a dense mass lurking beneath fresh stone. She was here to quietly sniff about. "That's what we'll tell them," Pallas had explained over breakfast. "And their reactions might tell us if anyone else has inklings about oddities and marvels."

Convincing as can be, Pallas fed that backstory to the boy, and he couldn't stop smiling at the blue girl when he said, "So you're here to dig."

"Every way but with shovels," she answered.

The Waywards were the largest nation, spread wide and happy with their native chaos. And Pallas might well be one of Till's favorites. Not Mere's. That's how convincing she was.

With the mysterious hill revealed, the Wayward boy surrendered what he knew. Nothing. Certainly nothing about anomalies or secret missions, and for that matter, he didn't have much heart for buried mysteries either. He was just a common lad honored to meet this important girl. The next several minutes were filled with his giddy chatter, including offers to help, but plainly not expecting to give anything more than free noise.

Then Pallas spoke again, and that's when a soft, swift attack was launched.

The Waywards didn't sense irregularities.

"I haven't seen anything odd in these hills," the boy leader repeated.

The blue beauty agreed, saying, "This was a long-range scan and not my scan, and I'm just following orders."

"Probably a big vault," the Wayward boy suggested.

He wanted to sound pragmatically ordinary.

Pallas nodded about the vault and then laughed when she said, "No, no. It's probably the Bleak rising from the core."

That made everybody else laugh. Evil was everywhere. That was true regardless where you happened to stand in the world. But the worst malevolence lived in the center of Marrow, and Waywards called it the Bleak, and invoking the unthinkable was the most reliable path to nervous glee.

Laughter rolled along nicely.

The quiet attack accelerated, taking more chances. Surely the light swift touch of electric fingers was noticed, yet none of the kids reacted.

Three Wings gave his leader an important nod.

Pallas played for more time. With a hard tone, she said, "By the way. We don't trust you."

"What's that?" The top boy was short and thick, strong in a host of ways and obviously proud of his service to his people.

"Mere," said Pallas. "She's famous for running little liars in our midst. They look and smell authentic, right up until they bite."

That Wayward had thick golden hair and pale golden skin.

"Just look at me," the boy under the hair insisted. "I'll show you everything."

He was too much of a child, even for a routine patrol. Defending his good name meant opening up his field glove and every nexus to a full examination.

Tyley was another one of Pallas' lieutenants. When that white skinned, exceedingly elegant creature completed her conquest, she shouted, "Done."

What was never a fight was finished inside a quick breath. Bodies were shot full of holes, minds trapped inside temporarily useless husks. That should have triggered every alarm, but the Waywards had lost hold of their gloves and nexuses as well as every local sentry, each of them chattering away with streams of believable data as well as the occasional anecdote to whoever monitored them back home.

Three Wings knelt over the proud boy.

To the wide, furious eyes, he said, "I like mementoes."

The punctured chest was healing, but not fast enough.

"Give me an excuse, and I take trophies from an enemy." Three Wings lifted the golden braids. "But you, little fellow. You don't qualify.

Enemies have bite, and you aren't any species of challenge."

Frozen iron and igneous skin had built the crust, and every sample of ground, no matter how tiny, was punctuated with fissures and lava tubes and porous cavities beyond count. Many of these holes were infested with steam or groundwater, plus masses of thermophilic bacteria thriving in edible darkness. Liquid iron churned below, and that's where the surviving vaults would hide. Elaborate machines woven from alternating shells of hyperfiber and perfect vacuum, vaults used slugs of degenerate matter to maintain their precious neutral buoyancy. A few were labeled according to contents and age, but most went unmarked, and those with failed camouflage had been harvested aeons ago. But if sensors identified a large, appealing specimen … well, that might still leave hundreds or thousands of kilometers of molten metal between the prize and you, which was the same as being lost on the other side of the sky.

Yet as impressive as the iron ocean seemed, it was really just a weak fluid churning over Marrow's mysterious core. What wasn't geology and wasn't machinery was believed to be rigid, and according to ancient accounts, as cold as deep space. Yet the core was also the tireless generator of heat and new iron. Some single minded force existed at the center of the world.

Maybe it should be called the Bleak, maybe something else. Either way, that force demanded Marrow's endless growth, and every time the sky burned and every time the present cycle crashed into oblivion, that cold hard impossible core was left larger and even more powerful than before.

In a world built on endless battle, exactly one war was worth waging, and that was happening today beneath Pallas' bare feet.

Cycles ended when a dragon died. Mere could be struck by that blast from a juggernaut, or the last dab of subterranean microbes died beneath the crushing sky. In every case, life was the fuse, and when the fuse was spent, the sky turned into plasmas that generated neutrinos, each one of those ghostly particles focused on the malevolent core.

The iron between was only hammered and only stirred. Otherwise it was left remarkably untroubled.

That's what Marrow's first inhabitants had learned. To cope with their wars, humans and the various aliens built deep, elaborate bunkers. At least that was the standard explanation offered by standard histories. Those first colonists either learned about the great cycles, or they were very lucky, and after surviving inside the iron, they showed the later generations reasons to build more elaborate escape pods, out-thinking those ancient rules.

But to be that living person, floating blind in the molten metals ... that was a scheme easy to improve upon. The best strategy was to suspend life and put an end to time, crossing several cycles in an instant. The same engineering worked for every form of life, for AIs and simple data dumps. That's why it was smart to build the vaults. That's why there were millions of them when Pallas went into her vault, and the numbers had to be even greater now. Invisible and patient, the average vault had no plan but to wait. Yet the iron ocean had its own ideas, the molten metal pushing a little harder than usual; and that's when something quite old and useful would rise into the light of a new cycle, trapped inside the fresh-made crust.

Pallas' sharpest nexus gave her the full analysis of that little hill, and more importantly, it offered studies of everything trying to hide beneath it. Just now, while they were fighting the Waywards, she finally spied something vast pushing up another ten meters. Why wasn't this anomaly noticed before? Rising like a balloon from the depths, the object was gaining velocity and maybe gaining size, and the entire world was going to take notice, probably in another few minutes.

"Except nobody else sees it," Pallas whispered. "Only me."

Which made her happy. Utterly, drunkenly thrilled. The best kind of day had brought her a spectacular mystery, and how could any other day in the next million years match this wondrous thrill?

The world appeared busily ordinary.

The world was lying.

Three Wings' pack was jammed with heads, plenty more heads dangling by their braids, and the cargo was ready to be lifted. But first he had to laugh at his captives while reminding them that they would recover soon enough. Embarrassment was the worst wound, and nobody ever died from shame. "No killers here," he added, fingertips drawing circles around opened eyes. "But let's hope your dragon adores you. Because I always demand too much for my ransoms."

Oxygen and nitrogen and insects. That's what Marrow's atmosphere was made from. Except the usual bugs were being replaced by ravenous dermestids -- beetles and flies that craved what didn't die properly or even pretend to rot. Human flesh was packed with multiple classes of energy, and all these little mouths had evolved tricks to enjoy the chemical and electrical potentials. The dermestids bothered Three Wings more than he'd ever admit. The original Marrow was simpler and much less creative. In those times, humans were alien in every sense, and a mindless body could lay untouched for years. Who would know about those times? Besides the dragons, that is. Pallas. That girl might well have been born inside that remote age. Unfortunately she swore ignorance, which was more evidence that she had to be incredibly old. And wasn't there something lovely about that? Your leader being more ancient than the species chewing on these easy meals?

Those severed heads didn't want to be lifted, or Three Wings wasn't trying. Either way, he fumbled with the strap and let the pack fall again, and the exposed mouths kept moving, laughing at him and insulting him. But with no air behind the teasing, they were easily ignored.

On the second attempt, the pack felt lighter, and after the buckles tightened, Three Wings began to dance, mastering the burden.

Tyley was enjoying her usual carrion work. Kneeling over headless leftovers, the tall girl searched pockets and body cavities for anything useful, everything pretty. Sealed niches and null-houses might supply intelligence, but her hopes usually centered on jewels and other beauties. Yes, Tyley was an elegant creature, and she was an easy catch for bright delights. But past all that poise, she was just as dangerous as Three Wings, with a viciousness and cunning that sometimes made him flinch.

Pallas had a third lieutenant. The purple boy was named Broken for good reasons. Definitely not sweet, yet the kid had a gift for suffering doubts. Soldiers shouldn't carry too much uncertainty, but he was the clan's exception. In the field, when trouble came and there was time for thought, Broken could devise ten ways to avoid the fight. That vigorous, reflexive caution was why he was entrusted with their only juggernaut. Kick heads and gouge out eyes and let the dermestids eat away every shred of soft tissue. That was just ordinary brawling. But bioceramic brains were invincible. Nothing but white iron or a juggernaut could kill the soul, and in this little group, only Broken carried the means to murder.

The three lieutenants stood together, waiting for the girl who was actively plotting their next hard walk.

This group, this clan: The finest in Mere's potent little nation.

That's what Three Wings was thinking when all of that happy self-congratulation was washed away.

Zero warning. One moment, this was an ordinary vault hunt. Then a different moment arrived with a vivid EM scream. "Scream" was the only word. The uninvited transmission covered broad portions of the EM spectrum, and just as odd, there was no hint about meanings. No images, no coded telltales. Just raw spectral brilliance emerging from the ground almost under their feet, reflecting off the hyperfiber sky and then off Marrow again before racing back into the sky.

The entire world heard what made no sense.

Three Wings cursed, and the entire clan turned to Pallas.

Who was already pointing at the unnamed hilltop, and taking a deep breath, their leader used every nexus as well as her mouth to shout her next order:

"Run."

And again, she told them, "Run."

As if legs needed prompting. The power and that rich mix of frequencies was unique. Senseless, yes, but blunt urgency made the transmission sound like an alarm. Voices across Marrow shouted obvious questions: "What is it, why is it, where does it come from?" Waywards were asking, and Mere's people, and then the distant nations too. But fascinated, ignorant conversations accomplished nothing, and that's why the dragons interceded.

"Quiet," six voices commanded.

And the rest of Marrow fell into obedient silence.

The transmission's source was the mysterious hill, two kilometers of rough ground waiting between them and there. Being barefoot like a Wayward wasn't the same as being Wayward. Bleeding and healing. Running was a slippery wet mess. Pallas soon amended her first order, falling back to a quick watchful walk, and then she went looking for good reasons to hold that pace. They didn't know what was waiting for them. Caution was almost never foolish. Most likely there was a large vault beneath the hill -- hyperfiber embedded with extra talents, packaged criteria deciding to announce its presence Now. That implied a high-end machine, primordial and possibly broken. There were historical precedents, and Pallas considered how to approach each situation. Which was what everyone else in the world was doing. Pre-built contingencies were rising out of long sleeps. AI savants massaged ancient databases and encoded zircons, while every expert as well as self-described enthusiasts fell into a project that didn't exist five minutes ago.

Yet data remained scarce. Pallas had sensors focused on the hill, and maybe there was a rising mass, but what she saw was just a distorted picture of reality, and ignorance was always the best reason for prudence.

Her clan walked hard for eleven minutes, field gloves feeding them preliminary numbers. The hill was small and unremarkable, capped with a slab of hyperfiber but otherwise empty. Starting to climb the slope, Pallas happened to give her toes a glance. That's when the EM roar vanished. And lifting her gaze, she realized that a collection of mismatched strangers had appeared.

She ordered her people to stop.

These newcomers looked as if they had dropped from the sky: Seven creatures, unclothed and unimpressive. Eyes watched and sensors probed. The slab was high quality hyperfiber, but thin. Probably a fossil left from some past cycle, lost in the churning iron but pushed to the surface during the last round of eruptions. And six creatures were still standing on the slab. Through one trick or another, the smallest stranger had vanished before the first focused scan began. But the largest visitor proved intriguing. It resembled an enormous baboon, except there wasn't any baboon flesh or bone inside a long body jammed multiple signatures. Which could happen inside old, failing vaults. Individuals on the brink of death would bleed together and merge, leaving an ad hoc chimera. But where chimeras were inevitably crippled, those eight identities had enough unity to pick one direction, and then with urgency and a certain grace, run away.

The remaining strangers were bipeds. The tallest wore living armor and a defiant pose -- the hallmarks of every harum-scarum. The other four were human in one rough fashion or another. One human boy was already running down the slope towards them. Was he a danger? X-rays and microwaves dug into his bones, into his mind, while nanosecond lasers turned skin into whiffs of easily scrutinized gases. Nothing about that child was remarkable. It was the other three who were spectacularly odd. Half-formed and frail in the worst ways, each creature was deeply out of place, and that's why the sensors, particularly the x-rays, had to throttle back, trying not burn or poison what couldn't stand the rough touch.

The running boy shouted. At Pallas, apparently. And the other strangers were yelling at one another.

Not one sound made sense.

Through nexuses, Pallas ordered her clan to spread out.

Through nexuses, Pallas asked everyone, "Where's the chimera?"

The baboon-built oddity was galloping away but plainly visible.

"And the little one," she added.

Several claimed that the alien had disappeared, probably going back where it came from. But someone mentioned that no, maybe it had sprouted wings and flown away, and the nightmare was how easily it had vanished, which was why Pallas threw most of her resources into that frustrating hunt.

Mere had to be briefed.

And Pallas was making ready to do just that. But then Tyley pulled the most unexpected signal from the data. A detail nobody would have looked for, certainly not inside those wild seconds. Gentle sensors were weighing what was odd and dangerous about the various bodies, and when an unexpected word was sung, nobody but Tyley noticed. And she repeated the word, as she should, wrapping it inside astonishment and large helpings of doubt.

"Dragon," she called out.

Half of the clan laughed, convinced this was a joke.

Except Pallas' nexuses fed her the same telltales -- shadow matter signatures that always meant that she was in the presence of a genuine dragon.

Mere had to be warned. But warned about what? Pallas wasted another moment inventing a ridiculous explanation for everything. Today's adventure? An elaborate training exercise. Pallas and her people were being tested. Indeed, Mere herself could be waiting in plain sight, disguised as one of those lost, archaic children. A test or a joke, or both. Wasn't that a fine idea to carry you forwards?

The running boy acted starved for attention.

Through a nexus, Pallas asked her lieutenant, "Dragon?"

Tyley had already given him hard study. On the most encrypted channel, she said, "No." Then with her mouth, once again, she shouted the impossible word, "Dragon."

Because nothing was ordinary, data had to be scrubbed and weighed, parts discarded and then sometimes brought back again. One candidate after another was dismissed until only one remained viable. The verdict was unthinkable, and awful, and Tyley cursed, sharing what she knew with the rest of the clan.

Wayward gloves sang the data.

Sang, "Dragon."

And Pallas gave new orders.

The running boy was immortal and ordinary. He meant little or nothing, and Three Wings could deal with him, the same as he dealt with Waywards. What mattered was reaching the dragon before one impossibility led to an even more incredible scenario.

No long after that, the harum-scarum threw two rocks at Pallas.

Her leg was cut, and then her head, and neither mattered. But Broken was bothered. Nothing made sense and the soldier was already scared, and being fearful as well as profoundly cautious, he decided that this situation demanded readiness. That's why he pulled the juggernaut from its holster, breaking a host of codes and traditions as well as his leader's blunt orders.

"Put that plasma to sleep and the gun away," Pallas warned.

The running boy wasn't running anymore. Limp on the ground, he was building a new heart. The multiple beast was charging towards the horizon, but winged sensors were overhead, watching its progress. And the little stranger that might have flown away? One more useless glance at the sky, and with Pallas' people mostly in position, she delivered her orders.

"Do not hurt any of them," she said.

The impossible dragon was mortal. That truth ruled all others. This new dragon was an oddly built, oddly pretty girl with long arms and big shoulders. She looked as if she would be happiest climbing, but there were no cliffs or trees in sight. Dark eyes and that broad thin mouth revealed some species of anguish. Old pains or new, Pallas couldn't decide. But stepping onto the hyperfiber, she stared at the strong arms and the sadness, and she suddenly felt nothing but sorry for this lost creature.

Hands had to be offered.

Pallas offered hers first.

How the girl grabbed her pistol was easy enough. Pistols were not weapons. In a world of immortals, bullets and knives were tools of debate and sometimes rough jokes, and nothing mangled would ever stop healing. The rest of the universe was unreal, legendary and lost, but Marrow was a wonderland. Burnished by time -- a paradise built from everlasting flesh -- it held enough beauty for a thousand millennia of exploration and little adventures. Pallas was going to have children and multitudes of grandchildren, and all of them were going to enjoy profound thoughts piled upon mountains of lovely thoughts, and overseeing this splendor were a few dragons endowed with pragmatic souls and a genius for enduring.

But this dragon wasn't immortal. She was a sorrowful creature thrown from an unknown vault, and of course Pallas tried to help her spirits. The empty hands were her honest attempt, and then her pistol was claimed by the girl's hand, and the new dragon turned the barrel and shot herself and the blood came fast and Pallas spent that next useless moment waiting for this dragon's last breath, followed by the white, purifying fire that would consume every future.

THREE

Bad news, gut wounds.

Young soldiers were taught that lesson early, usually the same day they were told that shooting your enemy in his belly was perfectly acceptable. But while Karlan wasn't one to carry sentiment or sorry nonsense, he didn't like what he was seeing. What the girl just did, she did badly. Intestines had absorbed that loud little bullet -- not her head, not the heart -- and that was pretty much the worst way to suicide yourself. A suicide that belonged to her; Karlan didn't want to second-guess the girl. But if Elata had come to him for advice, he would have put a straight finger against her temple, shouting, "Boom."

A helluva a lot wanted to be noticed right now. First among the obvious crap was that Karlan was standing naked in a very peculiar place, surrounded by youngsters wearing skins and talking gadgets. And not only was Elata dying ugly and slow, but nobody did shit to help her. Least of all those long-legged natives. The blue-skinned girl whose pistol did the damage … it was all she could do to grab her gun off the gray ground that wasn't steel or tile or anything sensible. Her face was bluer than before, and those blue eyes were huge, practically glowing. She acted like any kid who had done something real stupid or real wrong, and staring at her mess, she was begging for time to run backwards, if only to make this badness go away.

Then all at once, those wild kids were talking. Singing. Songs made from gibberish, with one word was getting repeated hard and fast. Knowing nothing about meanings only made the moods easier to read. This gang was crazy with terror. Half of these colorful faces were crying. Hands covered eyes, keeping bad things from being seen, and other hands tugged at braided hair and the brains beneath. Dozens of people wearing guns, but crap-sure, not one of them was acting like a respectable soldier.

"This is a mess," Karlan muttered.

Talking to nobody.

King heard him. Of course. And King agreed. Stepping close, the giant reached for the wounded belly, that big hand likely to slice flesh if it wasn't careful.

Which was probably why the alien pulled back again.

Elata offered one word.

"Cold," she complained.

Sure. The girl was dropping into shock.

Her complaint kicked Seldom into action. "Help her help her help her," the boy chanted, words butting against words while he whipped the air with his skinny arms.

It was funny, being the only one who could see things for what they were. Which happened in just about every chapter inside Karlan's biography.

"We can't help her," said King.

Talking to Seldom.

Which made the wiry boy louder and more desperate.

"Diamond!" he shouted.

There was no purpose in worrying about Diamond. Their sometimes-leader would recover nicely from his little stabbing. Karlan understood that better than anybody. But he took the trouble of looking down the slope, wondering if the boy had healed enough to stand. And there he was, reliable as shit. Running across the rocks, Diamond was moving slower than he wanted, carrying what looked like genuine pain but not the knife. The boy who stabbed him had taken back his knife and now was ahead of him, chugging along. Hearing Diamond closing, the wild boy decided to stop and look back. That's when Karlan saw the overstuffed backpack with all those bloody sacks dangling and swinging. Except they weren't sacks, were they? It took a lot to startle him, but this place had its tricks. And that was when he realized that these weren't kids, no. They were monsters who liked chopping the heads off other people.

Karlan cringed. A soldier who had accomplished more than his share of gruesome mayhem.

Then a groan leaked out of Elata, and he turned back to her. The girl never had much talent for being happy, particularly after her mom and old home were murdered. Sad as she acted some days, it was hard to see how she'd survived this long. But then again, these monsters didn't act especially eager to finish what the bullet started. It was almost as if they wanted to save her, what with all the wild gestures and the words stripped of meaning, plus that sharp panic and runaway grief.

Then the purple fellow shouted. Once and loudly, and he yanked off his leather vest, getting on his knees, shouting again while pressing down on the flowing blood. Which looked like a saintly act, set against boys and girls who marched around their world, carrying severed heads as trophies.

Watching purple hands turn red, Karlan's slow brain finally clicked. Sure, sure. These short-armed babies were the same as Diamond. You could cut them deep, maybe even chopped them into pieces, and they grew back just fine.

And Elata wasn't like them, which they knew and that's why they were scared.

Karlan let out a big curse and laughed.

Seldom hadn't stopped dancing and sobbing, begging strangers to please help his sad little girlfriend.

Lifting his brother by the shoulders, Karlan put his mouth to one damp ear. "They're unbreakable, and they're idiots. They don't know first aid."

The boy had weaknesses, but he was always quick to understand what left others baffled. As soon as Karlan set him down, he turned and said, "So you save her."

"What?"

"You're trained. You know wounds. You're going to help Elata."

Karlan's first instinct was to walk away, giving the miserable child what she craved. After every misery that had happened today, death had to be a relief. Then he reminded himself that Diamond was supposed to be the big hero, and they should wait for their sometimes-champion. Except just when the day could never grow stranger, a different mix of ideas and words came into Karlan's skin. Looking at the patient's sorry face, at the warm blood stealing away her body heat, he pulled in a big breath, and with a half-laughing voice, he asked himself, "Why the hell not?"

Elata was on her back, pale and shivering, and the purple boy was pushing his bloody vest into her middle. The Eight were missing, and Quest could be anywhere but probably wasn't here. Standing alone, spines high, King stared at the wounded girl. Seldom was kneeling and weeping, one trembling hand reaching for the wound and then pulling back. And Karlan stood behind his little brother, squinting hard, his tongue flipping back and forth inside his half-opened mouth.

For Diamond, thoughts usually came too fast to be noticed. Some tiny piece of his brain would fall in love with one possibility, and sometimes the body responded before the full mind could consider every competing idea. That was a pitfall to being Diamond. His will was too quick, and there was always the risk of sudden mistakes. One of those blunders was so large that a war began, and all these days later, his endless mind still couldn't measure the ramifications that came from pushing one blood-colored button.

Elata was more dead than alive, and nobody was helping her. That much was obvious. The purple boy didn't know how to stop the bleeding, and the gray boy with the big pack and severed heads had stopped short, not wanting to help. Meanwhile the blue girl couldn't stand any stiller, a little pistol in one hand and a shifty-shaped glove glowing in the other. Her and that pistol were connected to Elata. That was the story that took hold of Diamond, and that's why he charged the blue girl.

But his brother saw him. King was a statue and then he was a flash of silver, slapping

Diamond's wrist, shattering both bones before flinging that little human body aside.

Diamond slid across the gray and into the rocks, and then he sat up, the broken arm busy in his lap.

"First," Karlan was saying. "Stop the flood."

"I can push too," said Seldom.

Seldom's hands were next to the purple and black hands.

"And she's going into shock," Karlan said, looking at the strangers. At the blue girl. "So get her warm," he shouted.

Nobody understood.

Karlan looked at Diamond. "Nice if you could share your healing powers." Then he laughed without laughing, the face making jokes while the rest of him was thinking.

Karlan had tried to kill Diamond and maybe more than once, depending on how the incidents were counted. It was perfectly reasonable to be afraid of him. Except this seemed almost smart, putting the murderous man in charge of his friend's care.

"How would you stop the blood?" asked King.

"Burn the wound," said Karlan, looking at Elata's pale face and the listless eyes. "There's no time, but fire and iron might work. You know, shove a hot poker inside, cook the blood vessels to cut the flow."

"Ohthatwouldkillher," Seldom blurted.

"Unless she fools you and survives," said Karlan. "The scar would never stop hurting, but she'd have a few thousand days of spectacular misery. Provided she didn't get the urge and find another gun."

Those last words had to be digested.

"Find another gun," Diamond repeated.

Nobody reacted.

"Who shot her?" he wanted to know.

People looked at the patient, not the blue girl.

"Elata tried to kill herself," Diamond proposed.

Nobody denied it.

Diamond got on his feet, cradling the broken wrist while walking in a half-circle, purposefully keeping away from Elata and the others. Some idea was going to rise, something smart and easy. He imagined bonfires and coal-hot surgical tools and the girl screaming until she passed out. Then new thoughts dragged him inside a hospital room full of doctors wearing milk-colored clothes, the patient sleeping painless on a bed made of down and rare silks. Imagination built that solution, accomplishing nothing. Time was lost. With his good arm, Diamond grabbed the tall milk-white girl. "Fire," he shouted. Then he pulled back the hand while lifting his injured arm, fingers wiggling like eager flames.

The milk girl might have been staring at a strange bird, as little regard she had for his earnest suggestion.

But King grabbed his brother's idea long enough to dismiss it. He pointed down the slope, aiming at a clump of what didn't look like trees so much as soot-colored umbrellas. "Carry her and we kill her," he said. "Or we drag the wood here and make it into her funeral pyre."

The promise of fire had wasted more time.

Karlan waved at the blue girl, gaining her attention. "We have to close her wound," he said. "With bandages, fire. Anything."

Words were incomprehensible, but her expression and the alert, faraway eyes showed that the girl was listening to someone. The steel pistol needed to be pushed back inside its holster, and the other hand lifted its glove. Like soft metal being pressed flat between invisible rollers, her glove grew long and thin, and threatening to vanish entirely, it pulled free of blue fingers, hanging in the air but as steady as glass locked inside a wall, turning into a window peering inside another room.

A woman was in that window. Her face was as smooth as any baby's, yet the hair was silver like an old lady's, long and not braided. Eyes that held age and something that might be wisdom were focused on things out of sight. That face sang words, and then she was silent, and the blue girl sang one word and another two and then repeated the first word. Which was the same critical word repeated all those times before.

Diamond tried singing the song.

The blue girl glanced at him and waved, pulling his eyes towards the floating picture.

The silver-haired lady was small now, floating above an image of Elata.

Except.

The dying girl wasn't alone. Something else was lying with her on the gray ground. Under her? No, inside her. The most peculiar object, and Diamond wondered how Elata swallowed it. Which was a ridiculous guess. The girl's skull held an object that looked like a bottle, but a very particular bottle. The shape pretended to be simple, yet it was really quite impossible. Diamond recognized it. The bottle was a puzzle teachers used to make bright children realize that they weren't so smart after all.

The blue girl spoke.

The silver-haired woman seemed to agree.

The impossible bottle was transparent like thin glass, and it was endless. Its body opened on top and then tapered and bent, reaching back inside itself, and becoming the bottle again, it formed the same neat round hole on top.

Master Nissim, teacher and mentor, had used this illusion to explain amazing things, and at the same time, explain nothing.

"Imagine a tiny spider walking here," the old man had said, one crooked finger drawing a careful line. "The spider walks and walks and walks, into the bottle and out again. But the journey never ends. From the spider's perspective, the bottle has how many surfaces? One, yes. A single surface, inside and out, and this preposterous business is sitting in whose hand?"

In Elata's hand, and Diamond remembered everything about the classroom and that day, including who stood where and what each person said in turn.

He forced his thoughts back where they needed to be.

Once again, he sang the word that he didn't understand, but giving it all of the passion he could muster, working to be noticed. The blue girl and silver-haired woman stared at him, and again he yelled about fire, fingers dancing while he mimicked the crackling of wood.

The silver-haired lady understood. Unless she spoke loudly and clearly for entirely different reasons. Either way, the window turned back into a glove that deftly dropped onto the girl's hand, and the lady vanished, and the blue girl reached with her empty hand, a different gun pulled out of the purple boy's holster.

That boy acted scared, or furious. Either way, he sang a couple sour words before standing up and backing away. Then the blue girl aimed the wide barrel at Elata, and that's when King reacted, his armored hand beginning to take a swipe. But the girl was weirdly quick. Jumping back, she shot nothing but his hand, the flash bringing thunder and a horrible stink that wasn't meat cooking. No, the smell was acrid and chemical, as if the hand was dropped into a furnace, torn into to its tiniest ingredients.

Even Karlan flinched with the blast.

The blue girl quickly adjusted the gun with fingers and words, and she delivered a strange little kiss to the barrel, as if wishing the weapon well. A warning yell and a kick to Seldom forced him to back away. Then she yanked at the leather vest and the barely clotted blood, exposing the wound. This blast was faint, more sizzle than thunder, and it was carefully aimed and very brief. But there was so much heat that Elata screamed until she had no voice, eyes closed and mouth wide, all of the blood cooked along with the meat of her punctured belly.

Diamond assumed she was dead.

Again, one swift thought took hold, and he rushed her.

But the blue girl was quicker than his reflexes. The press of the thumb readjusted the awful weapon, and she began by evaporating Diamond's hands, and then to keep him from being any kind of distraction, she carefully burned away his mouth and nose and his tear-filled eyes.

Only one person could be the first person to see the Diamond standing outside his home.

That was one reason among many why Elata was special.

One hundred days after they met, sitting politely bored in school, Diamond gave himself permission to play with unusual ideas: He was never discovered inside the belly of a corona. No, he was born as a notion, a hope. One empty room inside a very large home looked as if it needed a child, and with magical wood and imagination, two old people built him. The boy could exist inside that room and nowhere else, but Diamond foolishly went through the door and left the house, finding his way outdoors. Except he still wasn't real. Only the world was real, and the real was always ready to wash away dreams. If Elata hadn't been there, and if she hadn't put her eyes on lost little him, and just important, if she never believed in his existence, Diamond would have become nothingness. Haddi would have lived an ordinary day, and Merit would have come home to kiss his wife's cheek, and maybe at dinner one of those old people would say to the other that it was strange how quiet and empty their home felt, and what should they do with the big storage room, nothing inside it but air and potential?

There was no point in confessing those odd thoughts. Diamond kept most of his games hidden in tiny corners of that busy, busy brain. And in that, he was the same as everyone else. People needed to play with impossibles and untruths. Envisioning the secret notions inside the children sitting beside him -- that was another good game. Everyone was racing through a world that was too real and far too magnificent to genuinely know, but if you could guess a person's daydreams, you won a clear view of their soul.

Lying on the smooth ground, blind and without a voice, Diamond listened to songful voices full of senseless, jumbled lyrics. And inside the chaos, familiar voices came and left again.

"Diamond," said Seldom.

"Alive," King said.

Karlan cursed before saying, "Quiet. I'm hunting the pulse."

"I hear the heart," King said.

Elata's pulse and heart?

"Yeah, she's living," Karlan agreed.

Diamond tried to speak.

Stupidly tried, because there was no jaw, no tongue. Twin stumps reached for the burnt face, two flavors of pain pressing against one another.

King said, "I hear," and paused.

Diamond sat up.

And Seldom vomited bile and air and wrenching gasps.

"Engines," said King. "Coming fast."

The wild children kept singing to themselves or to distant faces. Unless they made noise because their voices were so pretty. What bizarre daydreams did these people hide? Diamond shoved that question inside its own tiny box.

What King heard became everyone's sound. Machines roared as they dropped from the bright gray ceiling. The aircraft weren't jets or rockets either. Like enormous tuning forks, the vibrations ran through Diamond's bones, and trying to smile, the scorched face turned upwards, new fingers playing with the sockets inside his skull, trying to coax his eyes to reemerge, fresh and ready.

Quest glided in a wide circle, watching horrors unfold. Elata had shot herself and the barefoot animals had burned her and she was possibly dead. Almost certainly dead. Karlan wore a laughing face while his brother threw up mouthfuls of acid. Diamond had tried to fight and the foolish boy was mutilated for his efforts. King stood with feet apart, one hand regrowing, but otherwise he did nothing. Nothing. And meanwhile, the Eight were running into a gathering of inky black growths that might be trees or might be mushrooms. But if they were trees, they were growing wrong, pushing up from of the barren, filthy glass.

Hope. Quest was a world of hope just moments ago. But then Elata died and Diamond was maimed, and the grimmest possible idea took hold: Everything that she saw was ordinary. Was routine. This world was relentless and vicious, and each of these miseries weren't just inevitable, they were small. And what kind of world would that be? Both tree-walkers and the papio enjoyed talking about the happy afterlife where the virtuous dead would feast forever. But that paradise had its fraternal twin, a realm where evil souls suffered for their sins. And that was what this was. The corona's children were dropped here because they deserved punishment. Because the Eight and Diamond had kindled an endless war. Because King stood aside while his father waged the war.

And because Quest had stupidly extinguished the sun. They were criminals sentenced to an eternal prison. And the three mortal humans? Obviously they wouldn't have to remain here much longer. Shot and burnt, maybe Elata was already climbing in paradise.

Too low. Quest had glided too close to the others. Working her silent, invisible wings, she regained altitude, slipping away just before three giant machines descended on the little hilltop.

Quick as possible, the barefoot children formed three tidy groups.

The aircraft were sleek and black, tiny nozzles spitting out heat and buzzing whines. They looked like giant beetles and acted more alive than mechanical, and Quest wasted moments wondering how to approach one of them, masking her presence long enough to risk a taste and touch.

That bravery needed to die.

She had to leave. Now. The Eight could run a little ways and try to hide. But a creature like Quest could glide forever, and she could hide forever, and safety was waiting somewhere else.

She spied a flock of hunting insects. The big six-winged predators had jeweled shells and furious, idiot voices, their wings battering the air as they flew. Quest slipped among them, changing her body and her stink, and indistinguishable from her new family, she flew away. A wind that might belong to the morning or the afternoon helped her move, and the Eight continued running under the upside-down mushrooms, heading for a round lake, and that's where Quest would drink too. A long sip of water before she glided to some better part of this Hell.

Wind rises and the guttering flame rides the bent tip of a wick. But before the flame turns to smoke and dies, the wind breaks. That pathetic excuse for fire manages to survive until the next gust or the first careless breath, or until the molten wax drowns what cannot survive, regardless how much you want and need to see a furious blaze.

The dragon was the guttering flame. Her bleeding had been stopped, but the blunt cauterization bought them minutes, if that.

"Get her to me," Mere implored.

She was speaking to Pallas. On public channels, barely encrypted. These three stealths weren't trying to hide, and none of the nexuses pretended to be Wayward. Because among the mandatories was the critical need that every nation, and particularly every Wayward citizen, appreciated just how shitty this mess was.

"Medicals are coming," said Mere, her voice quiet but tight. Quiet but undeniably stressed. "They're making ready, best as they can. But you have to bring her."

"Forty seconds, we launch," Pallas promised.

"And bring the others too," the ancient dragon added.

Not an easy trick, since two strangers were unaccounted for.

"We need all of them," Mere said.

"Yes, madam."

"They'll help us understand." Which was obvious. "And if necessary, we can borrow pieces from them."

Borrow pieces? Looking at the naked children, Pallas felt sicker than ever. Squeamish and grieving. Which was idiotic. If they didn't save this weakling dragon, everything and everyone would cease. Given that choice, the decent person would enthusiastically hack apart a thousand mortals, looking for the one heart that would keep beating until the next crisis.

"Do you have all of the strangers?" Mere asked.

Again, this was a nearly public channel. "Yes," Pallas said. "Everyone from the hill is with us."

Blunt lies were often the best encryption.

"Hurry," her dragon implored.

"We'll do our best, madam."

The three stealths deployed hatches, the landing gear not bothering to sprout. The fourth stealth was circling at the fringes of the atmosphere, still shrouded, its tiny crew begging for any excuse to cluster-blast the first Wayward to intrude.

"Load and go," Pallas told her people.

Pure routine, save for one dying dragon. How to transport a creature so insubstantial?

Broken depowered his field glove and threw it down as trash, and now with both hands empty, he was ready to grab the patient. But the strangers were also busy. The harum-scarum spoke, and the largest human answered him, stepping up beside Broken, smiling as he gave the lieutenant one hard shove. Just for the fun of it, apparently.

Everyone but Broken considered shooting the man.

The big human knelt, reaching under the dying dragon.

"Let him," Pallas ordered.

The boy with the burnt face was standing, managing one cautious step towards the nearest stealth. Then with his half-grown hand, the harum-scarum took hold of the boy's shoulder. The new flesh was scaleless, pale and humanly soft. The hand's two thumbs squeezed while the speaking mouth offered more words, and watching the strangers, Pallas found an odd insight. Three mortals wearing the same long-armed bodies, and she couldn't tell who was related to whom. Yet those immortals seemed very much like brothers, the one with eyes guiding his blind sibling, following their companions up into the armored hold.

FOUR

The aircraft jumped off the hilltop, or the strange engines tossed the world away. In either case, Seldom cried out when his legs buckled, and Karlan laughed and fell and laughed harder. But not King. Standing strong, he held Diamond's bare neck with his new hand, keeping both of them upright. Which was important. Pride was power, and power demanded poise, and there was no poise in allowing your knees to fail beneath you.

Diamond had new hands, tiny and hot, and new eyes that found colorless light and lazy shapes. Yet he felt worse by the moment. Every thought about Elata brought anguish, and that was before considering anyone else. This was a cruel place, and did their captors even realize it? Fear came like wind, each gust stronger than the last, and that was why it was important, even critical, to play with nonsense.

How fast could he heal?

This was a race, Diamond decided. Hands like bandages, he covered his eyes, stubby fingers feeling the nose grow and the progress of lips and teeth and the squishy wet tongue.

Then the aircraft accelerated even harder.

Diamond crumbled and King settled beside him as the very hard floor grew pillows, soft and embracing.

Everybody laid down.

Five breaths. Diamond counted. Then the engines lowered their pitch, and the acceleration was a little less crushing.

Five more breaths, and he could smell the children, odd sweat rolling across unwashed, weirdly sweet flesh.

Six more breaths, and his mouth felt mostly whole. Pulling back his hands, the lidless, freshmade eyes found a blue face framed by gray-white light.

The face sang one word.

The girl pointed at herself.

Again, she surrendered her name.

That was Diamond's guess, and sitting up, he offered his name.

Each repeated the other's nonsense. A preliminary step to what mattered. Then Pallas gestured to Elata dying under several blankets. That pointing finger was asking the question.

"Elata," said Diamond.

Nodding, the blue girl looked at her purple and black friend. Looked but said nothing audible. That boy was cradling one of those limp hands, and quietly, urgently, he began to repeat the name. "Elata" was a chant. The purple boy was hoping to kindle magic. "Elata," he said, stroking the back of the hand, and then he was almost shouting, "Elata," while squeezing the wrist and that pale, mostly-dead arm.

Karlan sat on the nearby pillows. "Funny," he said. "You should be the prize. But no, our sad girl is the soul who matters."

"There's something inside her," Diamond began.

Karlan glanced at Elata, his tongue rolling inside the mouth. But the others preferred to watch Diamond.

"Inside her," Seldom repeated.

Diamond described the infinity flask. Except when it was told, the story turned ludicrous. He was mistaken, or worse, he sounded stupid. There was no reason to believe what he had seen, and Diamond was ready for any excuse to throw that crazy business into the trash.

Yet nobody offered doubts. Only Diamond. So he quit talking, and they sat, quiet as could be, feeling the aircraft rising higher. Otherwise, nothing changed. For fifty breaths. Then everybody was shaken hard, and the machine stopped climbing, find an altitude and pace it could love. Standing was easy enough, which the four of them did. And that's when one the wild children approached, folded and clean new clothes stacked on his filthy arms.

Seldom grabbed the gifts, eager to dress himself. Except the clothes were ready to dress him instead. A couple breaths was all it took, and that despite the boy's hard battle against the animated fabric. Trousers and shirt crawled around him and sealed, and thin sandals waited like rats, bent and cocked, happy to leap onto feet that couldn't have kicked at them any harder.

Karlan cursed, but he didn't fight his clothes.

King watched the belt and shorts crawl up his body, seams vanishing without thread or glue.

Diamond was ready to feel astonished or squeamish. Yet even as the trousers and shirt engulfed him, far stranger impossibles began. The aircraft's belly was one long and very narrow room, and it was crowded with boys and girls removing their clothes. But once the leather vests and shorts were lying on the floor, what looked like glass knives were brought out, and these naked people swiftly cut into their own bellies and bare thighs, the empty hands following along, yanking at the exposed edges, skin and tiny threads of red blood lifting before the glittering blades, all that flesh eager to be peeled away.

"My new eyes are lying to me," he hoped.

But this was real. Sheets of skin fell and the braided hair was cut loose, and the carnage dropped to a floor that was hard again. The pillows had been absorbed and everything that fell was absorbed, and once the children had stripped off everything they could reach, they helped one another. Neighbors generously carved the flesh off each others' backs and off their faces. Nothing could be more ordinary. If there was pain to feel, it left with the skin. Removing the feet was like yanking off tight boots -- a chore demanding focus and speed. And even those horrors weren't as fantastic as what happened next. Those stripped bodies healed. In twenty or thirty breaths, the blue and black and white skin grew back. Diamond didn't recover this fast. His brother didn't either. And King was just as mystified by the carnage, a tight small wary voice saying, "Listen."

The healing was so vigorous, and all of that new flesh was covering so many bodies at once, that the room was filled with a busy wet sloshing noise that was awful to hear, and wonderful, and then done.

Only one youngster didn't skin himself. The purplish-black fellow was too busy stroking a dying girl's hand, and he alone still held that peculiar sweet smell.

New clothes appeared, but instead of being brought, they fell from the ceiling. Another ten breaths, and the trousers and shirts had dressed everybody, the garb utterly simple, without pockets or buttons, the fabrics yellow and sometimes white and often black shot with dashes of gray.

Then it was dinner time. The ceiling squeezed out little cakes and colored pouches of juice. Some children ate and drank, sometimes they sang softly, but the mood was obvious, the interests narrow. Everyone kept watch over Elata. Faces that would never scar were deeply concerned. Underneath the different cheeks and endless skin colors, every face had little noses and big eyes. Maybe that's why Diamond could walk among them without being noticed. And Karlan was right: Elata was very important, while Diamond was nothing but another familiar beast.

The gray boy who had stabbed him stood at the back of the room, and when he wasn't watching the dying girl, he made himself busy, tying heads against a wall that was meant for nothing else. His flesh was gray as always, the black hair growing a little longer before it stopped. He watched Elata and then glanced at Diamond, smiling as if he expected to be happy. Except he wasn't happy. The smile was a habit, and his hands couldn't stop working with the bloodied trophies.

Every head was alive. Which shouldn't have surprised. Every mouth was moving, saying nothing, but it was easy to assume strong words, and the dull, undying eyes were throwing their hatred at the gray boy, and probably everyone else onboard this spectacular vehicle.

There was just one window in that very long room, and the tall milk-colored girl with a short fringe of red hair was standing beside it. Diamond stopped short, and she looked at him. The girl was gracious or she was too exhausted to care, and stepping back, she waved a hand, beckoning a stranger to look out and down.

Diamond's old home always felt enormous, but this world dwarfed that left-behind Creation. The landscape resembled the reef country, hard and twisted everywhere and sharp in the highest places. The forests were mostly black, but there were spots and long reaches of ground wearing other shades, including familiar greens. Five distant hilltops formed a sloppy line, each one of them burning on top, and a wide body of water passed under Diamond's feet, gray where it was deep and greenish black in the shallows. Great hands had erected a dozen glass towers beside that water, each as large or larger than bloodwood trees. And stranger still, land and water were covered with what looked like an enormous blanket. This was the world's air, Diamond realized. Spent breaths and untaken breaths were mixed with dust and smoke and whatever else didn't want to settle on the ground or water, and the blanket reached almost as high as they were, but not quite.

The visible atmosphere had a boundary.

A border.

This impossibly swift machine had carried everyone far above the world. Yet the gray ceiling was still much higher, smooth as polished metal and unmarred by any door. At least Diamond couldn't see any doors, using eyes that never stopped feeling new.

The smallest voice; the simplest name.

Kai.

Little Kai enjoyed tidy, unadorned beliefs: The Creation was built from busy particles and coincidence, and every mindless object was happy to follow its predictable path. In the same spirit, each species was loyal to its innate trajectory, and regardless what they claimed, the Eight were just as simple. True, they had never met a body with two minds, much less eight distinct, often warring personalities. Yet as smart and unique as each of them might be, in the end, they were the same as any eight papio or eight tree-climbers. Every group had to bow to its leader.

Chaos ruled the Eight when they were babies, but then Divers took control. The most human among them, in blood and attitude, she gave that shared body one voice and a strong purpose. Later, after learning of Diamond's existence, it was Divers who declared him to be the great enemy. With that human voice, Divers asked what would happen to the Eight and to this world if the abomination was allowed to mature, siring hybrid children filled with all of the human flaws, and invincibility too?

True, the future refused to be seen. But the threat of unpredictable change filled her audience with reasonable, easily shared fears. That was how Divers won the other Seven's cooperation, and showing the world her voice and her will, she convinced key humans to attack the boy while he sat inside his tree-walker school. But Diamond survived the assault, and that disaster brought the fighting to the reef, to the Eight, and finding herself standing before the boy's adoptive father, Divers used the shared hands, yanking the man's head off its frail, old body.

Every human understood fire, and they were masters at finding vengeance. When given his chance, Diamond lashed out at the Eight, flinging them into the coronas' world. The cool comfort of the human realm was lost. They were lost inside a barren realm rich with energy and pain, and the shared misery might be a justice. Perhaps. But one of the Eight had orange blood that loved the heat, and that's how Tritian saved the others, and given another million days, they might have prospered. But the sun failed suddenly and the coronas died, and Diamond came down to the wastelands, looking for the sun but finding his enemies instead.

There must have been, should have been, days when the Eight lived eight distinct lives. Each of them still carried half-recollections. Favorite smells, half-heard sounds, and occasionally spirit would rise out of memory, revealing nonsense while whispering nonsense, offering useless portraits of other realms.

Existence without history: That was the boundless past.

Diamond found the Eight, and against every expectation, Diamond allowed the Eight to follow him into a little room and then into a new world. Surrounded by glass and fire, there was no sun below or any dangling lights, yet light was everywhere just the same. Each one of the Eight expected one its siblings to feel at home. Yet none of them did. Nothing in these circumstances was remembered or felt inviting, and very little seemed sensible. Fleeing was the easy choice. Run away from the wild children, abandon Diamond and the others. And during that hard first sprint, each of the Eight carefully listed the same respectable reasons for this desperate strategy.

They had already survived two worlds -- realms built from small ingredients and tidy, inescapable rules. This new ground resembled the reef country where the Eight were born, except that every surface was harder and sharper, and everything alive was different in appearance and voice and in its stink. Yes, this was a horrible realm. But the Eight endured hundreds of days among the coronas, which was far worse, and more importantly, this world was blunt evidence that the Creation was too large to measure. The Eight needed nothing but to survive. All they wanted was to find the next plunge and another new world, and another plunge and world, and eventually, if just a little luck fell with them, they would reach a soft, cool room with food in the larder and time to rest.

Freedom and time. That's what the Eight were chasing. Except their body had barely recovered from its earlier wounds. Limbs felt heavy. Fatigue stole away their speed. And worse, the razored ground tore at fingers and toes, lost blood and flesh marking their route. Ten days of running would shrink them by half. Kai laughed when he offered that calculation and imagery. Sisters and brothers responded with scornful chatter. They wouldn't outlast this day. They told him so, trying to scare one another into running faster. But there was no faster inside them. So they imagined fat animals squirming inside the shared mouth and long drinks of sweet water, and later, once they were full of nonexistent nourishment, seven of them launched into elaborate arguments about priorities and schemes certain to leave them in charge of this awful world.

Kai listened to the talk and ignored the talk. The Eight weren't planning a conquest. No, this was the battle to decide who would lead next. And what good had come from that instinct? For all their genius and endurance, this shared life remained miserable, and that wouldn't change until they found the voice that understood the power inside true harmony.

Kai could be either gender or both. Unless he embraced nothing at all. But there were four sisters and three brothers, which was why he had always declared himself to be the fourth brother.

Balance enticed harmony.

Divers was a dangerous girl who didn't know why she carried that particular name. The others held the same ignorance. As babies, each found some little sound that felt more pleasant than others, and that sound became their identity. Names gave comfort, and comfort brought balance, and what could matter more inside the inexplicable life?

Kai was the exception.

Vivid, ancient memories gave him every reason to take this name.

Kai meant Water.

Vast deep and roiling hot water.

There was a Kai before this Kai. Enormous and powerful, the ancient Kai never stopped moving, and unlike tepid rainwater trapped inside a bowl, His great self was filled with light, with crackling energies and vast busy organs. The imagery was too vivid not to be true. And shouldn't the splendid be shared?

Yet the fourth brother rarely mentioned those visions. Partly because his siblings refused to believe him. Which was reasonable, sensible. Wise, perhaps. Kai was the driest creature among them, his body wrapped around machinery, his biological portions having an electricity-and-gear logic. Nothing about Kai was large, and he certainly wasn't a deep roiling body of water.

Divers was happy to mention her brother's limitations.

"You're a puddle, if that. Rainwater resting inside a shallow footprint, and two moments of heat would boil you to nothing."

She meant to be cruel but true. Which was Divers' genius.

Yet quite a lot was cruel and true. For instance, they were running across a new world, water in its air and water in the footprints. What if a giant footprint waited beyond the next ridge, deep enough and wide enough to hold the magnificence embodied in this very simple name?

Kai.

"Me," he thought.

Happiness like a thread wove its way through desperate, exhausted muscle. A happiness best kept secret from the others, at least until the ridge was crossed and tiny Kai would see his glorious future.

Diamond was standing near the very tall, very white girl. He was staring through a window, watching the world or looking into another room. Seldom wanted to join his friend, distracting himself with anything else, but those severed heads were hanging on the nearby wall, eyes open.

Seldom didn't want to be watched.

Remaining beside Elata. That should be most important, he decided.

Except Seldom couldn't serve as her nurse. The purple boy had the patient's hand, which was what Seldom should be holding. The group's leader stood over both of them. That girl had dropped her leather clothes, which was one kind of interesting, and then peeled away her flesh, which was extraordinarily grim. But the blueness had already healed, bright yellow hair growing longer every moment, and she was wearing plain white clothes that acted alive. The unthinkable kept happening and happening, yet every event felt common and easy for these human-shaped creatures, as natural as breath was for Seldom. He watched the important girl saying nothing, blue eyes looking one way and another and then a third, but never changing focus. Then she stared at Seldom. He had been painfully self-conscious until those clothes crawled up across body, curing the nudity. Except the girl still made him bashful. She stared past his eyes, her mouth ready to speak. But not to him, no. She was watching ghosts that nobody else was allowed to see.

"Any of this yanking loose memories?" Karlan was talking to King.

The alien stared at the long room, listening.

"Maybe you came from here," said Karlan.

"No, nothing's familiar."

Laughing, Karlan said, "I like that trick of skinning yourself. Ever consider trying that?"

"Yes," King answered, and the subject was finished.

As an experiment, Seldom attempted to remove his shirt. The living fabric was soft and warm and nearly weightless, and it was full of strength and stubbornness, resisting his first tug and the harder second tug. Infuriated, he grabbed the bottom edge, all of his strength fighting to peel away what had no interest in leaving his body.

And then the leader spoke. To him. One word rode a single soft note, and she came close enough to set two blue fingers on his shoulder.

"You shouldn't," those fingers warned. "Leave your shirt on."

Seldom stopped struggling.

And she left him.

Smiles could mean anything in this baffling mess of a world, but the blue girl had smiled at him, which felt wonderful. And that single touch gave Seldom so much courage. Several more odd children were kneeling beside poor Elata, wrapping padded belts around her waist and chest. Seldom couldn't help one sick person, and he couldn't undress himself, but he was ready to brave those disembodied heads. So he began walking as the aircraft began to shake. Then three steps into his journey towards Diamond, new magic arrived. Seldom weighed nothing. Suddenly free of the floor, he sailed upwards and not slowly. The boy felt flung, and that's when his new clothes changed their nature, inflating like balloons, pulling around his head and body, burying him inside a mixture of cloud and steel.

Striking the ceiling, he felt almost nothing. Bouncing softly, he rolled in the air, laughing at all of this casual oddness -- a nervous, misplaced giggle that couldn't last, quickly turning to sobs.

His clothes were clothes again.

Nobody had weight. Except for Elata, everyone was floating.

Diamond called out, "Seldom."

The boys started to wave at each other, and then the aircraft lurched upwards. Slamming against the floor, Seldom's trousers turned into a rigid skeleton, an insect shell. Nothing hurt him and he was tempted to enjoy standing again. But no, the room had to drop once more, slower this time, and drifting towards the ceiling, Seldom imagined the drunken pilot happily flinging them across the sky.

A bright wet sound burst from King's eating mouth.

Karlan laughed, and Seldom looked down.

The cabin floor was missing. The aircraft's belly had been stolen or eaten, or maybe it never existed in the first place. In a dreamland, everything was possible. Strange children and lost children were floating above a second, much larger room, that new space filled with machines and more people and what looked like empty beds waiting on the long sterile floor.

Imagining a hospital, Seldom let himself feel relief.

Then a mechanical arm reached high, nabbing him like ripe fruit plucked from the bakebear tree.

That wet heart was still beating, but only barely. A never-hot metabolism was suffering catastrophic organ failure. Highlighted knots of data caught Pallas' attention, and anticipating her questions, the diagnostic AI offered an odd word:

"Disease."

The patient was a zoo filled with bacteria and viruses and fossil viral codes. Much of that menagerie was benign, but a vibrant portion was parasitic or outright infectious. And even if the internal enemies could be vanquished, the patient's archaic genes were programmed to mutate and breed, and after a few decades, die.

This disaster began with Pallas' gun, and that blunder triggered a different kind of sickness inside her immortal heart.

Freshly built and fully-equipped, the hospital had risen up to meet them and then merge with their little stealth craft. The medical staff were as prepared as possible, only these were impossible circumstances. No protocol dared imagine any disaster like this. Multitudes of contingency menus had been drawn around late-arriving dragons and weak dragons and even dragons that emerged from obscure vaults. But nothing like this girl. "Elata." That's why the first duty was to rip away expectations. Doctors had to appreciate their phenomenal ignorance. The most benign tonic might stop that wet heart, or arriving with a touch, the blandest local microbe would poison Elata's blood. Marrow was a world full of potential hazards, and the world was dying on that tiny bed. Stakes and consequences couldn't be higher. That's why Mere dispatched her best available vehicle. Fusion engine after engine had come on line, the hospital rising from the atmosphere but not into the surrounding buttresses. Riding that thin layer of safe vacuum, it had circled Marrow once before slowing and dropping, making the rendezvous. Codes were offered, traditions named, and every dragon studied the flight path as well as the emergency declarations. Mere's panic was compelling. That's why weapons weren't launched. Not even warning blasts from the Waywards. Just queries and invasive data probes, friendly words and diplomatic insults, and from underlings, personal attacks on the little dragon who was responsible.

Mere was a thousand kilometers in the future. With no orders left to give, she showed herself to Pallas. Neither mentioned shared fears or guilt, and offering encouragement wouldn't help either. Words and wishes meant nothing in a place like this.

The combined ship had retained the stealth's simple floor plan: A brightly-lit cabin, longer than before but just as crowded, with the single window near the stern. After charging through the vacuum, the ship had grown wings and was now settling into a careful descent. With feet on the floor, human doctors set to work, and the AI doctors grabbed up the two other mortals, quickly examining sick bodies and wet brains for clues about … well, clues about everything.

And Pallas? She was famished. Cakes of electrified lard were ready to eat, wrapped within that fabulous smokey flavor used nowhere but inside field rations. She was gulping her third cake when the initial reports offered themselves. Only Mere could see everything. A stoic expression claimed that nothing was remarkable or alarming. Just intriguing. The ancient lady scanned data streams and preliminary conceptual schematics, some of her focus and bits of her time invested on this unwelcome puzzle.

"Will I ever sleep again?" Pallas secretly thought.

Which was everyone's question, and there was no point sharing that either.

Then Mere nodded, confidently saying, "Well. It's always good to know what we shouldn't do."

"What shouldn't we do?" Pallas asked.

"Freeze her. For example."

Freezing was the obvious measure. Drench the body in liquid helium. That was the best trick to render a dragon harmless: Flesh and fluid turned into a human-shaped glass sculpture, the critical mind trapped but still alive.

Except dragons weren't supposed to have water-and-fat brains.

"She's too fragile," Pallas guessed.

"Or maybe not," Mere allowed. "But we've only got guesses about how that poor body would react. Cease all molecular motion? A worthy experiment when nothing's left to try. But I'd like to trust that an official account can be written afterwards."

Elata might well have be frozen, so little was happening.

"That poor body," Mere repeated. Then the lady fell silent, her mouth open, eyes turning away and then pivoting back, looking again at the vault-born girl when she said, "We need to know about the boy."

One strange boy was lying passively on a nearby bed, while the much larger fellow beside him was restrained with multiple straps as well as an invisible buttress. Intrusive wands pushed where they wanted to push, and Pallas felt obligated to be positive. "I'm sure we're learning a lot about them, madam."

"I mean the other fellow," said Mere. "The one Three Wings tried to murder."

"Because he was ordinary and in our way," Pallas said. Defensive, loyal to her own. "Sensors said he was normal, and Three Wings barely hurt him."

"Sensors." Mere shook her head. "Machines that spit numbers and dream up relationships between those numbers, and we call that data, and data, I need to remind you, has no voice or soul."

Did they have time for life lessons? Pallas didn't believe so, but being suitably irritated, she saw what older, more seasoned clan leaders would have recognized at once.

"The stabbed boy," she said. "He's their leader."

"Or feels he's in charge, yes."

"So we shouldn't have cut him."

No time to chastise. It was enough for Mere to nod while saying, "Every sound made by each of these children. We're throwing the recordings against libraries and code vaults. Every resource in my reach is being used, plus help from three other dragons."

The immortal boy and the harum-scarum stood together on the hospital floor, watching Pallas. Busy doctors had finished poking at the mortal boys, releasing the one and coaxing both to stand and move aside.

"I want to talk with the child," said Mere. "Except we can't place the language. AIs and linguists are trying, and failing. Which is remarkable, or it means nothing. Even that little judgement is too much."

Electrified fats churned inside Pallas' belly.

"But there is a workaround," Mere said.

"Yes, madam?"

"You are there, and you can speak for me."

Pallas didn't need to ask, "How?"

Two steel limbs unfolded. One limb was reaching for Pallas, the just-born hand turning to reveal a tiny bioceramic cyst.

"Shit," she managed.

With no time to waste, new fingers jabbed the base of her skull. That cyst was fabricated to fit perfectly into a pre-carved cavity against her brain. And the immortal boy suffered an identical, if rather more delicate assault. Mastering his language was impossible. Teaching him the Marrow dialect was impractical. But a new language, freshly cooked and phonetically similar to the boy's rough barks, could be shared with two people at once. And if they were taught just enough to trigger genuine conversation …

A prosaic, half-easy venture. In principle.

Except the trick meant shaping billions of pico-links between cysts and minds, and that involved electrical storms and surgical plasmas. A million years might have been lived without experience this particular misery, the entire universe made blazingly, excruciatingly white.

Invisible again, gliding low over a warm gray lake, Quest ate whatever was slow and small. Every meat in her former world shared a very particular flavor, proteins built from the same few amino acids, sweet fats and bitter sugars woven into the mix. But this world refused to be simple. Bug shells looked like bug shells, and jointed bug limbs worked the same as any beetle leg. Except instead of keratin, exoskeletons were silica. Hundreds of amino compounds built the local alphabet, lipid membranes were puzzles changing from from bite to bite, and even the simplest carbohydrate was tainted with alcohols and esters and iron. Iron gave every mouthful the taste of living rust. But even though nothing in the menu was familiar, there was genius inside Quest's guts. She skimmed the lake twice, growing as she ate, and once her body felt too large, she ate more before sloughing off what was weak and least effective. Fuel was essential. Speed, unused but barely restrained. And an even greater capacity to vanish. Camouflage meant bending light and eradicated odor, and that required still more power, which was why every other meal was shunted into her invisibility as well as a sequence of half-born bodies carefully folded and tucked away, ready to be used with the next emergency.

Weaving a sleek body and fins, Quest dove beneath the water's gray face. The lake floor was glass barely touched with silt. Waterborne insects tasted like those in the air, but there were lineages of fish and bodies that couldn't be confused for fish. Unique genetics, bizarre skeletons. This busy world was infested with multiple Creations. Making legs, Quest scampered across a beach and into the black forest. Every leaf was a half-dome catching the sunless light. Every tree grew taller by the breath, trunks creaking as new wood was built. The forest was full of crawling and running citizens, some burrowing through the hard stone ground, a few rolling like little wheels with brains. Quest sampled some of each. One fat citizen had two mouths like King and the same hard eyes, and Quest's sonar showed a robust King-like skeleton. But this was just an animal, delicious looking and foolish, and that's why she bit hard enough to stun it, then swallowed the oddity whole.

Her brother had a distinctive taste. The air surrounding King was full of lost cells slathered in fragrant oils that existed nowhere else, dipped in odd salts and rare metals.

This little monster tasted exactly as she imagined King would.

What's more, it was immortal. Razors inside Quest's throat slashed through the scales, but the wound healed quickly, turning into fire, and when her genius-stomach attacked the foreign tissues, her meal slashed her with spines and a dumb-animal roar.

She spat it out.

And in thanks, her prey tried to chew the head off her newest body.

Quest retreated, bending light and purging herself of every new stink, and then cloaking every sound with its mirror.

She was nowhere and nothing.

In a place where nothing would ever hide, she became the warm litter of dead black foliage.

Large feet were approaching.

And Quest jumped high. Devoted to one direction, the Eight had never seeing their sister, racing into the lake as the exhausted body collapsed. Then the long head dropped, giving up the luxury of breath in order to drink water and swallow alien bugs and at grab one lazy serpent-beast that twisted in smaller and smaller rings while being sucked down.

Not softly, Quest landed on the Eight's long back.

They were startled, and then they relaxed.

Relief, was it?

"Nine wise souls," said the long mouth. "We had the good sense to run."

Quest lifted, hovering in front of the face, only her voice exposed. "Do you want to know?" she began.

"Know?"

"What happened to the others."

The Eight said nothing. Which was sure evidence that eight opinions were struggling to find the best answer.

"Yes," was the final response.

"They were killed," Quest said. "Those rag-wearing children murdered everyone but you and me."

Another silence. Then, "Even King?"

In the old world, Quest never heard tenderness within that shared voice. But there was concern now, woven tight around a shifting point of pain.

"Those rag-wearers had a strange weapon," she reported. "A hotter, more awful fire than anything we've seen."

The Eight absorbed that sorry news.

Then she teased them with bright laughter. "No, I'm lying. Those children didn't hurt any of us too seriously."

Silence.

"But the tree-walking girl … she shot herself, and she's probably dead."

"Why did she kill herself?" the Eight asked.

"Because she couldn't run away."

Death was another escape, yes.

"The strangers tried saving the girl. I saw that much. Then everyone climbed inside winged machines, and I don't know where they went."

Another long pause.

"We ran for respectable reasons," her companions said finally.

"Tell me three reasons."

A halting, self-conscious voice attempted to explain itself, and the invisible Quest silently flew away. Yet the foolish Eight continued their confession, even as important noises were approaching. Aircraft were descending from a new direction. The Eight were about to be captured. But not Quest. She made that critical promise to herself, believing it well enough to build confidence. Flying for a long while, she carefully circled the gray-topped hill where Elata had died, uncertain what she needed until the moment she discovered a little battlefield. The oddest corpses that she had ever seen were baking in the brilliant, shadowless daylight. But nothing about the dead was dead. Immortal flesh insisted on flinching and twisting, mindless heads sprouting from severed necks, simple mouths breathing slowly while blind hands swept away a gathering of bugs and bright black worms, those smarter mouths relishing this wondrous bounty.

Every nation had its cadre of human and AI "doctors." True, flesh never aged, disease was all but impossible, and only the most catastrophic wounds refused to heal themselves. Except bioceramic minds relished a good calibration, and the most ambitious souls always craved vibrant, fashionable bodies. And true surgeons? They were the rare exceptions. Singular, narrowly devised specialists, the surgeons were tasked with butchering and patching imperiled tissues, and inside that elite profession, Padrone was one of the very best: An AI designed and dedicated for one job of consequence, which was to keep his dragon alive.

Mere was his dragon, and he should be with her now. But the dragon broke every protocol, ordering her surgeon's full consciousness uploaded into the hospital mainframe. Padrone's mission was simple, his orders explicit. Mortal dragons didn't exist, not in history or even as an irrational fear. Yet children in the wilderness found a mortal dragon -- a tiny thread of biology that might die within the next few moments. Only Padrone could save the world. That was obvious, and he accepted his responsibility. Gladly. Chance put everyone in peril, but chance also gave him this opportunity to prove his mastery and ensure his legend.

Padrone was a psychopath. The best surgeons always were. Empathy might be a laudable skill for lesser physicians, but compassion and understanding were banal distractions too. The soul floating beside the operating table didn't seek distractions. Patients were collections of body parts, and the surgeon needed to recognize how the various pieces fit together and what was broken and what was deadly. Concern would do nothing but burn time, while grief and doubt were even more dangerous. These were suffering bags of intricate and occasionally beautiful pieces, but the consummate healer was willing to torture those pieces, using every tool and in the most savage ways, because cold brutality was often the only way to save the Whole.

After the hard flight and rendezvous, the hospital was returning to Mere. But surviving the descent seemed unlikely. This new dragon was pathetically, inexcusably weak. A female. Age: Almost nothing. Asymmetric and decorated with scars, the body was already festering with microbes fought to stalemate by an immune system that was temporary and stretched thin on its greatest day. Trying to murder itself, that brain had revealed its own deep weaknesses. This suicidal creature was made from water and slow, despairing fats, the blood ancestral in the broadest fashion, yet full of specific proteins and key markers never mentioned in any literature. This patient was an insult of improper flesh, and that's what Padrone announced, cursing furiously in every known language.

The other doctors, machine and human, didn't physically retreat. Yet there were other ways to give his anger distance, and for the next moment, Padrone enjoyed the freedom to make gigantic decisions.

He was Mere's surgeon, after all.

Until now, she was the weakest dragon in the universe.

The silence ended when he announced, "Well, so be it."

"Yes?" the others asked. Or thought. Or no one spoke. He heard nothing but his own crucial thoughts.

"We will put this one through the oven," he declared.

Which had never been done and might not be possible with this kind of tissue, and suddenly these doctor-mechanics were united by their doubts.

None of that mattered.

"As fast as possible," Padrone said. "We turn the raw into the half-finished, and we'll do it properly, and when we land, a smiling dragon walks upright into her million-year life."

She didn't sing, she spoke. A small distinctive sound.

"Pallas."

Her name, and the name didn't need explanations, just as the following noise was understood suddenly and easily.

"This is a new language," Pallas explained, pointing at her mouth.

"My name," he said. With fresh words, not the old.

"Yes?"

As before, he said, "Diamond."

The name's significance went unmentioned, but Pallas nodded enthusiastically, her finger aiming at the bed.

"Elata," he offered again. Which wasn't adequate, and he added, "Elata's one of my best friends."

The newest strangers wore white and acted like doctors, examining the brothers as well as

Elata. Except they were backing away from their patient now. Maybe they were silently directing the busy machinery, except they stood like fiercely interested spectators, nothing more. And how could they matter? Elata was surrounded by an army of marvelous machines. New arms sprouted fingers of every shape, every purpose, while needles by the dozen were shoved inside the chest and stomach, the largest of them plumbed into bladders of colored liquid dangling from a distant ceiling that never stopped producing marvels.

Pallas repeated the name, "Elata."

Suddenly the human doctors found important work.

"Elata," one said. Then all of them sang in one perfect, shared voice, trying to encourage a girl who could hear nothing.

"Diamond," Pallas repeated. And winning his gaze, she made a pistol with her hand, pointing the straightened finger at her own belly. "Why?"

"My friend has been sad," he offered.

Pallas didn't appear satisfied.

"Sadder than anyone should be," he added.

That was a weak answer. Sadness and grief shouldn't make anyone give up. Diamond certainly wouldn't. Witnessing his father's murder, the boy became furious, and then energized. A good rage now would help give him a larger, more compelling voice. Except he was mostly sorrowful, carrying loss and helplessness that could only partly cover up the anger that was directed at the girl he could barely see beneath those swift mechanical arms.

"Why is she sad?" Pallas asked.

"Elata's been … " The new language was large but tidy, making it easy work to find the best word. "Melancholy. My friend has always been that way. Then bad things happened in her life, and everyone else's life, and that was before we came here … "

His voice trailed off.

Pallas looked at Elata, and maybe she was silently speaking to others.

"You're nice," Diamond said.

Surprise. "Am I nice?"

"For doing so much for my friend, working so hard to save her."

But Pallas didn't want compliments. "No, Diamond. No one else would deserve this. Your friend is just that important."

"The infinity bottle," he guessed.

She stared at him.

"Inside her. I saw it. You're talking about the bottle that never ends."

"The klein," she said.

"What is that?"

"The klein is a marker."

He repeated the new word.

Pallas opened her mouth but said nothing, perhaps listening to someone else's important voice.

"I'm important too," he said.

She considered him.

"I'm exceptional." The statement felt true until it was noise. In this place, surrounded by marvels and by unbreakable people like himself, Diamond's voice was the most unexceptional detail.

Pallas said, "Maybe," and nothing more.

Diamond waited.

"The klein is a marker," she repeated, fingers drawing a bottle in the air. "By itself, a marker means nothing. But as a symbol, the klein is critical. Woven from shadow matter, permanently tied to the bearer's mind, kleins can't be faked or stolen. And once set, they can never be removed. Every klein serves as a warning to everyone else. The bearer is a genuine dragon, and we must appreciate what she is."

A new word had arrived, without context. "What does 'dragon' mean?"

"In its oldest form? The dragon is a giant beast that spouts fire."

Diamond imagined wood burning, a jet engine throwing flames, then corona bodies blazing inside a sunless world.

"Your friend is a dragon," Pallas said.

He said, "No." And after some hard thought, Diamond said, "No," again, with all of the authority he could muster.

Pallas gestured at the ceiling. "There's a special fire, Diamond. A heat and light so large that they will incinerate this world. And all that it takes to bring the fire is for one dragon, any dragon, to die."

That was ridiculous. Pallas' explanation felt impossible, and worse, it was silly. Obviously Diamond's newborn language was already broken.

From inside his old language, he said, "Elata isn't like that."

"I don't understand you," Pallas said.

Back to the new words again. "She's just a human girl. I'm the one who matters. And my siblings."

"Elata isn't your sister?"

He had misstepped. Said too much. But could any secret remain secret? These people knew everything about everything, their magic woven from metal and light, including the blurring machines weaving a cocoon around his comatose friend. Having no idea how they would save her, Diamond had no doubts that they would. And it was obvious that these sorcerers read each other's minds, which was why telling them everything was inevitable.

"She's not my sister," he said.

"We saw others on the hilltop," Pallas said.

Maybe everything should be told. But Diamond would give away only what he wanted.

"I am important," he insisted.

The blue girl smiled suspiciously, her teeth even whiter than Diamond's teeth.

"I was born in a very different world," he explained. "Not Elata's home, but somewhere else. My original parents hid me inside her world. Because I was so important, and because I had to be kept safe. But my real father told me that I had be somewhere else … and I think this was where I belong."

"Your real father," she said.

"I remember him."

Diamond wanted to sound certain, but he knew very little. A father remembered inside a few dreams wasn't close to being real. What Diamond understood best was that he was deeply ignorant about everything.

"Elata shouldn't be the dragon," he said. "I should be."

Pallas was watching and listening to people nobody else could see. Or she was exhausted, too numb to pay attention to the slippery delusions of one unimportant captive.

"Monsters of fire," he said.

The blue face ignored him.

"Who are these dragon monsters?" he asked.

Her eyes shut and then opened slowly. Only a slice of her attentions found him. "We have six dragons."

"Show them to me."

Her eyes closed again.

Elata's bed and body were enclosed inside the new cocoon, and the white-clad humans were hugging and weeping, sharing joy or misery.

"Show me the dragons' faces," he insisted.

Pallas seemed to ignore him. But then a curtain appeared beside the two of them, flat and silver and almost pretty. Diamond saw his own reflection standing inside what wasn't solid and possibly wasn't real. Then he was gone, replaced by six distinct faces.

Pallas was watching the crying doctors.

Diamond poked her and then pointed.

And with even more confidence, he pointed again.

"That's my father, and she's my mother," he said.

That blue face looked at him, at nothing but him.

"Save my friend," said Diamond. "Save your world and Elata too. Then I will tell you the rest of what I know."

FIVE

The weak enjoyed one grand blessing. They were
free to believe whatever they wanted to believe.

No one alive today was remotely weak.

Strength meant seeing the dangers that
were everywhere. Marrow was built on hazards and
pitfalls, failure and everlasting terror, each of your
enemies standing ready to do battle, and the worst
enemy was the deep past. True history once
existed -- some proud, clear-eyed account that
could be trusted. But honest story was built on
details, and the aeons had stolen away the critical
minutiae. Every account was dipped in murk,
tainted evidence twisted into knots. Even the
eternal mind was sick with mistakes and hope and
other failures, making it unreliable. "Memory is
happy only when it lies." A dragon had no choice

but to believe that, and only a precious few tricks still existed that might reveal the lost, inescapable past.

Sleep. That was one route to reclaim your history. Not because sleep gave rest, though the fresh head was often less incompetent than the exhausted kind. No, what sleep offered was moments when the spirit forgot its tension, when she found herself drifting between endless life and something else. That was when genuine memory might offer its service. Great reaches of time became transparent. A life larger than worlds was small again, and you remembered some honest thing. A detail vivid genuine and true. Untold ages of falling into sleep had taught you that precious skill. That's what this game was about. Eyes closed more easily when the soul appreciated that every left-behind moment could be wrung out of a brain that always woke again, and probably in a very little while.

Of course another consequence of sleep was dreaming, and dreams were something else entirely. Lies, more than not. Obvious and toothless, and if you were lucky, fun. There was some first mind in the universe, and she fell into sleep, into dream, and then she woke again, refreshed by nonsense. A tiny soul was roused by the false memory of a meal or mate or perhaps both of those joys wrapped inside one delicious body. And billions of years later, dreaming souls still relished feasts never eaten and loves never endured.

How old was this dragon?

Perfectly rested, undistracted by circumstance, her mind was helpless before that preposterously simple question.

"Ancient" was inadequate in so many ways.

Every dragon began brilliant. That was what they told one another, told themselves. Bioceramic minds could hold the richest life, plus a little room left to grow. There must have been days when the dragons told fresh jokes, perhaps over good wine, and they laughed with new lovers who weren't exactly like old lovers. What could be more perfectly reasonable? Yet those grand times had been buried beneath routine and death. The sameness that must endure, nothing new given its chance. But at least you still had the freedom to fill a narrow cot inside what passed for your home, eyes closing and the immortal mind eager, summoning that face that you haven't imagined in a hundred million years. Not a special face, no. And there is rarely a name attached. Just one human face warmly smiling at you, and you smile back at him, and you sense, you know, that he has to be genuine. Which is when sleep comes and maybe the first dream involves that man's face, and a dreamed feast, and your uniform melts away, and you aren't a captain anymore.

Washen had just closed her eyes when Mere roused her.

"Madam," said the nexus reserved for the littlest dragon. "A situation has stumbled into my people."

It had been a very long time since she had been a captain. Why think of herself that way? The dragon sat up, blinked and breathed, and then waking completely, said, "Ready."

Yet Washen wasn't ready. A fierce little briefing was delivered. As outlined, the situation sounded frantically peculiar. An unmapped vault had spat out several odd creatures. That wasn't unheard of, by itself. Marrow was full of oddities, and the roiling iron never tired of bringing up relics and lost children. But Mere claimed that one of these new children held a klein, the universal symbol of the dragon. Which was an utterly, madly ridiculous.

That briefing ended with a promise for more news.

Was this the best nonsense Washen could dream about? Apparently not, because Mere soon returned with another fantastic claim: The new dragon had tried to kill herself, and she might well succeed. That familiar voice laughed in despair, and then Mere said, "I'm going to shake myself awake now, happily ashamed."

Washen knew the feeling.

"I need help," said Mere.

Washen had already authorized a hundred actions, each obvious and a few of them genuinely useful, most of those orders involving the discovery of old knowledge to fit inside the new.

"Everything I have," Washen promised. "The others?"

"I'll speak to friends next."

Two more dragons belonged to their tiny alliance. Aasleen, the Great Engineer, and Washen's closest friend and occasional lover, Pamir.

"As for the others," said Mere. "Warnings without detail, urgency without explanatory noise."

Questions begged to be noticed.

Washen stroked the back of her head. Hyperfiber was fixed to her skull, the focusing bowl and a plasma cyst perpetually ready to annihilate her and the world. Selecting one obvious question, she asked, "Do we know this dragon?"

Mere said, "No."

"You're certain?"

"A barely human little girl. Purely and unequivocally mortal."

"No."

"Yes."

"Never."

"Until this moment, I would agree with you."

Data were shared, and Washen yanked open her personal libraries, inviting scholars from Mere's camp to digest her inadequate records.

A larger question was offering itself, just as urgent and unanswerable. How could a dragon appear now? Marrow was loyal to its rules. Mere and Washen and the Marrow natives emerged only when the face of the world became cold enough to walk. That's how it had always been for Washen. Some dragon died, and if she wasn't the dragon, then she was present when the sky exploded. Either way, technologies barely mapped and never mastered made her live again. One infinitely brief death ended when she found herself standing on warm iron or fresh rock, or maybe ankle-deep in boiling water, lungs always empty but eager for that first scorching breath.

In principle, yes, a dragon might be found frozen inside an old vault or walk out under her own power. But that hypothetical figure had rarely shown up in history, and who ever bothered to imagine a fragile creature like the child who was dying right now?

"This vault," said Washen. "Is it remarkable?"

"Odd enough to see at a distance and send people to have a sniff," Mere allowed. "Something massive is underground, and it's old. Novel signatures, hints of unregistered technologies. But no, until today, nothing about this mission was crazy-abnormal."

Washen had no choice. "What is mine is yours," she promised.

"Thank you, madam." That was the undiluted habit. The subordinate verbally bowing to the one-time Great Captain.

And in the same vein:

"Save that girl," Washen ordered.

"I'm sending a full hospital and my personal surgeon, madam."

With that, Mere vanished into urgent work, and Washen launched her own tasks. Making ready for the end of the world: That was every dragon's existence. But with the situation so urgent, this particular dragon invited her son into her quarters, sharing the critical feeds with him.

The man was no dragon, and this Locke certainly wasn't her son. Not directly. Reality was built on endless variation, but reality was also lazy, preferring to draw from the nearest and the most likely. This particular Locke was a mirror of the man Washen gave birth to, persistently happy and stubbornly loyal. Found inside a high-grade vault, he was frozen and alone and thrilled to be rescued from the cold. He was also devoted to his quantum-mother. The underground aeons had stripped away most of his memories, which was a blessing. Those gaps in experience letting him enjoy novelty and any fresh path into experience.

"The girl will survive," said her son. "Or."

"Or?"

"She's someone's very big joke."

That was the happier notion.

Mother and son watched Mere's ships drop to the hyperfiber hilltop, snatching up the patient and her four companions.

"Is that all of them?" Locke asked.

Video pulled from a stratospheric drone said otherwise. Two more bodies had appeared on that hilltop. A fact never mentioned by Mere. And in the same spirit, the little dragon didn't share what was happening inside the stealth, or later, any critical events onboard the hospital ship.

"She'll tell you everything, if you insist," Locke said.

When Washen was a captain, Mere was hers to command. But no more. Each dragon had her own nation, and sad to say, all had compelling reasons to doubt the commitment and good sense of her peers. The alliance between these two ladies might feel as if it had lasted forever. But history and memory -- flawed as they were -- warned about past disasters. Was this why Mere draped her vessel in every kind of security?

"That little hill," Locke mentioned.

"And the vault below," Washen said.

They nodded, knowing each other's thought. These unexpected children might be very valuable. The new dragon might even be real. But just as intriguing was the relic that had brought them here, and quite a lot more might be waiting underground.

"The Waywards missed their chance," Locke said.

Important vaults surfaced where they surfaced. No reason but chance was responsible. Yet the Waywards' ambitious dragon tried to claim everything that sprouted from his ground and across the rest of the world too.

"Till has to be furious," Washen agreed.

Locke nodded, and he waited. Then at the appropriate moment, he asked what he could have asked ten minutes ago. "When will you call 'her'?"

The name itself had magic. That's what the cagey phrasing meant. But on the principle that nothing was magical, despite appearances, Washen said, "Miocene doesn't need my invitation.

She already knows more than we want her to know, and we'll see her face when it needs to be seen."

Whatever his past, Washen's son was a pleasant, ageless fellow, handsome and tall and strong in the best ways.

Washen was taller, dark and pretty without losing that serious, sober nature.

These two much-the-same people said nothing for a long while, studying feeds as well as their own thoughts.

It was Mere who interrupted the silence.

"That immortal boy," she began.

A child had galloped down the hill and was gutted for his trouble. "What about him?"

"He's made an intriguing claim."

Washen felt herself waking but then didn't.

"He believes that you are his mother, madam."

Washen glanced at stoic Locke.

"And his father happens to be another dragon."

"Pamir," Locke guessed.

Washen assumed as much.

"No. He claims Till."

Miocene's son, Locke's half-brother, and the eternal leader of the Waywards.

"Base genetics?" Washen asked.

"Analyzed," said Mere. "And I've looked at microchine markers and the brain's topologicals. The evidence suggests a boy who deserves all the pride and all the burdens that come from belonging to the two of you."

Time was finished. Breath and heartbeats and the dance of clocks were finished. This was Death, and the soul wanting peace had been given its peace, and Elata was happy. To cease. To be complete. Her life stripped from useless bone. That body was a gift to every other life, scavengers and rot and fire. Let some passionate beast take what the former tenant left behind. Her flesh would be another's responsibility, and free of burden, nothing would happen inside the boundless black.

Except for thought, it seemed.

Elata was definitely dead, yet a sprinkling of ideas continued to form. Images simple and quick. Words clotting around the clearest notions. This had to be the afterlife. She had proven the afterlife real. Which was a surprise and not a surprise. Here was one turn that she had imagined, and she was careful not to celebrate. The persistence of thought meant that the drearies were coming. Boredom was inevitable. Stubborn, useless thoughts cutting grooves into her ghost mind. Some color of insanity was inevitable. Elata was quite sure. An utterly terrifying end without end, undeserved and unfair, and to bolster her courage, she tried to laugh and then to curse, and hearing neither, she cultivated deep silence, hoping to fool the afterlife into believing that she must have slipped away.

And then change came.

What wasn't pain or pressure pierced a body that should feel nothing. Except the knives seemed real, tiny teeth in a thousand mouths gnawing at her organs, and what certainly felt like a voice drenched her with nothing but her name.

"Elata," she heard five times, and then a sixth.

The afterlife knew who she was.

Laughing again, she discovered her mouth.

Brittle, possibly pissed, the voice said, "Elata," a seventh time.

Something in the tone was familiar.

"Diamond?"

"Yes."

She barely recognizable him, and Elata certainly didn't sound normal, a bleached breathless voice asking, "What's happening, Diamond?"

"Not very much," he said.

Then he laughed, sounding sorry and happy too.

A fresh thought came.

"I'm alive."

"Yes."

"But not for long," she added.

"Maybe not," he agreed. "But Pallas told me --"

"Pallas?"

"The girl with the gun. The gun you stole."

Elata didn't care about any girl's name. "But I can't be. Alive? How did I survive?"

"Because they're saving you, Elata. We're inside their hospital, flying I don't know where."

"Those wild babies? How can they have aircraft?"

Diamond didn't answer. The boy who never had to think long about his next words. Then he finally allowed, "Things are complicated."

What wasn't complicated?

"You have a doctor, Elata. A machine doctor. He's smarter than any of us, and quick. Which is good, because he's doing surgeries nobody has ever tried before. Medicine that may or may not work. But if he succeeds, then you won't be wounded anymore. In fact, your doctor is going make you the same as me."

"I don't want to be a boy."

"Don't tease," he warned.

"I'll heal like you heal?"

"But faster."

This new, unanticipated reality deserved a good angry laugh.

Diamond spoke again, but to someone else, crisp little words making no sense.

A shudder passed through her body.

"Are we landing?" she asked.

"Not yet," Diamond said.

"I felt something."

"But you won't much longer," he said.

"Won't what?"

"Feel. They have to put you into a special coma. And when you wake, you'll look exactly like you should look."

"Dead?"

Exasperated, he said, "Stop."

"Apparently I can't stop anything."

"This is difficult to understand," Diamond said. "But you have to realize. Appreciate. This world can't let you die."

"That's what the blue girl told you?"

"Pallas. Yes."

"Oh, Diamond," Elata said, finding her sharp, teasing voice. "I'm dead for one little breath, and you already found yourself a new girlfriend."

The man wore a wide muscled body and wide brown eyes, bright black hair stolen from his mother, and a narrow face that was all his own. That was a memorable face that always rode the narrow borders between handsome and pretty, and average and plain. Standing on the Great Round, he sang to his enduring people and his AIs. He sang about heroes and sacrifice and the endless struggle to preserve everything everywhere and for all of Time. The most powerful creature on Marrow had the stamina to fill every day with soaring lyrics about commitment and pure objectives. Except nothing good came from overbearing stagecraft. No matter how right and compelling any truth might be, the audience eventually became too familiar and comfortable, and too smug, and worst of all, lazy in the presence of pivotal matters.

The singer always knew when fatigue was stealing his audience. The drift in the eyes, the reflexive quickness of the passion. That's when the dragon delivered some new flourish -- a cutting insight or a jolt of humor that left the multitudes engaged. Charisma. That was a piece in how Till inspired a sprawling nation, and charisma was why he stood above all other dragons. Except this eternal man didn't carry much fondness for leadership and its trappings. Charm could win any day, but the days rarely mattered. Unity was an ally in defending a frail, aging universe. But perpetual unity was never the goal. That's why the daily performances only came at the cycle's beginning. Weave unity into the cultural center, then step away, giving that passion ample room. Outside eyes, looking down from some high ignorant place, might consider the Waywards as being a half-coherent mob of fanatics. "Because we are," Till would sing, praising people and machines alike. Standing on the Great Round, watched by shameless proselytes, he cultivated the best kinds of mayhem. No leader could shape every mind. Who knew that better? And that's why every Wayward child was free to shape his beliefs and her beliefs, and more importantly, discover personal doubts and disbeliefs too.

There was direction. Despite appearances, orders came from the top. But Till didn't batter his nation with commands and ultimatums. There was only one inarguable mandate: Waywards were always making ready for the next annihilation and rebirth. If the details were in flux, so be it. The citizen had as many children as wanted, or none. City-states could be erected wherever their citizens wished, complete with dialects and customs to help them stand apart from neighboring Waywards. Ten sects might possess ten interpretations of an ancient text, giving rise to enthusiastic, ritualistic warfare. Because every cycle was entitled to its own history, and Wayward history had to be interesting. Havoc and corruption were spices, criminality was calibrated to remain just out of view, and there were even a few ambitious children who tried to carve away some of their father's ultimate power. And Till always had children. No other dragon was profligate -- another reliable proof of his embracing of the maelstrom.

Three-hundred-and-nine. On this very ordinary day, that's what Till claimed as his own seed. Two young daughters stood behind the singing dragon. Today's epic song was reliable, beloved. Outsiders invading Marrow: Till was singing about a holy war waged so long ago that it wasn't history, was barely legend. Yet this was the oxygen in every breath, and the enemy had a name, and singing, "!eech," gave humans and AIs the necessary chill.

Marrow was a great world riding inside the hold of a great starship. And the !eech were rapacious monsters in legend and fact and everywhere between. The Greatship was once a human possession, but the !eech stole it and then attempted to conquer Marrow. This song was a vibrant description of one battle inside the uncounted sequence of wars. In that, nothing was unusual. Every morning had its song, and Till was in the midst of his performance when those early reports arrived. A Wayward patrol had been ambushed, enemies beheading some children in the wilderness, which was a bit of bad news but not worth ending the performance. And his voice didn't break when the EM signal arrived, so bright and wrong that it shook the world. That signal came from near the headless boys and girls, emerging from a barely-worth-a-hard-look hill. Two events and maybe the ties weren't coincidental, but he kept singing. Because every response was obvious. Scouting parties launched themselves. Local probes were shaken out of their stealthy garb. And the nearest Wayward city decided to mobilize, in the off-chance that hill proved worthy of a name and a battle.

Then, even as little Mere threw an enormous machine past the sky, Till sang. The poorest dragon was spending a lot of fuel and trust for no defined purpose. Words about a mercy mission leaked out with the general intelligence. Which was intriguing, of course. But even these cascading events were barely more than curiosities. Nothing mattered but finishing the next verse, and that's what the Wayward dragon was accomplishing, with verve, while one of his daughters vanished inside a mobile command center.

Till happened to be a character in this glorious song, but he wasn't the protagonist or the funny observer or the soul destined to be the final hero. Yet he gave his younger self an exceptionally funny line, knowing his audience would roar its approval, and now there was time for updates to be piped through various nexuses.

Seven visitors were seen on the hilltop. Born from a vault that had ridden up from Marrow's interior. Perhaps. A vault of respectable size and mass, plus small or large hints of mystery. Lifting his arms, Till's rich voice delivered a single long note, and that was when he ordered the mobilized city to claim the hill and vault. "For Waywards everywhere," said the venerable script. While through a second nexus, he demanded briefings about these seven newcomers.

Details emerged slowly, which was unusual.

Two of the visitors had tried to vanish, though the largest was found again, on foot and appearing easy enough to catch. As captives or guests, the other five were riding back to Mere's capital, and there were hints and signs that one of them was … no, that wasn't sensible at all.

"A new dragon," one source claimed.

Then another twenty spies repeated the crazy claim.

Offered the impossible, skilled leaders were quick to shift tactics. A new crisis demanded focus and experience and energy. But confidence liked to overstep its talents, and Till refused the temptation. Till refused panic or to change course, and while he seemed to embrace chaos, whether inside his territories or throughout the unseen universe, he could remain stubbornly immune to events that threatened to distract him from the everlasting Ordinary.

A long, especially lovely verse had to be navigated, lyrics wrapped around dead heroes and dead enemies. Meanwhile, Till's daughter remained inside the command post, seducing a compromised machine that happened to belong to Mere's camp.

"You are beautiful and please talk to me," she purred. "With your beautiful voice tell me what you see with your beautiful eyes, what you hear with those lovely ears please please please."

The impossible dragon had been found. What's more, the machine claimed that the girl was mortal and injured and very close to death, but Mere was fighting to drag the creature back into some measure of health.

That news had to be shared with the singer.

Shock and disbelief. Till allowed himself both reactions. And even though the song continued, pauses and little stumbles in the lyrics were noticed by millions.

Then a stolen rumor arrived. Till had a new son, some odd boy fresh from the ancient vault, and it just so happened that Washen was the child's unlikely mother.

Measured against the new dragon, this was a less incredible story.

But only barely.

More data continued to arrive. Thousands of camouflaged AIs worked the wilderness, and one of them had just uploaded its logs from the last three days. Inside the useless and the magnificent was a snatch of peculiar telemetry. A more robust mind would have instantly recognized the importance, but this wasn't a major scout, just a stupid drone pretending to be a stupid insect. It dutifully reported meeting another pretend insect that had bit into it, and in response, the drone chewed on the offender. One of Mere's machines? No. The rude entity was shown to be organic, yet shifting its nature one way and then somewhere else entirely, and not only did the scout report what was seen and tasted, it also confessed deep puzzlement. The experience was very odd, and could it please enjoy an upgrade or two?

Analyzed and encrypted, the results were delivered to Till and only Till.

He was singing, mid-verse and at the epic's grand climax, when he suddenly fell silent.

The universe was glorious and mostly invisible, and Till appreciated that every mind had to be brilliant, and not just because of neural connections and the velocities of bioceramic thought. No, the functioning brain was blessed with hyperfiber wisps and flecks, and it was the nature of hyperfiber to reach across what was real. Every endless universe was just a single facet in the boundless array of existence and possibility. One old man, particularly a dragon immune to death, was forever in contact with his mirror-selves, and that was why a trillion Tills were standing upon the same Round, singing the same proven song, and why this one Till felt his universe shudder with the horrible, inevitable news.

The greatest dragon stood like a statue. Millions heard his song and then his silence. What was wrong? Something was horribly wrong. Then the handsome pretty ordinary face was filled with calm authority.

"I have news," he announced.

To his nation, he shouted, "The !eech."

He roared, "The !eech have returned to Marrow."

And in the next moment, with his boldest smile, Till announced, "And now the Waywards are at war."

Doctors tested flesh and mind. They wanted to know how Diamond was built and see if and how he was lying. Working fast was important, unless these people and their thinking tools were always so quick. Or maybe Diamond was seeing a careful, deliberate pace. He didn't know, could only guess. He wanted to ask quite a lot but Pallas was elsewhere, doing much or nothing and presumably at the proper pace. So he kept still while myriad fingers touched his skin, fingers of sound and bright light embracing his heart and rolling down his guts. He was electrified. Then for an instant, he was asleep, and waking, he was convinced that machines were in charge and people were their compliant helpers. Unless perhaps Pallas and the others were nothing but elaborate phantoms invented for the sake of a few young people cast into this furiously mechanical world.

The hospital was descending, but slowly. Elata lay inside her cocoon and her coma, while Diamond's other friends stood beside the window. Something was happening outside. Astonishment in the faces proved that. Seldom stood beside the glass, Karlan directly behind him, hands on his brother's shoulders, while King was the armored wall behind both of them. Each stared at things that were surprising and impressive. Even Karlan wore the wide-eyed shine of someone who couldn't believe what vision was offering him.

Warm glass fingers were pulled out of Diamond's mouth.

He called to the others. "Come here."

This was a worthwhile test. Who would abandon the window for him? Diamond assumed Seldom would rush over, but he hoped for King. Then he hoped for anyone. But nobody was willing to abandon the view. Glancing at Diamond, Karlan made a pistol from one hand, aiming at the distant, bewitching spectacle.

A human doctor approached, brandishing a bright little knife and mirror. When he was very young, Diamond used a knife to mutilate his own skin, trying to give himself a noble scar like his father's. But that knife was only steel. This blade was bright like glass and nearly weightless, the edge exceptionally sharp. With the mirror set floating in the air, the doctor's hand attempted to scar the boy's face. Blood flowed from the cheek and then stopped, and the wound's neat edges found each other, mending in moments.

With the same knife and motion, the doctor slashed his own face. But his injury healed so much faster, exactly matching the knife's pace.

This was no medical test. Diamond was being shown that he was painfully slow at patching tissue, which led him to wonder in what other ways was he inferior.

The knife was hidden away.

Thinking about that bright blade, Diamond called out, "Pallas."

She wasn't there and then she was beside him.

"I thought of something else," said the feeble, lying boy. "Maybe it's important. I don't know."

"Tell it," she said with their private, newborn language.

"No," he said. "I want to look outside first."

The blue girl considered, or she was asking for advice. But it felt like her voice and her decision when she said, "Come."

The window grew wider as they approached. An enormous city waited below them, flat lands covered with giant glass buildings. The buildings were like tree trunks, except they rose straight from the ground instead of dangling from the world's ceiling. Genuine trees stood between the towers, dark blue instead of green or black, and wide paths ran where people would want paths. Everything about this city was lovely and sensible. Shared purpose, a common plan, and Diamond couldn't stop thinking about the home forests that he missed more and more.

Long and heavy and full of dozens of bodies, the hospital ship nonetheless hovered weightless inside that brilliant air. The pilot was searching for a landing field. That's what Diamond assumed, and looking down as if to help the hunt, he mentioned his impression to Pallas.

"Except we aren't landing," she said. "We're waiting for others."

Seldom turned to him, asking, "What did she say?"

Diamond looked at the friend who hadn't come when prompted. "She says you're very handsome and she's claiming you as her husband."

The boy flinched, then smelling the joke, laughed.

"She says we're not landing," Diamond explained to everyone. "We're waiting for other ships."

"Not ships," Karlan said. Grabbing the idiot by the head, he forced Diamond's eyes into the distance. A dozen of these magnificent glass towers had uprooted themselves. Slowly and gracefully, they were tearing away the transparent walls while new pieces danced and then pulled together, weaving winged machines and quiet fierce engines that bent and then shattered the blue trees underneath them.

Seldom looked at Pallas when he said, "This city can fly."

"My friend says you're very lovely," Diamond said.

"He's right, I am beautiful," the blue girl agreed. Then she glanced at the ceiling, listening to another inaudible voice. A smile sprang out, and it was easy to see and hear the relief when she said, "The patient is saved."

"Elata?"

"Everyone is safe." Pallas touched Diamond's hand, her fingers hotter than his hot fingers. "And it's decided. We're returning to where we found you. To find whatever else there is to find."

Now the nearest buildings began uprooting themselves, the entire city finding wings. In the face of that astonishment, Diamond said, "I wanted to tell you, Pallas. In my world, there are these few bits of a very beautiful stone, and that stone looks something like the knife the doctor used to cut my skin."

Pallas stared at him while speaking to the invisible others.

"I was named after those rare gems," he added. "That's what 'Diamond' means."

She squeezed his hand, and with a firm voice said, "No."

"No what?"

"You're talking about a simple mineral. Made from carbon, and carbon is cheap, and if you know how, you can catch a person's breath and build nations out of diamond sheets and fullerene weaves."

And with that, Pallas pressed his cool palm against the gemstone window.

The women meant everything to each other, but they were not friends. Friendship would be an encumbrance, another vital task requiring relentless attention. No, they had a negotiated union and zero choice in everything important, and while each held the same station and rank, they weren't colleagues either. Colleagues belonged to some greater organization, and should one die, the organization stubbornly persisted. But that wasn't true about dragons. Each was her own organization, and the death of either ignited the sky, and then time would leap to a different moment when they would return to life, each stumbling across a different portion of the blasted, marginally liveable landscape.

There was no escape from what wasn't duty or a noble calling, much less any job. That was that nature of existence. Each dragon would be reborn on the next Marrow or the one after, or maybe she wouldn't emerge until some distant incarnation of this utterly familiar world. But with zero choice in these matters, each let herself become smothered inside the relentless business of ruling whichever piece of the iron ball came to her cursed soul.

These two were allies and better allies than most dragons, but they were distinct in character and outlook, insults and slights and more than a few wars dotting their shared past. Washen loved the Greatship more than she loved any living soul. How many times had that been established? But love demands devotion, and devotion invites certain species of failure, beginning with sentimentality and predictability. While for her part, Mere was far too enthralled with exploration. She was the dragon who compulsively pried open vaults, studying the residue of past ages, and there were days when it was better to be Washen: A smart ageless lady following the script, ignoring mysteries waiting inside another dragon's trash.

But today brought the exceptional. A new circumstance had found them. No script was in hand, and no impulse seemed wiser than every other. An impossible dragon was fixed to a buried marvel, or she was fixed to nothing, and this situation demanded smart actions taken while sidestepping debates or confusion that would waste critical moments.

"Eight sleeps and fifty percent," said Mere.

"Eleven to make fifty," Washen said.

A dragon owned the ground beneath her capital city. These two were estimating how quickly they could transport half of their capitals to that anonymous hill.

"My hill," said Mere.

The simplest declaration of ownership.

Washen skimmed the official claim while documents were forwarded to her scholars. "I'll contest your claim. On parentage, probably."

If Diamond proved to be her son.

"And Till?" asked Mere.

"Is free to claim the boy and everything associated with him." Legal onslaughts would leave a huge muddle, and muddles meant time to find fresh ideas. "What about the harum-scarum?"

"A depleted young male with archaic signatures," Mere said. "Unrelated to every harum-scarum on Marrow today."

"Pamir will make his claim."

"Absolutely."

The ladies were equals and friendly allies, today and presumably for another million years. Unless mistakes were made. A shared past full of alliances made during huge campaigns and little battles, and who could trust any count? But one war stood apart. Only four dragons were born on that unlikely Marrow. The insects and three humans ruled the iron, and the human nations appeared divided and weak. This was the rarest circumstance. That's what their enemies saw, and that's why the !eech attempted a lightspeed invasion. Three holes pierced the sky, and the !eech descended, trying to capture the quarreling dragons. But weakness was a lie. Till and Washen and Mere had set an elaborate trap, complete with false selves and hidden armies. The slaughter was magnificent, and thorough. Even better, there was one long day when three dragons, working together, could have lifted the fight into the Greatship. But Washen scuttled the attack. Defeating the !eech wasn't as important as her love for the ancient machine, and that's why she held back her forces, refusing to burn and blast those high strongholds. And despite a trillion blessings and the endless kind words, Mere couldn't forgive the woman that she had mistakenly admired.

More wars were fought, hard-won sometimes but more often ugly-lost. Lost meant that one dragon died or all died and Marrow burned itself and the invaders. But while the pattern felt eternal, it was not. Time passed and the !eech invasions became less likely, and then unusual, and at some ill-measured point, no one came from overhead anymore. Their enemies grew cautious or turned weak, or the invading !eech had realized that the only wisdom was to wait, doing nothing but nothing, trusting the ages to give them a remarkable Marrow born without human dragons.

Whatever the cause, ages and aeons had passed since the last invasion. The Greatship was still above them, or it was not. Either way, the sky was sealed, and the fabulous starship existed as an abstraction, just as unknowable and unusable as a universe punctuated with suns and living worlds, species beyond any census and a furious vacuum growing colder by the moment.

How long since any dragon had left this drop of iron and rock and stubbornly living souls?

The days refused to be counted.

"Aasleen," Mere prompted.

"Nineteen sleeps to make fifty percent," Washen reported.

The Dragon of Machines presided over the most distant nation. But her people were AIs, often tiny and swift, and nineteen days revealed a distinct, rather surprising sluggishness.

Mere said nothing.

Washen nodded. "Twenty sleeps and one hundred percent for Pamir."

Pamir was fond of small cities full of aliens, particularly harum-scarums and other robust species.

Intelligence reports and long conjectures demanded study. The next pause stretched out for several moments before Mere said, "Your new boyfriend is beating all of us to the target."

Till, she meant. And bless her, Washen had the grace and ease to laugh at the little dragon's joke.

"The Waywards are mobilizing," each woman reported, inside the same moment.

The scale of the preparations was what impressed them.

"Even if he knows that Diamond is his," Washen began.

"On the basis of just that."

"He wouldn't."

The largest nation was a disunited, many-minded tribe. Unity was an easy trick when ten million bodies were ruled by a retired Ship officer. But five hundred million Waywards was a good estimate, and hard work was required to make chaos walk a narrow path. Yet Till's children weren't just donning guns and launching fleets. They were ripping open the new earth, weaving what looked like munitions factories that would be finished in another ten sleeps, each of them capable of spawning new fleets even before the other dragons could transplant their capitals to that mysterious hill.

What made Till so decisive?

One answer offered its service.

"My new son's father," said Washen. "He imagines even more interesting treasure inside that vault."

She paused, and Mere joined the silence. Then.

"Those two missing children," both said.

Both said, "Perhaps."

Deeply familiar with one another, linked in too many ways, the immortals anticipated each other's mind.

"I'll meet with the five babies I have," said Mere. "Then fly them back ahead of my people."

To help establish her claim.

"But I'm a very poor girl," the little dragon added. "And if he wants, Till could fill the Blisters with people and towns and rounds and gun emplacements."

"You need help."

"Always."

"One choice."

"Which means no choice," Mere agreed.

"I should be the voice," Washen said.

"Make our plea, yes."

As a captain, Washen had ruled by consensus and empathy. But those two beauties weren't going to be particularly helpful now.

"You have Miocene's respect," Mere said.

There was no denying the fact. With a sigh, Washen allowed the conversation to ebb. No other dragon had the resources, the power or the will, to inject a compelling force into the middle of the Blisters. Would either woman dream up a better plan? Not likely. And that was why Washen agreed.

"A personal appeal would be best," she said.

"Remind the lady just how much she loves her son," said Mere.

"And hope her affections won't spark war."

On the thinnest edge, the world was pivoting, yet the old women made time to enjoy some long and hard and very grim laughter.

SIX

Deep dark purple found Elata's eyes. Except the
color was wrong, overcooked and ridiculous. Even
the richest purple wasn't this intense, and in the
same fashion, these eyes felt like mistakes. Too
sensitive, too acute. Elata tried to close them but
failed, and not having hands to cover her face, she
couldn't shut out the purple that was beautiful but
definitely not the same color that she loved in the
old world.

  Was this the answer? Did every world's light
bend in its own particular way, and was this world
drawn from fancier shades?

  That idea was scary and fetching and made
her a little happy, which was another oddity.
Happiness. That was one of the more peculiar

qualities percolating through a mind that didn't belong to her anymore.

Then the purple was lost, a soul-searing blue filling the void, and Elata quit trying to shut the stranger's eyes.

A tone began. Deep and low, the sound seemed to rise from her middle, shaking a body that felt just a little familiar.

Elata wanted to talk. One word, that's what she managed, her voice enormous and the word completely wrong. "Hello," she intended to shout, but an unexpected noise came charging from the mouth. That single bright note meant, "Hello," and she knew that without trying to know it, and another wrong word followed after.

"Blue," she said.

"Is that what you see?" a man sang.

Startled, Elata fell silent.

"Elata," said the man.

He used her birth name, said it properly. But even though every other word was wrong, she couldn't stop understanding this very different language.

Once more, she sang, "Hello."

"Now tell me what you hear, Elata."

Music, but not one song. Three tunes played together, and she heard each well enough to follow rhythms and the lyrics about love, which was as silly as anything that had ever happened in Elata's life.

She laughed.

Thankfully that sound hadn't changed.

"What do you hear?" the man asked.

"A stranger asking questions."

The man introduced himself. "My name is Padrone."

"Hello, Padrone."

"I'm your surgeon," he said.

"You saved my life?"

"I gave you life."

"So I managed to die after all." That was a victory. Her goal had been reached, and then this foolish doctor yanked her back again. Which was probably an easy trick inside a realm with impossible blues and purples.

Padrone ruined the celebration. "No, child. Your suicide failed."

"So you're keeping me alive."

"No. I made you live."

"I don't understand."

"Because you misunderstand life." Flat, unsentimental fact. "What you were before was simple, Elata. The most rudimentary organic existence masquerading as true life."

"True life," she repeated.

"The anaerobic bacteria burrowing under the black floor of a lake," he said. "You were a little more elaborate than they are."

Elata had never seen a genuine lake, yet she understood. And she more than imagined water. The muck and stink turned real in her thoughts. What looked like a black blanket was stretched across the bottom of the water, the blackness filled with furious little sacks of water and busy chemicals. Which triggered the memory of sitting in the classroom, sharing a microscope with Diamond. Sharing squints at tiny sacks busily making new sacks, and the moment was as real as that day had been.

"Diamond," she said. "How is he?"

"That boy happens to be alive."

She said, "Good," and then saw what the doctor meant. "Diamond is the same as you. True life."

"Nobody is same as me," Padrone said.

Was he proud? Elata couldn't decipher the voice.

Her surgeon continued. "Diamond and the harum-scarum live in the expected ways. But the other boys are unaugmented, which makes them frail and temporary. And true life should never be that way."

"Temporary," she repeated.

"Life gazes on the Eternity," he said.

"I thought I could," she said.

"No, but now you can."

Multiple thoughts fell into one searing idea. "I wish you hadn't."

Padrone said nothing. Her saviour might be conferring with others, except there was no evidence to support that impression. The girl who couldn't close her eyes saw nothing but a rich shimmering green, and the three songs had ended, and someone's heart was beating slowly, but with enough strength to be felt against ribs that certainly felt like her ribs.

"What are you doing, Padrone?"

"Making ready," he said.

"For what?"

"All of you must be alive."

"Oh."

"And this very important work requires additional resources, far more knowledge, and a rigorous, creative plan."

"You sound like a smart person."

"I'm not a person."

"But are you alive?"

"More than ever, yes. And thank you for that gift, Elata."

Others were talking.

"Children playing with a ball," said Kai.

Every voice was busy.

"And we are the ball," he added.

Which no one seemed to notice.

But he was loyal to the image. "These children are kicking us exactly where they want us."

After the foul water, after meeting and losing Quest, the Eight were still intent on escape. Aircraft had passed high overhead, but those pilots didn't pay attention to a solitary figure charging across the twisted landscape. Lower, slower aircraft had circled, but they soon dropped behind the hills. Only one band of feral humans bothered chasing the Eight. Sometimes they screamed in that singsong language, sometimes they shot into the galloping body with guns that did no lasting damage. But they never ran fast enough. The beasts were inept, or they didn't care. Or Kai was right and this was how it felt like to be a rubber ball driven by expert feet.

The next slope lifted them, and reaching a long ridge, the Eight slowed. The black trees were fewer and smaller, and feeling exposed, most of the voices began to argue for a change in tactics.

"Suggestions," Tritian said.

"Hide," some wanted. But where and how? And assuming they could disappear, what would that accomplish?

Others wanted to confuse their enemies. Taking control of one arm, that alliance tossed a stick high, declaring that the sharp end would decide their new, unexpected course.

The plan died before the stick hit stone.

"Listen to me," Kai begged.

"Say something useful," Tritian said.

"We can't escape. So we surrender on our own terms."

Some laughed. Maybe at Kai, definitely at their own fears. But the Eight were lost in a world filled with violent monkeys. These were circumstances where Divers always excelled, and that's when her voice returned, tyrannical and smart and convincing. Not only did she give her full support to Kai's suggestion, but then offered a scheme better than anything he could have envisioned: An elegant surrender; the declaration of Self.

Without a whisper of debate, the decision was made.

The Eight fell into a determined walk. Glassy black blocks and razored shards looked as if they were thrown from a furnace yesterday, yet trees were already growing inside the deep cracks. Black trees with parasol black leaves squeaked and moaned, chasing the shadowless light and the gray ceiling. But there was one white tree considerably larger than the others, and dead. Killed by some outrage and conveniently stripped of its bark, the exposed wood as smooth as the finest paper.

Two shards of glass became happenstance knives. Slicing into the wood, the Eight drew a quick picture of the vertical realm full of monsters, below and above. This was their former world, and they put themselves floating between, but instead of carving a single body, each hand was shared four ways. Pale dead sap bled as lines met lines. Sketch after sketch. All their days of life, and the Eight had never attempted this simple, blunt exercise. They drew themselves as individuals and then cut that shared body wherever their own blood was richest, dabbing their distinct color and chemistry on these rough little self-portraits.

Nobody resembled anyone else, yet none seemed convinced by their own shape. Even Divers, carrying so many human traits, gave herself an upright, monkey form, but with eyes standing on stalks and a stern, tooth-packed sucker in place of the simple human mouth.

They worked, and fleets of aircraft conspicuously ignored them, and the living trees grew higher and deeper, and from several directions at once, gruesome babies moved on bare feet, stealthily pressing closer.

Kai and Tritian were last. Tritian dabbed hot orange blood onto what looked like a squat human. But without any blood of his own, Kai shoved bits of black glass into a many-legged serpent that never stopped disappointing the artist.

Even as the children came out of the forest and down from the treetops, Kai was adding flourishes to this inadequate image.

"I need to show what I am," he told himself.

Show whom?

"I need to see me," he muttered with the long mouth.

Then a flash brought one thunderous crack, and the borrowed hand was gone, and while the other Seven screamed in outrage and misery, the tiniest of the Eight fell silent, watching the white wood burn, the carved lines erased and the careful dabs of mismatched blood peacefully boiling away.

A building had climbed into the air, and for no reason but to swallow the hospital ship. Yet this marvel couldn't be more routine. It wasn't just the colored children who ignored what happened outside. Seldom wasn't watching, and neither was Karlan. A diamond-skinned building was eating them whole, yet the brothers sat on the floor, one laughing and the other crying, but neither throwing much energy into those efforts.

"The monkeys won't stop talking about you," said King.

Busy people and singing voices filled the hospital, and Diamond heard his name in the clatter.

"And don't believe the smiles," King added. "There's fear here. Wrapped around Elata's name, not yours."

"She's the **dragon**."

"And what in vomit does that mean?"

Diamond's fingers danced like fire.

His brother didn't care about silly fingers. "Do you remember any shadow of this world? Do you half-understand what you're seeing and why it has to be?

"No, no, and no."

"But you keep trusting what you hear."

Looking past the window, Diamond let his thoughts run. The airborne building was floating, unaided by gas bags or propellers. Crystalline walls had torn themselves apart, every shred moving with purpose, reforming into a mouth or doorway, or something else. What name was best?

"My parents are here," he told King.

"Point them out."

"On this world, somewhere."

"I know what you meant."

A wry smile broke loose. "Both of them are dragons."

King stared at his monkey brother. Threats everywhere and those scales had to remain extended. Yet nothing else about the giant was menacing. "I know your mother," he said. "And Haddi would tell you that you're a foolish boy running on a narrow tree limb."

The great doorway closed over them, the hospital gently shuddered, and standing on the trembling limb, Diamond fought to keep his eyes dry.

"Look," said King. "The blue girl wants the dragons' son."

Pallas was standing beside the Elata's cocoon. Diamond joined her, effortlessly summoning the new language. "How is she?"

"Healthy and growing strong."

"Good," was a small word that couldn't be repeated enough.

"Come with me," Pallas said.

But Diamond touched the cocoon first. Its surface felt like a fancy ceramic pot, slick and hot enough to scorch normal flesh. His friend was wrapped inside this heat. But should he believe what his fingers told him? Every one of these impossibilities might be a lie.

"Come on," Pallas said. "Someone wants to meet you."

She walked, but Diamond remained where he was. He wasn't sure why, and then he was. "The others," he said. "I want them with me."

"They won't understand what we say."

"So we talk slow and I explain."

The blue girl thought hard or pretended to think. Then she waved at the tall milk-colored girl while giving an inaudible command. The milk girl pulled King by the arm, then kicked the sitting brothers until they stood. A door had appeared inside the hospital's hull. The flexible walls were humming when Pallas and her lieutenant stopped short, waving them through, and Diamond entered a room built moments ago, woven from a shredded building, or maybe from a million anxious breaths.

The door closed or never was.

A silver-haired woman was waiting beside the far wall -- the woman that Diamond had seen inside Pallas' floating screen. Or she was someone else. Maybe a thousand important people wore that face, like soldiers sharing the same reassuring uniform.

Using the new language, the woman said, "Little."

"What is?"

"I am. Too small. Too slight. That's what my name means." Wide dark eyes defined a face that appeared badly starved. She was tiny, yes. But not insignificant. Wearing a simple smock, silver like her hair, she stood on bare toes, tiny feet unwilling to touch any more of the floor than necessary.

Diamond smiled at those feet.

"Mere," she sang.

The word seemed simple, but there were flourishes, depth and history. Or this was just noise, and Diamond was being foolish.

"Mere," he repeated, badly.

Then with a wink and an inquisitive smile, she said, "Diamond. Named for the gemstone."

"Yes."

"Who named you?"

"My parents."

Mere stared at his eyes, but he was certain that she was watching quite a lot more.

"Can you read my thoughts?"

That earned a tilt of the head. "Like words on a screen?"

"Words on paper," he preferred.

"Would that help our situation, cracking open your brain like a book?"

Diamond mulled that over, aware that the room and presumably the entire airship were beginning to climb.

"Well, we have played with telepathy," she continued. "Tricks and cheats have been invented. The head can be left transparent for every other head to peer inside. And how badly do you think that ends?"

"I don't know," he said.

She didn't explain. "I need to know everything about your home. About diamonds and your parents and all the rest. But your mind isn't a book. You'll have to sit down and tell me."

"All right," he agreed.

Seldom was leaning against Karlan, while King looked like an insect shell, discarded by the molt and left empty.

"But biographies must wait," she added. "I need to understand the heart of what's happening."

"What is happening?"

"The young woman. Elata."

"Yes?"

"Inside her … "

"The infinity bottle," he said.

"An excellent name." Mere let her heels drop to the floor, for an instant. Then she rose again, and somehow her face became even more intense. "We call it the **klein**. An ancient word, and it means nothing. Infinity bottle, the klein. Like any name, a sound given and then worn, and the name should mean quite a lot, but usually doesn't."

He nodded politely.

Seldom grabbed Diamond by the elbow. "What's she saying?"

"I don't know," he confessed. Then to Mere, he said, "This is a mistake."

"The klein?"

"It should be mine," he said.

Mere said nothing.

"I'm very important. They told me so."

"Who told you?"

"My mother. My father."

"The couple who named you?"

"No, they adopted me. And I don't know if my name is good or silly. But my first parents put me inside another world. I remember that much. They hid me to keep me safe." What else should he admit? "And my brother too. King. We were found together."

Confessions and half-truths were absorbed. Then a hard slow voice said, "This is an old game for me."

Again, Diamond offered polite nods.

"I've never known the klein to ride the wrong body," she warned. "And nobody has seen it emerge this late or inside a fragile piece of tissue."

Seldom yanked his friend's shoulder. "Is she talking about Elata?"

"Yes," Diamond said, never looking away from the little old woman. "You've never met anyone like us."

Mere said nothing.

"There is another world," he said, one finger confidently pointing down. "My brother and I came from there. With our three friends. I don't know why we're here, but King and I were babies when we were hidden. Millions of days could have passed before we were born, and that's why we can't remember details or the very good reasons for everything." He paused, considering. "Teach King this language. He'll tell you the same story."

"That your memories have degraded."

"The oldest memories have."

"Yet you're certain about your significance," Mere said.

"Yes."

"And the klein simply got stuffed inside the wrong body."

"Yes."

Two long steps, sudden and effortless, and then Mere was perched on her toes, the top of her head close to Diamond's chin. He smelled the woman. This person ate remarkable foods and lived on a different, very peculiar world, and she smelled different than any other person. Nothing had ever felt so alien as the human smiling up at him. Then she turned around, and a stern voice gave a simple command.

"Touch me," she said.

"What?"

"Put your hands on my skinny back," she insisted, leaning against Diamond.

The silver fabric was slicker than silk, her skin as warm as Pallas' skin. But the machinery rooted inside the skin was hard and cold. Mere wanted him to feel these knobs and bumps, and with hands shaking, he couldn't let go.

Seldom was offended. "What are you two doing?"

Then King reached out, one hand covering half of that willowy back.

Two steps and Mere was beside the wall again.

Facing them, she said, "My life began like yours, Diamond. A baby without parents. But strangers found me and adopted me, and maybe we are similar. I was living on a world of mortals, but I didn't die easily. That's why my adopted home considered me to be special. I was a god. But a very tiny god, as you can see. Weak and silly, and that's why they named me 'Mere.'"

Barely the beginning of a story. But this was an orphan's tale, and happiness enveloped Diamond, unexpected and comforting.

"For a few thousand years, I lived as a god. Which is not a long while. And then I left home, and for tens of thousands of years I served as an officer for a great vessel. A ship like no other. But that life ended, and next I became a dragon. Which is a much more important job than being an officer or a god."

"Why?" Diamond asked.

"Because. With a gesture or a secret thought, or perhaps even by mistake, I can obliterate this world. Everything you see burns to nothing, and I leave behind a barren hot blister. Which is how the world begins all over again. A process that has happened … well, a numbing number of times … "

Diamond flinched.

"What's she telling you?" Seldom asked.

"We fell off our branch," Diamond said.

"I don't understand. What's that mean?"

Diamond covered the boy's mouth with his hand.

"Now let me explain why this little dragon needs to be scared." Mere said that and then paused, waiting for Diamond's eyes. "Your Elata is genuine, or maybe you are. But the klein is just a name, and the marker inside your friend could be a lie too. Maybe there aren't any new dragons today. The very simple test is to kill each of you, starting with her, and watch what happens to the world."

"Please don't," said Diamond, in both languages.

"And there's another situation that wants me frightened. The old dragon standing before you, and all of these millions of innocent people who might die before their next breath … we're terrified by the other two. Those brothers or sisters who stood beside you when you first arrived. Maybe you don't know them. Maybe they emerged from a different impossible world, and that's why you avoid naming them. But I'm guessing that's not the truth. And if you can lie, then you must know more than you claim. Which is why I confess that I can't remember anyone, not in the last ten million years, who seemed half as dangerous as you, little Diamond."

The corpse looked like a short girl with a thick, stubborn body. The head had regenerated, complete with monkey jaws and a working tongue and bright imbecilic eyes. Corpses were reliable keys to any species, and Quest needed a key. Clinging to her invisibility, she dragged the prize first beneath a grove of black trees and then inside a deep crevice, and after eating the carrion flies and their eggs, she carefully peeled apart the treasure. Nothing was familiar, except for the very human architecture of the feminine body. The dead flesh was more vibrant than any fly, the bones bright white and tough to break. This was what would happen if Diamond's brain was stolen, or King's, or perhaps even her own. Quest knew how to build an auxiliary body and fill it with small, simple behaviors. Did the corpse hold any ideas? That freshly sprouted head was certainly trying to be normal, nostrils breathing and the yellow hair growing long. Maybe the body was waiting for its owner's return. But as she cut into the skull, finding spongy masses of fat, a more horrible possibility offered itself: The girl's true soul was hiding inside the stubborn heart, inside the white femurs and vivid red blood, and Quest was doing irreparable harm.

She paused, fingers turning gentle. Every mind had its mark, a visible signature of delicate, interplaying energies. And no, the only minds inside the carnage belonged to the maggots burrowing deep into their new home.

Speed was critical. A family would come hunting for their missing child, and Quest had no intention of being discovered. Her next disguise had to convince everyone. Yet it was unsettling, dismantling these vigorous organs, tasting them and studying what they did and then carefully fitting them back together. But always retaining a little of the deathless tissue, weaving a home where her true self could hide.

Quest put on this girl's vest and breeches, and on a whim, licked the soft leather and the bone buttons. These flavors surprised her, and she chewed at a hem and sucked on the girl's bone knife and then her dirty dead thumb. What kind of beasts made their clothes from their own immortal skin and carried bone knives carved from their own self-renewing legs? There was no way to prepare for that revelation. If one of these monstrous children appeared now, full-brained and strolling down the forest trail, Quest would have surrendered. Instantly, without hesitation, she would have laid down before the monster's bare feet. How could anyone resist demons this strange, this driven?

But nobody happened along, and the panic receded.

Quest imagined giant wings and rockets, her great new body racing across the world, chasing lost brothers.

A wonderful, ludicrous daydream.

Aiming small, Quest finished her girlish body and the new face, that warm flesh imbued with its own tastes and odors.

What next?

A skilled seamstress had given the vest pockets. A thin slab of something that wasn't glass was waiting inside the largest pocket. New fingers teased the object awake, and colors swam, sounds fighting for attention. A human was singing. Singing to her, nobody else. He was a handsome monkey, and the lyrics were more complicated than bird songs, impenetrable and frighteningly quick. But inside that ridiculous song, one word was repeated and repeated and repeated.

"!eech," she heard.

Some words were never allowed to change.

"!eech," he called out.

"I know that word," Quest muttered. To herself, using the human mouth.

Then she repeated what she recognized, a click of the tongue followed by that very simple "eech" sound.

The handsome man was replaced by a new creature. Three crystalline dome-shaped eyes rode a low-slung animal, jointed limbs carrying an armored carapace divided into five distinct sections. Quest had two eyes and three sections. But in every other detail, this could be her.

Once again, the girl would have surrendered. An unarmed child wandering past her little hole could have taken her prisoner. But nobody came and the enormity of the moment faded into a general, useful terror.

Past the trees, along a sweep of ground where molten rock had recently flowed, Quest found a much deeper, blacker cave. On bleeding bare feet, she ran underground, and eyes that could only pretend to be human watched images of the !eech. Then the handsome man returned, and she sat with him and listened to him as he sang about impenetrable matters that could be nothing but momentous.

Every doctor always asked the same unanswerable question:

"How do you feel?"

Except for Padrone.

"You're strong enough," he announced. "The cocoon is going to shatter, and you will stand."

Elata had eyelids now. She closed her eyes to the darkness and opened them. "You're done with me?"

"Hardly."

"Good. Because I don't feel finished."

There was a mind behind the male voice, and that mind was silent. Padrone was trying to decipher what his odd patient had just said. Unless responding to Elata was last on a list of priorities. Which she didn't like or accept.

"I feel odd," she said.

There was no reaction.

"I'm scared," she added.

"You are not scared," said Padrone. "And you'll master your new existence soon enough."

"Now that I'm alive," she said doubtfully.

White light appeared to her right, narrow and brilliant.

"Should I look at the light?"

"Or look away. Neither choice is wrong."

Elata was discovering how any inspiration always led to five more ideas and another fifty possibilities after that. A storm of notions that disagreed with one another, but that didn't matter. Every idea seemed thrilled to be sharing the same fabulous head.

"Padrone."

"Yes?"

"I love you."

"You don't."

"How do you know? Can you read thoughts?"

"I read very little," her doctor said. "I watch. The best knowledge comes from the informed eye absorbing the full ocean of data."

"Ocean," she said. "Oceans are giant bodies of water."

"They can be, yes."

"You gave me a new word."

"And thousands more," Padrone promised. "A bioceramic scaffolding has been applied to your tidal pool brain. Not a complete mind, but the local tongue is just one of its gifts."

"That's incredible."

"Quite incredible," he said. "Common physicians would have required surveys of the patient and hours of slow, well-mapped surgeries. But I had minutes, perhaps less, and you should be thankful that I'm far from common. I am the reason why the world survives."

"Well, congratulations. And thank you, Padrone."

Silence.

The white brilliance grew hot. Elata was ready to blink against the pain, except the nature of pain had shifted. Discomfort couldn't blunt the joy when radiance and its fire poured through these wonderful eyes.

"Padrone."

"Elata."

"Do I love Diamond?"

"Perhaps you do."

"Why do you say that?"

"The name induces fond reactions from your tissues. And in the next moment, fear. Human love is often manifested in those terms."

"Are you always going to watch my thoughts?"

"As I explained, I see your body's reactions to stimuli. But thoughts are something else entirely."

"But you'll keep watch over my reactions. Yes?"

"No."

"Why not?"

"Because you won't interest me for much longer."

And then the cocoon dissolved, thick hot fluids falling away from her new body. Elata heard the splash and she heard singing. Some of the noisy people were nearby, but most stood in the distance. Their nonsensical tune had become language, each voice full of rhythms that would have been unnoticed before. Yet the sum total wasn't as delightful as she would have guessed. Everybody sang but nobody made any effort to link their songs, and finding no chorus, Elata tried to offer a few notes of her own.

She failed. Hot syrup emerged with a hard cough, and then she vomited sticky threads of bright pink that wasn't blood.

"Stand," said Padrone.

She couldn't see any likely machines. "Where are you, boyfriend?"

Her first words with the new mouth.

"Who is your boyfriend?" her doctor asked, speaking from nowhere.

"You," she said.

"I am here."

Elata sat up, legs dropping over the table's edge. But she didn't want to stand. Hands resembling her hands played with new legs and the perfect, unscarred belly, and she thumped her chest, enjoying the hollowness of lungs, and she discovered a pulse that was far too slow to be normal, particularly as excited as she felt now. Yet even as she focused on her body, Elata remained aware of her surroundings. This was a huge long and very crowded room, and some of the people looked like children, others might be grown, and there were busy machines or objects meant to look like machines. In an instant, as a reflex, Elata counted every face, human and otherwise. Most of the strangers were staring at her. And one after another, they called her, "The new dragon."

"Dragon," triggered surety. Every craziness that Diamond had told her was true. Elata went to bed dead, and now she was one of the most important people anywhere.

Important girls could give orders.

"Padrone. Show yourself to me."

The adjacent floor was smooth and white, and then it was black and twisted. A concoction of black metal ropes and bits of colored fire rose up,

topped with a face built from ghostly nonsense --
wide luminescent eyes and a matching smile
gazing at the most important patient to ever enjoy
his brilliance.

Inside an ocean of ideas, Elata saw the
humor.

"You're making a joke."

"A minor talent," Padrone said, laughing
along with her.

"And now I can't die anymore," she said.

"Only after the most exceptional effort."

Watching faces, the new dragon
remembered who met her gaze and who nervously
looked away.

"My other boyfriend," she said.

"Diamond."

"Where is he?"

"In an adjacent room."

"And now I'm like him," she said. "Our cuts
always heal, and we think in a thousand directions
at once."

"No, Elata. Your recuperative powers are
markedly superior."

"And our minds?"

"Roughly equal. I presume."

Again Elata thumped her hollow chest.

"But I'm making surveys and making plans,"
he continued. "More surgeries will be necessary, for
you and for the others. I need to prepare each of
you to live here."

"'Here.'" Repeating that word caused a second word to offer its services. But she didn't say, "Marrow," aloud.

Instead, she told her savior, "I have two questions."

"Ask."

"Where are my other friends?"

"With Diamond, and you'll see them. As soon as you stand for me."

She leaped off the table, and out from the floor came a long robe that covered her in black velvet.

"My second question," she said, grabbing her jaw.

"Yes?"

"Does this new mouth have to tell the truth?"

The question baffled the machine, or the moment was so wondrous that he let the silence play out. Then very seriously and with a hint of scorn, the AI surgeon informed his exceptional patient, "I gave you this life. But my dear, your soul is, and will always be, your own."

Mere claimed to be terrified, except her face wasn't scared. She had stopped talking, that flat keen gaze fixed on Diamond while he thought about the Eight and about Quest, lining up their lives inside his mind, from now back to the beginning. What would he tell, and which pieces should be pushed to the front? The Eight murdered Diamond's father.

The easiest story was to paint that mishmash creature as evil. Except Divers had been in control, and how could you blame the heart and lungs for what the mind does? And maybe Quest destroyed the sun, but as the worst kind of accident -- one innocuous touch resulting in catastrophe. Ignorance was the villain, and a thousand other stories about his sister would give this ancient woman plenty and nothing inside the same breaths.

The best explanation? The mind snapped back to the most critical memory: Inside a dream, Diamond's biological father told the sleeping boy, "Bring everyone." The corona's children included the Eight and Quest, and Diamond had obeyed his father. And if he told just that, maybe this little god and ship's officer and world-burning dragon would understand, and every question would be answered, and instead of that hard stare, Mere would smile at him, singing another fancy song that would leave everyone feeling wonderful.

"I need to tell you," Diamond began.

Mere closed her eyes.

"Everything," he lied.

Then she opened her eyes. "You left one world for this world." Was she skeptical? Not at all. A flat statement, perfectly ordinary. "That is what happened, is it?"

"Yes."

"Describe your world."

"A round room," he said. "With trees."

No reaction.

"The forest hangs from the roof, and the sun is below us." Just that much, using this simple, newly-carved language, Diamond was ready to talk for days, celebrating a realm more vivid and alive than the dark, suffocating world left behind.

But it felt safer to close his mouth.

A reassuring nod. "Numbers," Mere said. "Measure this other world for me."

The numbers he knew best meant nothing here. Diamond stopped one kind of thinking and found another, a fresh mathematics offering its help. "This far," he said with his voice, his arms. "This is a meter."

The little dragon nodded.

"A thousand meters is important," he said.

"It's familiar, yes."

Shutting his eyes, one kilometer was obvious.

"What are you doing?" Seldom asked.

"Measuring the Creation."

Without hesitation, Seldom offered school-worthy figures. But those were distractions. Diamond summoned the reef and hanging forest, and inside his head, carrying this new kilometer, he measured that very long line from his last bedroom out to the reef and to the Papio.

"The radius," he began.

And paused.

"A thousand kilometers and we lived on top. Our world is a cavern, four thousand kilometers across and much deeper than that. With one kind of human in the hanging trees, and the other humans living on the reef."

Eyes open, he found Seldom throwing his arms through the air, enthusiastically drawing the Creation.

"But it can't be a cave," said Diamond. "You would have seen us. A room that enormous and so close to the surface … "

"What are cackling about?" King asked.

Diamond explained.

And his brother stomped on those doubts. "Don't tell her what's impossible. We're idiots and she isn't, so let the lady decide."

That felt true enough.

"In this world of yours," said Mere. "How many people?"

Diamond turned to Seldom. "She wants to know our population."

His friend looked at the floor. "Zero. Everyone's dead."

Karlan scoffed. "You don't know that either."

The four of them stared at the same piece of the floor, working with the awful thoughts. Then another voice, loud and familiar, said, "All right then. If you don't want to welcome me, I'll leave."

Elata, wearing a knee-long black robe.

Seldom and Diamond hurried to hug her.

Karlan held back, smiling and not-smiling when he said, "Don't bother thanking me."

"What did you do?" she asked.

"Just saved your life, and all that shit."

Still as a statue, King listened to everything, including Elata. "Your heart has changed," he said.

"Slower and a million times stronger," she said.

Elata looked the same, except for the joy and purpose and a convincing sense that this girl was an entirely different creature, every grim idea washed away, leaving her happy and not just about little matters. She pulled at her thick hair as she strode past them. Here was the Elata fearlessness, only more so. She walked straight to Mere and sang, and then the two dragons winked at each other before Mere shook her head.

"No," she meant.

Another reason for those two to laugh.

"What?" asked Diamond. Asked Seldom.

Elata grinned at each of them. Again, the hair needed to be yanked. Almost savagely yanked. "What surprises me most of all," she began. Then she fell silent, waiting for someone to prompt her with the obvious question.

Seldom.

"What surprises you?" he asked.

Seldom's wrist and Diamond's right elbow needed to be grabbed, and like a mother talking to thousand day-old children, Elata told them, "Touch my head. Feel the new brain working."

Two hands lay on her hot skull.

"King," she said.

The huge hand dropped lightly on top. And without permission, Karlan pushed fingertips against the back of her fever-hot neck.

King pulled away first.

Retrieving his fingers, Karlan laughed at some part of this game.

Only a thumb and finger held his wrist, yet Seldom couldn't make his hand move. Diamond tried to free his arm, but only once. He was happy with the vice-strong grip. Built to climb trees, this broad-shouldered, profoundly rebuilt girl was stronger than he had ever been.

Staring at an empty corner, Mere offered busy whispers to nobody.

With his huge feet apart, King was ready to resist the next surprise.

Elata let go of Seldom and let go of Diamond. Then she stared at Diamond until he matched her gaze, and a voice that couldn't have been more joyful said, "I'm a dragon."

"I told you."

Beaming, she said, "They've never seen anyone like me. Or like any of us, for that matter."

Except Diamond should be the dragon. He couldn't shake that idea. With hope, and then without it. Wanting the power, and then thrilled to be free of at least one terrible burden.

"What should we chat about next?" Elata asked.

Her expression held layers.

"I was going to tell her about the Eight," Diamond said.

Elata turned to the lady, a question rolling out of her.

Mere offered a nod and some swift music.

Then Elata translated that song into a surprisingly thorough lecture. "Waywards. They're a big tribe or nation or religion that looks like wild kids. Mere's people were pretending to be Waywards when they found us, and the genuine Waywards just grabbed up the Eight."

Diamond's thoughts ran to Quest.

And Mere spoke to Elata again. A much longer piece of song, this time.

Elata absorbed all of it and turned to the others, her smile warm, amused. "Okay. I've been given a job. Something needs to be explained, and I'm your teacher. The mark inside me? Unexpected and unprecedented, and it could be a mistake. Maybe Diamond is the dragon, and I'm just the thief who stole the label he should wear. Which sounds like me, doesn't it? Or maybe it belongs somebody else even more deserving. Karlan, for instance."

Karlan cursed and laughed.

"Or me," Seldom whispered.

Elata wrapped her arms around her waist. "Precautions. A lot of precautions have to be taken, and that means with each of us. Since any one of us might be the real dragon, we need to be protected from accidents and the idiot actions of a girl having a very wicked day. And that's why my new best friend, Dr. Padrone, is going to rebuild everybody. Including you, King. And you, my boyfriend. All of us need the best bodies and the most wonderful minds."

"They can do that?" Seldom asked.

"This world is built from iron and surprise," said Elata. "The many-colored children and us flying over everything and back again? That seems incredible until you see how easy it's done. Like rebuilding an old-fashioned brain. You know, my head always felt simple because it was simple. But fat can be measured and mapped in minutes, then digested. Then Padrone pushes our thoughts inside the same tough business found inside King's head, and Diamond's head. A brain full of machinery that won't die easily or willingly, and maybe never dies."

"Good," was Karlan's assessment.

Seldom hugged himself, saying, "All right." He said it three times, skepticism surrendering to hope.

He began to cry.

"What about us?" Diamond asked.

Elata looked at him and then King. Two moments of intense consideration ended with a warning. "I have a voice inside me. It's called the nexus. Padrone, my surgeon and good friend, hasn't stopped talking to me. He's making ready to enhance both of you. When he's finished, he promises that you'll heal faster than ever. Like me, you're going to know the local language and some of its history. But your minds have already been built. Which is trouble. Hard machine brains don't grow old, but they're also stubborn about tinkering. Even the most spectacular doctor can't just eat your heads and poop out something better."

She paused, laughed, one hand hand brushing against Diamond's face.

"Just the first operation is going to take time," she said. "A full long sleep, which is how they count the days here. Since there's always daylight in this world, no darkness, they splinter time by counting sleeps."

The idea of a bed and closed eyes was appealing.

"If I let them work on me," King began. "May I come out with a new shape or fresh talents?"

"Good question." Elata turned to the other dragon, translating.

The woman seemed to listen, but she offered no answer.

"What would you want to be?" Diamond asked.

King rocked side to side. "I don't know," was the honest reply.

Then Mere lifted an arm, and the conversation ended. "The missing sister," she said to Diamond. "Before the surgeon takes you, I want to know more about her."

"Quest," said Diamond, in his own tongue.

"What about Quest?" asked King.

Elata looked at the giant. At Diamond. Then she wiped tears off Seldom's worn out face. But she didn't speak until she was staring at Mere, repeating the name, "Quest," before adding quite a lot more.

Diamond listened to the senseless noise, and when Elata fell silent, he simply asked, "What?"

Elata offered a faint smile and shrug.

"You lied to the lady," Seldom guessed.

"A liar needs the truth, and I don't know enough." She shrugged. "I just gave her fair warning. Quest can't be found. She's a marvel at camouflage, and if she wants, she's far more spectacular than the Eight and both of you combined. Oh, and I also mentioned that if anyone deserves to be a dragon, even more than you, Diamond … it's the girl who can make herself into anything … "

After that, everyone stood silent, waiting for their benefactor's reaction.

Mere was staring at nothing, and she did nothing for a long while.

Describe a secret world and millions of people hiding under your feet, and the ancient dragon didn't flinch. But praise one buggy little alien, and her face began to change. She looked simple, a little foolish and sad, arms lifting for no purpose but to let her stare at her own empty hands, the mouth opening and then closing again, nothing worth the air invested in just one plaintive, hard-edged note.

"!eech."

SEVEN

Washen flew without declared intentions. Riding a fusion plume, she crossed the Blithe Sea and Highpoint Mountains, and over the satin-black jungles of River Nine, she made one jarring course correction while transmitting a nominal text, surrendering nothing but a destination and arrival time. With every other dragon, there was a powerful mandate for protocol. Navigating Eternity meant that you and your peers never stopped offering respectful gestures and pleasantries born from ritual, from manners, from lazy habit. But pleasantries didn't apply to Miocene. Respect snuggled inside cordial packaging held zero importance to that dragon. Every agenda was obvious, and why dance with the obvious?

This dragon, their Miocene, wasn't the same creature that Washen had known. Yet they were very much the same women. The two Miocenes served for thousands of years as First Chair to the Greatship. Both were marooned on Marrow, and both had identical sons named Till, and after joining the Waywards, both became the Master Captain -- a very brief reign ending with the mutiny of the same ex-captains now serving as invincible dragons. Save for a multitude of tiny details, countless Miocenes shared the same extraordinary fate. Till tried to destroy the Greatship -- a seminal moment that Washen would never forget. Perhaps the boy wanted to free the Bleak trapped in Marrow's core. Maybe pure wild madness was responsible. But this Washen had watched Miocene change sides, fighting fiercely against her son. This Washen saw the plasma gun rise, and the Wayward's prophet obliterated his mother's head and mind, and that same ugly end happened inside a multitude of mirror universes. But at least once, somewhere within the carnage, one fortunate mother survived her son's attack. That Miocene was the one who escaped war and justice and every intrigue, and she was the one who outlived the first Wayward nation and the first human-witnessed cycle on Marrow. And being Miocene, singular and inexorable, of course she willed herself into becoming a full fledged dragon, matching ranks with that murderous, remarkable son.

Ancient duties and insults. Surely that's what made the woman glacially aloof. And oh yes, there was the tidy fact that this Miocene and their Till not only fought a thousand wars, but there was a count -- a count known only to the two of them -- of the moments when the mother killed the son or the son aimed well enough to end her: Gods clawing at each other's throats, and Marrow dying each time, and after a brief taste of Nothingness, the multiverse made Miocene live again, pissed and primed for more redemption.

Every dragon was born from a unique timeline. Which was inevitable, what with the extraordinary difficulties necessary to join this elite Few. And it was so easy to accept that history had invented this particular Miocene. But easy beliefs were often wrong. Smarter, less sentimental voices argued that time didn't make the woman cold and cunning, because that was how she was born, and approving of her own nature, she spent the aeons carefully improving her excellence. What's more, this dragon, the ultimate Miocene, had a singular genius for seeing the limits of Eternity. Minds were always small, and great minds knew that lesson best. But if a soul could strip the excess off her nature, what remained could lift even greater burdens. Inside the day and the centuries, the advantages would be tiny. But in circumstances where every dragon was talented and every dragon was magnificently lucky, the lady who didn't waste a calorie spitting out pleasant words would prosper just a little more.

One extra success every millennia: That brought a thousand victories inside the next million years. Then the hyperfiber sky would press down, hammer to the anvil, and Marrow would have to burn, and the cunning, chilled dragon would step out onto the new world, even stronger than before.

Till, the murderous son, ruled the prolific Waywards and their wide territories, his nation sinking countless vaults into the iron ocean, preparing for future cycles. Meanwhile other dragons enjoyed one another for alliances and shared resources as well as wasteful pleasures. But Miocene was the regal beast living apart. Outside her odd realm, she was friendless and mistrusted if not unconditionally hated. Yet she never failed to do well. Hundreds of dragons were known. Most were rare -- aliens and minor captains and AIs born with the klein inside them. But a single Till always appeared on the hot crust, and almost without exception, he found himself staring at the razor-faced mother who was eager to test the ungrateful son.

Washen admired this cold dragon but never mentioned that affection. Not to Mere or any other dragon. Because they would understand those affections, and the result would be fewer bouts of idle chatter, agreements and arrangements becoming a little more scarce. And if Washen was formally ostracized, even for a year here, a decade there, she would have no choice but apply Miocene's lessons to her own immortality, cutting away empathy and decency, sharpening the soul inside a situation that was as close to Forever as could be.

This was a thin slice of Washen's thinking.

Slamming into the atmosphere, descending into Miocene's territory, quite a lot more had to be considered. Every volcano was leashed, the landscape sculpted by a very particular hand. The grayness of low-grade hyperfiber was suffused with cultured minerals uncommon to the rest of Marrow. This scene always evoked ancient memory. Sensibilities born on the Greatship ruled this nation. Not just today's hyperfiber and the granite, but as the millennia passed, a maze of caverns and underground cities would be wrapped inside hyperfiber envelopes. With each incarnation of this iron world, Miocene made it her mission resurrect the starship that was once hers, if only for a few breaths, a few heartbeats.

And how long ago was that?

The mind was never brave enough to stand beside any reasonable number, declaring, "This is how much time has passed."

But having posed the question, Washen found one rough answer offering its service. And that number always made her tremble.

The Eight were moving.

Were rising.

A simple, indisputable sensation. Cloaked in heat and darkness, they felt themselves being carried aloft. Kai imagined a very large aircraft escaping from the twisted ground. Everyone assumed exactly that. Stout wings and roaring jets, and the Eight were laid inside the aircraft's hold, unconscious but restrained with leather belts and enormous steel buckles. Imagination invented armed guards wearing leather and bone, nervous human faces spellbound by this majestic entity. The Eight were being transported to some important place. The gray ceiling, or another portion of this world? Whatever the destination, a prison cell was waiting. Questions would be asked, pain delivered. Awful, awful miseries, and each prepared for torture with the plain truth: Nothing could be worse than everything else endured inside their shared lives, and these feral little beasts were going to suffer a sorry lesson, trying to sculpt the will of the Eight.

Then, just as they achieved a state of anxious readiness, their body fell.

A sudden, steep plunge.

One of the imaginary aircraft wings had ripped loose, and judging by the sensation, it was easy to calculate when the coming impact would arrive. Tensions built. Fine papio curses were offered. But the predicted moment came and was gone and nothing was struck, there was no explosion or fire, and then they fell faster, vast realms crossed in moments.

Madness needed its explanation. The Eight were being tossed into a bottomless hole, another world waiting below. Or the aircraft was magical, stealing away weight or perceptions. But Divers offered a simpler story: This was the anticipated torture. The aircraft was spinning through the air, those feral children trying to shred the Eight's courage with tricks of momentum and perception. And since weaklings deserved to fail, she ordered the others to regain control over their thoughts, recovering the best part of their poise.

Shared silence took hold. Which was noticed, or what happened next was coincidence. Either way, they resumed their ascent, the sensation more intense than ever, and the journey lasted far too long. Vast distances were covered. Half a day was consumed, maybe more, and every voice offered the same guess. Worlds were like hollow beads and solid beads, and those shattered black lands were only a stopover, because now a much greater world was ready to be revealed.

Blind in every way, Kai envisioned water. The water was smooth and a little warm against bare papio-inspired toes. He wiggled each toe and watched ripples spreading out and smoothing out, vanishing into the lovely liquid body. Then the imaginary eyes reached farther, discovering an ocean full of too many colors, full of shifting busy loud light, and in the extreme distance, an island shaped like a cylinder rising into a realm that refused to end. No ceiling stood above this world. Because this was the final world. Ocean was the end, nothing beyond but emptiness and blackness and a cold that Kai had never forgotten.

He told the Seven what he had seen.

They didn't react.

Undaunted, Kai depicted what had to be legitimate memory.

The climbing sensation ended.

Slowly and then quickly, Kai fell hard again.

"They're stabbing at our minds," he warned.

No one reacted.

Kai said, "Tritian."

What wasn't a voice came to him, whispering softly, failing to be understood. Then the whispers were gone, or never existed.

"Divers," said Kai.

Silence.

"Hello."

Which he muttered badly. Kai suddenly couldn't manage the simplest word.

Again, he tried calling to the others.

The answer was furious white pain. Then misery cut him and the blade stayed inside him, twisting slowly, carving his mind until strength was lost and hope was shattered and agony was the only future that could be contemplated.

Another moment passed.

And then all that pain slipped away, leaving behind the taste of warm salted water.

"Hello," someone said.

Kai didn't recognize the voice. But it felt human, sounded male, and if not kind, there was at a trace of warmth inside a word that shouldn't make any sense to him. Yet he understood the man's greeting.

"Help me," Kai tried to plead.

Kai's new voice was wrong, changed and wrong. Words came out as gibberish. That was his next thought, as mistaken as any today.

The stranger said, "I'm sorry."

"Sorry," Kai repeated.

"For your discomfort, for the need to hurry. But time is scarce, and we need to be able to speak with one of you. Ask questions, answer questions. And apologize for the fears we've caused."

White misery had been set aside, but what came next was even more unsettling. Kai felt two arms and two legs connected to his mind, and fingers making fists. The urge to move was overpowering. He expected to find himself inside the other Seven, broad leather straps holding all of them in place. But no, he could kick and swing at the darkness. Nothing stopped him.

"There's no need to fight," the male voice promised.

What was that?

"But pay close attention to my words. You're about to experience a considerable surprise, and it would help everyone, particularly you, if you would keep your wits when this happens."

"What happens?" Kai asked.

Using a new language. Kai understood what he just said, and with the same structure of sounds and silence, his companion asked, "Do you have a name? Of your own maybe? Yes?"

"Yes."

"If you wish, share it."

Kai said, "Kai."

"Very good," said the man. "Now, Kai. Do you feel ready for whatever happens next?"

"Yes."

"No, you do not," he promised.

Kai discovered eyes, and the eyes showed him a small, barely lit room shared by two creatures. One of them was human, male and grown. Black hair, reef-colored eyes, and a friendly, captivating smile. A voice that already felt familiar addressed the other entity, saying, "Hello, Kai."

Who was this second creature?

Kai was. Ripped from the Seven and deposited on the most ordinary chair, he had been wrapped inside a human body, and the terror grew worse as he rose up on unwanted legs, fingers digging at a bare chest that tore under his nails, nothing beneath the skin but more pieces of this helpless, horribly exposed self.

"I want to sleep," Seldom said.

"I bet you know how," said his brother.

"All right, I will."

They had met Mere inside one room and then the dragon brought them into another room. White chairs grew out of the white floor whenever a body wanted to rest, and Karlan acted happy to sit. But Seldom was back up on his feet. Sitting was painful. That's how tired he felt. Perched on a chair, he couldn't forget that his legs ached and eyes burned, and exhausted, useless thoughts ran through the most useless skull in the world. He was the clever boy in the old world. People liked him well enough, but it was more important to be reliably smart, piecing together puzzles while feeling helpful enough. But in this world, Seldom was an idiot, and he wasn't enough of an idiot to forget his limitations. Fatigue was just another one of his grave failures. But rocking from leg to leg, his exhaustion seemed glad to leave him alone.

Diamond was whispering to King, and both were staring at the brilliant people standing on that white floor.

The new Elata was speaking to Mere, singing senseless words.

Then a door appeared and the blue girl came through, long strides carrying her towards Mere. Three geniuses, two of them dragons, and the old dragon was silent. But the tilt of the faces hinted at secret conversations skittering under the words, even as Elata babbled along in that bright, half-musical language.

Seldom's legs decided to walk, carrying him closer.

The women didn't notice him. Elata pressed on with her one-sided conversation, and suddenly Mere laughed, loud and with joy. The blue girl was or wasn't speaking, but Elata fell silent, and turning, she offered Seldom a big Elata smile. Because she did notice him. Because nothing escaped her attention. Which wasn't all that much different than before, was it?

That observation made Seldom happier.

"You and Karlan are next," Elata said. "Padrone says that he's almost done scrubbing down the operating tables."

"Scrubbing down?"

"That's a joke." She laughed the same as always. Because she was the same person. That's why Seldom felt better. Elata was Elata, and he was going to be the same Seldom.

"I want to talk to your doctor," he said.

Her smile changed. Still a grin, but with more weight behind it. "You will. In a very little while."

Mere touched the blue girl, three fingertips laid against the chin, and the girl nodded and turned and ran. A flat-out sprint that not even Diamond could match. This new room was exceptionally large and growing bigger. People stood in the remote distance. Seldom had no idea how many people, but it could be hundreds, and they also watched the girl's impressive speed.

"Where's she going?" he asked.

"Damned if I know," Elata said. Then she hurried to Diamond and King, grabbing Diamond's hand while the other hand wrapped fingers around the longest, sharpest spine on King's elbow.

Seldom felt happy until he returned to Karlan.

His brother said, "Sit."

"No."

But the floor knew better. A fresh chair emerged before Seldom realized that he was falling. He expected his legs and thoughts to bother him again, but they were being nice now. He was comfortable. Sitting back, Seldom heard his mother warning him not to slouch. Her voice was clear and close, and warm, and she smelled like soap. But their mother died hundreds of days ago, murdered because the Eight wanted to kill Diamond. A dream was holding Seldom, and he would have happily stayed with the ghost but his brother pinched his hand.

"Know what they're doing?" Karlan asked.

Seldom's eyes were dry, even when he blinked hard. "Who are you talking about?"

"Pallas and her crew. Look at them over there."

Pallas was the blue-skinned girl. Karlan was always better with names than Seldom was. Would that stay the same, after Padrone was done rebuilding them?

"Those are her soldiers," Karlan explained.

Children had gathered around their leader. Except for the gray boy. A rectangular piece of wall had survived from the first little aircraft, and that slab stood in the middle of the vast floor, the severed heads still on display. But the gray boy was using a white-bladed knife, cutting the braids one after another, each of the heads moving its mouth, making no sound, all shoved inside a sack that happily grew bigger as more room was needed.

"Know what they're doing?" Karlan asked.

"Never. Do you?"

"Sure. Look how they're standing."

Seldom stared until he admitted, "I don't see anything."

"Soldiers have a look. That's my experience. Being ordered into a dangerous fight, they get pinched faces."

"Pinched faces?"

"You know. Bad news and no escaping it."

Seldom looked at his brother. "You're just guessing."

"Sure. But what people want is usually pretty obvious."

"What do those people want?"

"The hill we came out of. If I was their general, I'd order them to claim that ground and every treasure buried under it."

Diamond was a prize. And Elata. And the corona's other children had to be treasures too. But the Creation under the hill? "There's nothing left to take," Seldom said, his voice pained but confident. "Our world is dead."

"Know so?"

"What else do you know, Karlan?"

His brother liked that question. People didn't often ask for his opinions. "First of all, our world isn't buried inside anyone's little hill."

"Because it's deep underground," Seldom said.

"Shit, you think a giant cave stays hidden? From people who read thoughts and fly faster than cannon shells?" His little brother deserved a teasing laugh. "No, the hill's nothing but a marker. To a doorway. To some secret hatch back into our old world and maybe other places too. Which makes it precious and worth fighting over, and that's why Mere's sending her people off again."

The gray boy was shoving the final few heads into the sack. He didn't wear any pinched looks, smiling and whistling as he finished up.

"What about those heads?" Seldom asked.

"Offerings. Or hostages. I can't figure out those particulars." A big, arrogant shrug filled the next pause. "The thing is, Seldom. Answers like to be simple. Complicate your thinking just delays you getting to where you need to be."

"Where do I need to be?"

"With me, so I can watch over you. You idiot."

Seldom sat back, and with renewed determination, shut his eyes. Ten nights came and went, but not one dream. He slept hard until Elata was tugging at his arm, half-shouting when she told him, "It's time."

Karlan was already walking away, gladly abandoning him. Mere was conversing with Diamond, and when she stopped talking, Diamond spoke to King. King was being called a harum-scarum. Where did that name come from? Seldom didn't know or couldn't care. And what about Blue Pallas and the other children? They had vanished. They must have flown off on their important mission. Elata was walking after Karlan, leading Seldom across the giant room. There were thousands of people now, and everyone was disturbingly quiet. Panels and blocks of shaped light had formed what looked like the work stations found on the bridge of any large aircraft, and the crew manning these posts appeared busy, saying nothing as they did the important and impossible jobs.

A set of stairs led down into another new room.

Seldom caught up to Elata, asking, "What happens to Diamond?"

"He's harder to rebuild," she said. "So's King. Didn't we explain that already?"

Seldom was still half-asleep. He was only pretending to think.

She said, "Come on. Your surgeon's ready."

A smaller room waited beneath the bridge, and the entire room was Padrone. That was Seldom's impression. Metal limbs and bright eyes surrounded him, and sweet rotting flowers made the air thick. Puckering his nose, he said, "My name is Seldom."

"He knows your name," Elata said.

Two cocoons were waiting. Knowing the simple answer, Karlan didn't hesitate, crawling inside the first cocoon, giving his brother and the dragon a fine send-off wave before the machine closed over the opening.

But easy as they were, simple answers weren't good enough.

Seldom stopped short.

"No," he said.

A voice came from everywhere. It was quiet and male, and Elata nodded at whatever she heard. Then she turned to Seldom, saying, "You're going to be fine. You're going to be spectacular."

"And I'll get a better brain," he said.

"Of course you will."

"But ask him," he said. "No, tell him. Tell Padrone that I have one demand. I'll let him change me, just like he did you. But he has to give me certain kinds of knowledge too."

"You'll know the dragon's language right off. How's that?"

"I want more."

She smiled, laughing softly at some part of this. "Tell me what, and I'll convince my new friend."

What would make Seldom happy? What truths needed to find a home inside his vibrant new mind? And then his brother's advice came back to him. The simple, perfect answer found the boy, and the machine and the dragon both had to wait for his laughter to end.

Every foot stood on the impossible.

That's what children learned as soon as they learned to stand.

Beneath an envelope of liquid iron, the impossible core waited: Phenomenal densities coupled with inexplicable, eternal energies. All normalities left behind. One tiny portion of the universe didn't understand the rules, and that's why the rules couldn't touch it. Mass and power emerging from nothingness, or from magic, every million-year cycle ending with a shaped explosion, and every cycle compressing the core even more savagely than before. And the greatest wonder might be that the core and the pulsating Marrow were never reduced to a speck of black hole small enough to fit inside a woman's palm.

But a second explanation existed -- a barbed logic popular with quirky minds and AI savants. In that solution, the core wasn't special at all. The rest of the universe was what was magical. Iron and vaults and dragons had escaped the rules of normality. Stars and vacuum were a ridiculous mess, flawed from birth, sick in nature, and soon to die.

"But not today," said Washen, dropping a boot on the hyperfiber tarmac.

This was lowest-grade hyperfiber, more white than gray, spiced with tiny blisters where the curing process had collapsed. Yet in this very early era, with small populations and industries barely born, any hyperfiber was an indulgence, and this indulgence was being used as a landing berth for a visiting dragon.

That was Miocene's way. Flowing lava and black, iron-infused stone weren't welcome inside her nation. This dragon's cities embrace the logic of the Greatship, every room underground, connected by grand tunnels decorated with rivers and artificial light. Managed indoor spectacles were what mattered, while the surface was punctuated with gray domes, every gray doorway ready to be sealed ten different ways.

Any dragon's visit was an exceptional event. Even for Washen, and she came to Miocene's front door more often than anyone else. Yet despite a history of conflict, and despite the plain oddness of the resident despot, Washen looked forward to these moments. A very powerful illusion was in effect here. Standing on the tarmac, she had returned to another day and a better place. Washen was walking the Greatship, and the old duties were reflexes too embedded to be forgotten, including the simple act of eagerly looking about, hunting for the mirrored uniforms of her fellow captains.

But no, Miocene wouldn't push the conceit so far. Her officers wore trim suits, elegant but always short of formal. Her citizens were mostly human, and just like when she was the First-Chair, only humans were given the richest responsibilities. Which was rather like the Wayward policy: A rare similarity, since Miocene and her son presided over vividly opposite realms.

Two important souls approached. A tall dark man, and a darker, even taller woman. Smiles had been ordered, and they were robust, convincing smiles.

"This way, madam," the man said.

"We should hurry," his companion added.

"Our Lady has important news," promised the first.

"Critical intelligence," his partner added.

And Washen said, "The !eech have returned."

She expected one of several reactions. Professional worry. Professional panic. Stubborn, ill-considered bravery. But the news seemed to ambush the duo. Which was incredible. Miocene never quit eavesdropping on the Waywards, on Till. Of course the resident dragon knew about the !eech. And these had to be Miocene's best people, decades old and ready for a million years of duty and polish. Yet the man responded with pain in the face and open, shaking hands, while his partner refused terror, turning razored eyes on the messenger.

"If that were true, Our Lady would have told us. Which she hasn't done, and you must be wrong, madam." Then after a brief pause, she said, "Please, we need to run."

They broke into long-legged trots, newborns leading the deity. A steep tunnel led underground, and where the tunnel flattened, it widened, revealing false skies and gorgeously faked sunshine. Another hallmark of the Greatship: This compelling, almost perfect representation of a distinct world. The golden-white light of Sol was overhead, and Washen, who had never left the Greatship, found herself deposited on what looked like an important avenue on the legendary Earth.

Public mood was another surprise. Anticipating heightened security and layers of encryption, Washen discovered hundreds of citizens in the midst of ordinary business. Warm smiles. Polite smiles. Words spoken by happy mouths and shared between nexuses. And sensors woven into Washen's ribs felt the EM whispers, dense but utterly normal.

Her two companions knew nothing about an alleged !eech, and no one else on this long street seemed aware of unexpected dangers haunting the world.

An avalanche of questions was kicked loose.

"What's Your Lady's news?" asked Washen.

"We don't know," the man confessed.

"We do know," the woman corrected. "But we don't understand enough to explain the circumstances. Particularly to you."

"You mean the new dragon," Washen guessed.

Again, a simple declaration was met with astonishment and hearty doses of skepticism.

"What new dragon?" the woman asked.

The man was too puzzled or too frustrated to react verbally. Better to shake those nervous hands and pick up the pace.

Oddities kept accumulating. The !eech were the thieves who long ago stole the Greatship, countless wars fought against those horrid enemies, and now the !eech had returned, if only in the form of one little body. And if that wasn't remarkable enough, a new dragon had emerged long after she should have been born. Yet everyone here was dressed for comfort, not for military service. People were enjoying treats and holding hands and some kissed and most ignored the kissers, just like normal souls ignored everything that didn't directly involve them, including a visiting dragon gliding along a floor of bloody red cultured granite.

Looking back at Washen, the woman conceded, "She has found a marvel, Our Lady has."

"Like nothing ever before," the man said.

"And it's hiding underneath a hill," Washen offered.

Maybe yes, maybe no. Whatever the answer, they weren't eager to agree with an interloper. After glancing at her associate, the young woman explained, "It's alien in design, and profoundly so. Our Lady says. Matching nothing inside her archives, which are the finest anywhere, of course."

"A singular discovery," the man boasted.

"And where is Your Lady?"

The pace had slowed. "Close," he promised, offering an earnest wink and a half-pause, sending out a message through a public nexus.

Washen's tools had no trouble pulling out the meaning. The man was admitting, "We don't see you, Madam. Where should we deliver your guest?"

Miocene's voice was equally public, calmly pointing them towards an emporium waiting up ahead.

Washen ran faster, passing her companions.

Because it might look unseemly, chasing after another dragon, the woman slowed her pace and straightened her back. But appearances didn't matter to the man. He and Washen sprinted down the long avenue, reaching a single door flanked by various signs promising unique clothing at reasonable prices.

Miocene stood beyond the door. Regal, and ludicrous. That's what Washen saw. The shop's owner occupied the precise middle of a small, pleasantly decorated room, absolutely tickled to be offering her great dragon these modest garments to wear in bed.

"And it knows how to tell stories," the woman claimed. "For when you're awake, Madam. And asleep. And best of all, during conjugal moments."

"How very interesting," Miocene mentioned.

Washen approached.

Then her guide announced her by name, adding, "We mentioned the artifact, Madam."

The former First Chair, the master of power and rational vengeance, offered the thinnest smile. But she kept staring at the sunset-colored garment resting in her long hands. The narrow face and black hair were untroubled by age. The second most powerful creature on this world, and she said, "Thank you, no. You need to find a more worthy owner for this garment."

A ludicrous scene, and Washen was off-balanced, exposed.

Which was the plan, no doubt.

"Maybe my friend would be interested," said Miocene.

The laugh came easily enough, Washen saying, "Another day."

Taking back what no one wanted, the shop owner retreated. Then with a nod, Miocene warned her man to vanish as well, and he took the initiative to close the shop door before his stiff-backed partner could arrive.

And that's when camouflage and overlapping encryptions came to life. The sounds of commerce vanished, and the buzz of nexus gossip was gone, and what had been a tiny business became the most isolated room on the planet.

If she was in the mood, one dragon might try to disable another dragon inside a room like this. But according to every security system as Washen's disposal, she was safe.

"The !eech," she said.

"A little solitary monster. Yes. I know."

"And the new dragon."

"Who wanted to kill herself. Remarkable, isn't she?"

"Plus a mystery hiding under a Wayward hill. At least you mentioned that news to your people."

"To a few, yes." Eyes that never stopped hunting for weakness stared at a face she knew well. "My Intelligence cadres are fully briefed. Ten shock brigades are on alert, and they know why. And the absolute minimum of AIs are trying to carve the rational out of the madness."

"Till claims the hill," Washen said.

"But will graciously allow the rest of us some share of the wealth." With a warm light tone, Miocene laughed. And for several moments too. "We'll be allowed patches of ground fifty kilometers back and the freedom to watch while the Waywards make their investigations."

"Unless we contest the claim."

Miocene took a breath and held it.

"Your brigades are ready to move on him," Washen said.

And the other immortal let the breath escape.

But she didn't speak.

"You won't make alliances with us," Washen said. "Not until we have an agreement in place."

"Dear little Mere will sacrifice her people," said Miocene, "but the benefits will be thin and spent and then lost. You absolutely need my full, undiluted help. The !eech have returned. Till's going to make a war to catch that one bug, and even when he succeeds, the fight continues. Because it's just Mere and you and two other little piecemeal nations. Till has already won the momentum. So yes, I'm in a rich position. You need to give me every item I ask for, and then you should to throw more gifts my way. Because the only way you win this day is to make me happy."

"And what do you want?" Washen asked.

That triggered shrugs and a mocking shake of the head. "To begin with? I want one of the orphans. Someone that I can adopt as my own."

"Which one?"

"I'm not quite certain," Miocene claimed, a serene little smile building. "But I have heard, maybe more than once, that old ladies should be especially fond of their little grandchildren."

As a baby and toddler, then as a compliant boy, Diamond lived inside a set of locked rooms. He knew nothing about the surrounding world, save for what kindness and carelessness happened to reveal. Which was really quite a lot. Finally stepping into the open, Diamond already knew how people acted and knew what every word meant, and the differences between himself and everyone else were obvious. One great tree's wood had taught him about the living forest, a single dead bird hinted at the beauty of vibrant life, and even without windows, the boy was comfortable with day and with night.

This new world, this Marrow, needed a simple room where the ignorant boy could sit, watching tiny details, slowly absorbing the rules of a much larger realm.

He told King his thoughts.

"An important and powerful father," was King's assessment. "That's what the boy needs."

"Do you still hear Pallas?"

"Not her and not her people. They seem gone."

"I don't see Mere."

"Her voice is everywhere," said his brother. "Leading five conversations inside just this one room."

The room was enormous and populated with hundreds of windows. Each window floated above the floor, oval sheets of color and motion, and most had a stranger beside them, watching whatever was on the other side. Fingers touched controls made from smoke. Voices sang orders or suggestions or just musically muttered to themselves. This was the extraordinary crew guiding an enormous, unlikely aircraft, and while most of these neighbors seemed human, there were also creatures built from odd frames and odd hands and what might not be faces at all.

"She's coming back to us," King announced.

Diamond imagined Pallas. He imagined Mere. But no, Elata emerged from beneath the ship's bridge. Taking hold of his hand, she said, "The other brothers are being cooked."

"How's Seldom?"

"Terrified, but clever," she said. "Have you noticed? Clever people usually invent some way past their fears."

"What did he invent?"

"I'll tell you later. First, we have an errand. Our harum-scarum needs to meet a different dragon."

Confident about directions, Elata led them past windows and busy people and one beast that looked like a six-legged table upholstered in yellow fur. A narrow door emerged from the approaching wall, and the next room was small and lined with dark wood, and empty. But then the door sealed behind them, and one man was standing in the room's center.

"He's at the far end of the world," Elata explained, explaining nothing. Then she sang a phrase before translating. "'Pamir,' I told him. 'I give you King and his considerable little brother, Diamond.'"

Pamir was thick and muscular, and by appearance, as human as anyone could be. Nothing about the new dragon was handsome. The face looked like three faces pulled from unrelated strangers and carelessly slapped together. One eye was rich brown, the other a washed-out tan. Much of his hair had fallen away, and what remained had lost all color, revealing a lumpy, faintly shiny leather-colored scalp. Pamir wore loose trousers and sandals, the open vest carried by big arms and shoulders, and some sort of rusted-colored device was buried inside his otherwise barren chest.

"What's that machine?" Diamond asked.

Elata translated, or she asked the question for herself.

The dragon offered a single note.

"'Antimatter in a bottle.'" Elata shrugged, laughed. "Whatever that means."

This seemed like a quiet, windowless room where a boy, if he had time, could learn quite a lot.

Pamir offered more noise.

And Elata laughed nervously. "He says I shouldn't be. I don't belong here and don't deserve to exist and I don't need to stay."

"He said all of that?" King asked.

"And, 'You're ruining my day, little girl.'"

Pamir stared at Diamond. Except he wasn't here, he was standing on the other side of the round world, and this was a statue built from light and sound.

The statue spoke.

Elata translated. "You could well be Washen's kid,' he says. 'What I hear, you've got your mother's reflexes, right down to the misspent empathy.'"

Pamir had a growling voice and an unfriendly mismatched stare, and those thick arms crossed themselves over the boobytrapped chest. This was a blunt, disagreeable dragon.

"I don't like him," Diamond said.

Elata translated.

And the dragon laughed, loudly and enthusiastically. So real was the image that when he stepped close, his shadow lay at their feet, and then he peered at the only figure taller than himself. Nonsensical notes began with "King" and finished the same way.

Then Elata spoke, forcing Pamir's song into normal speech.

"'King, I'll wager that nobody has explained to you what you are. That you belong to a spectacular species, and your civilization is older than the oldest human species. You ruled a powerful, technologically advanced empire while my ancestors were flinging turds instead of insults. And do you know why you act as you act? Because your ancestors were born on a wet poor homeworld, and to survive, they had to stand on the best islands, battling for resources. Food. Mates. Status. Particularly status. Your worth means everything to you. Harum-scarum? A human name born from ignorance and the monkeys' envy. The monkeys won't ever understand. You have a lovely, consuming need to battle every foe, real and otherwise, and the best victories come without violence. Yes? Does that capture your nature, King?'"

Elata stopped talking.

King pulled himself taller, feet sliding apart.

A moment passed, and then Pamir laughed at parts of this or at everything. Diamond's impression was that it took time for what happened here to reach the dragon's room. Was it the distance, or maybe the wires between them were tangled? He began to ask, but Elata spoke first.

She sang and Pamir answered, then she turned to King. "I'm explaining your name."

Pair spoke again.

"He wants to know. Were you born carrying the name?"

King rose higher. "My father gave it to me."

Elata translated with a couple notes, then continued singing.

"What's all that?" Diamond asked when he could.

Shrugging, she said, "I told him about the Archon. Who sounds like a harum-scarum. Bluster and standing your ground and all."

King broke into a human laugh.

Pamir was studying all three of them. This dragon didn't seem as smart as Mere, which meant nothing. Diamond needed to stop trusting his impressions. Faces couldn't be believed, not even when the face pretended to be close enough to touch. These people were meat wrapped around their true natures, and meat could be shaped by need and wishes. Except in Pamir's case, who was caged light and the illusion of shadow.

The dragon spoke once more.

Elata translated. "'My new friend.' Yeah, he called you that. 'My new friend. There's a better name for your species. The Clan of the Many Clans, and doesn't that sound proud and perfect? And they have a word that translates into King. Only you don't want to wear that name. The king is the man or woman who rules everything that can be ruled. The king stands everywhere at once and protects everything at once, and for him or for her, there is one future and it means loss. To be overthrown, cast aside, vanquished as only kings can be.'"

A long pause.

Then King said, "Tell the monkey, 'Thank you. But long ago, I figured that out for myself.'"

On the reef, there were days when the very good ordered the abuse of the very bad. Thieves, murderers. Traitors to the Papio. Sometimes the Eight were invited to watch while professional torturers used pain to reveal deeply flawed souls. Their methods were simple, blunt. Tools pulled from a mechanic's drawer were usually adequate. Misery and repetition: That's how the prisoner's resolve was stolen, and only then would the official interrogation begin.

But this interrogation didn't need hammers. With nothing but a new body, the prisoner's strength had been stolen away.

Sitting helpless before this black-haired beast, it seemed as though only one escape remained. Shock himself badly enough, and Kai would fall unconscious, leaving him out of reach. That's why the new fingernails gouged at soft flesh, blood clotting but not fast enough, rolling down his bare front, pooling in his lap and then on the floor.

The man responded to the carnage with a smile. But it was an unhappy smile, and a sorry voice asked, "What are you doing to yourself?"

Then, unexpectedly, he said, "Kai, please stop."

The smallest, weakest piece of the Eight had been stuffed inside a carcass that could be savaged. Desperate to impress the enemy with his willpower, the prisoner gnawed at his own wrist, dull little teeth opening up a vessel that would save him from the next question.

Which happened to be the previous question, only the phrasing was changed.

"What the shit are you doing, Kai?"

Biting higher on the arm, Kai filled his mouth with meat that he spat at the floor between them. And with that drama achieved, he stared at his enemy.

"Till," said the man.

Salty warm blood filled the unwanted mouth.

"My name is Till. And I like to hear it said by others. So please, say my name. Will you, Kai?"

No.

Till was sad and increasingly worried. That's what the face promised. "You think you know what this is. You and I sharing a little room. And because you feel weak, you insist on believing the worst."

Kai closed his unwelcome eyes.

"I'm not trying to injure you, and I don't want to remake you, Kai. This body is a quick and sloppy trick. And the language between us? Invented today. I have no idea what you know or how to compel you to tell me anything, and unfortunately we don't have days to bridge the gaps. Later, I hope. I'll explain our history, explain this world and the worlds beyond. And when I'm talking, you'll be free to ask questions, demand clarity. Or to make no sound at all, if you'd rather. But you must listen to me now. You are going to pay attention to me now. And the universe will appreciate you a little bit more if you stop making such a mess out of your temporary body."

"Temporary," Kai repeated.

Till nodded. Nothing more.

And then the bleeding was done, every wound healed. That suddenly, that easily. And against every expectation, the whole and healthy body relaxed around him.

Kai glanced at his clean fingers, wondering if he could bite them off at the joints, one at a time.

"Let me offer a confession," said Till. "When I was young, I was horrible. Massively, passionately horrible."

Kai looked at the black-haired man.

"I made wicked, brutal, stupid decisions. Willfully endangered billions of worthy lives. Oh, and I murdered my mother too. Who richly deserved her fate, yes. But it was clumsy, passionate murder, and I didn't deserve to survive my idiocies. But to be alive is a blessing. That's what I decided, and with enough time left to catalog my blunders. Maybe you'll have that same kind of luck in your life. You know, with enough days left to make amends. But the two of us ... we might have only hours left to live, even minutes. Unless we're too late already. Our enemies are here, Kai. I don't know how or how many, but I want your help, and as soon as we finish, I swear, I will put you back where you believe that you belong."

"Belong," Kai repeated.

"Where you still are," said Till. "Because no, I wouldn't rip you away from her bodymates. That would be wicked, and I am not. I'm no evil man. Though make no mistake about this, Kai. If the universe needed, I would murder my mother every day and burn trillions of good people while devastating worlds beyond count. If that would somehow stop the !eech."

"What are the !eech?"

An intense, deeply unlikely story began, crossing huge reaches of time and unknown realms. And Kai listened. Every word inside this new language was fascinating, and the prisoner was focused, enthralled. Yet then in mid-sentence, without warning, Till stopped telling the story and then rose to his feet, saying, "This has to be enough for now."

An interrogator's trick. Kai was certain.

Except the room and Till had vanished, and Kai was suddenly falling again, the cold blackness above punctuated with tiny warm lights, while far below, rising to meet him, was an ocean twisted by the writhing of great bodies and a smothering hot lovely light.

EIGHT

Wayward knees squatted on the hill and every
portion of the surrounding landscape -- a thirty-
kilometer radius of iron and black stone, rainwater
lakes and hard-running lava flows. And how many
Waywards were there? Suppression. Camouflage.
Illusion. The first three soldiers in any army. What
Broken saw was believable. Sapphire bunkers tied
to reactors, railguns, and latrines, all serving
thousands of nervous bodies, while the bright air
above buzzed with encrypted chatter. Plus eleven
distinct signatures of juggernauts doing a
respectable job of frightening everyone. The only
good part of this day was that Broken didn't have to
be the only one who was afraid. Juggernauts could
always be decoys. Hopefully they were. But even
decoys delivered a message. Shielded nukes and

plasma cannons could be waiting for the first idiots to risk the hilltop.

Pallas and her clan were destined to be the honored idiots.

Pallas was explaining, and her audience knew to keep quiet. "That little stranger who flew away. Till believes it was !eech, and that's why he might drop every resource at the site. And he's right to worry. Elata and her companions describe what could be, probably is, a juvenile female !eech. But these children know nothing about the species' history. To them, she's just a shape-bending entity who happens to wear a self-given name. 'Quest.'"

So the incredible and the ridiculous were true. The conquerors of the universe had returned to Paradise.

Pallas' entire clan was squeezed inside one swift, new-built vessel. These were the soldiers who brought that dying dragon to Mere, and they were everyone else who had followed them part way home, riding inside other stealths while wondering if their next breath would ever happen.

Staring at her three lieutenants, Pallas said, "Comments."

Broken spoke first. Which was remarkable. The calmest voice he could manage proposed that Till should nuke the hill and the countryside. Then to feel a little more certain, every dragon should work together, obliterating every life form within a two hundred kilometer radius, including sterilizing the atmosphere and bubbling the ground. Although that might not be enough, he conceded. And that was why some brave dragon should finally turn a juggernaut on his or her own head. Burn everything. That was this fearful soldier's reflex. And having argued for the end of the world, Broken felt marvelous. Everyone was staring. One end of the continuum belonged to him, and it was hard to envision any plan half as bold.

Tyley rolled her eyes, rolled her shoulders. "Just one !eech," she pointed out. "And she crawled from below, not above. So this isn't an ordinary invasion. This doesn't taste like war. All we need is to find the girl and kill her and then call it a very good day. That's what I would do."

The middle ground was taken.

Three Wings offered his bright laugh, and questions. "Let's talk about what we don't know. Which is everything. Where did this !eech come from? And why now? And why that name? Mostly I want to ask about the name. Quest doesn't sound !eech, not from what I remember, and I want to know a lot more about the child. Before I burn her or the rest of this ignorant world."

Pragmatism in the midst of strife. Three Wings was the better soldier, and Broken was happily shamed.

"On the subject of ignorance," said Pallas. "What looks like a first-time dragon makes a convincing attempt to kill herself. But we have just enough luck. Two more drops of blood escape, and our six dragons are sitting between lives, unable to appreciate what killed them. Unprepared to take the Elata girl seriously next time. Plus there's other strangers dripping in mystery. Two mortal boys who seem ordinary, except for being great friends with a once-mortal girl who carries more power than any of us. And the durable lad who Three Wings so helpfully gutted. Diamond. Who claims to be in charge of their clan, and those in custody seem to support him in that. But instead of a klein, he carries a pathological sense of destiny. And oh by the way, he appears to be the love child of Demon Till and Madam Washen. Which makes the harum-scarum almost ordinary, doesn't it? King, womb-brother to Diamond, and I don't know any ripe details about this family's history. The Eight? A mess of minds trapped inside one body, and tell me if you understand how that happens. Tell Mere, please. She's desperate for insights. And now we're back to our little !eech. I'm telling you this: If you see her, be nice. Be sweet. Shoot her to restrain her. Chop off every wing and leg until the kid's too small to generate fresh limbs and flee. But never forget -- this mess is wrapped around a klein. Since we have no useful idea about how these creatures came here, it's not impossible that the dragon's marker was misallocated. Any one of these children could be the true dragon. Quest could mean everything, and small people need to be spectacularly cautious. Keeping the world alive means that every allied dragon is spending precious time and reasoning and probably a few lies too, trying to help Till appreciate this impossible situation."

An audible tone found them, and Pallas paused. Three Wings had his own mission, covert and undoubtedly fun. Pallas gave a simple nod, other soldiers wished him luck hunting Wayward heads, while Broken offered nothing but a shy glance wrapped around nervous silence.

With that, his friend slipped into a drop-sheath and vanished.

"One more mystery," Pallas continued. "The hill itself. This is no normal vault. Certainly not a box or tomb we recognize. Someone needs to understand this piece of ground, and that's why the Waywards don't get ownership. Our best case scenario, today and for the next ten thousand centuries? Every dragon gains a comfortable presence near this hill. Nobody excluded, and every nation pretends to work together. Nobody ever wished for this, but nobody can ignore the gift either, and we're going to leverage the conundrum into a grand alliance. That's what we're insuring now. Our little dragon gets her share, and we get too little praise, and half a million years from now, heroic hyperfiber statues of us will be guarding this hill. And so will we. For aeons to come, we will never stop talking about what we've accomplished today, between one sleep and the next."

And the speech was done. Pallas stood before them as the ship began its hard descent. Every nexus brought the "make ready" signal. Every means of exposing themselves was being utilized. Their clan was promising the world that they were lightly armed and riding a barely armored vehicle nearly two hundred kilometers above newborn crust and over a nervous, heavily entrenched army, and what Pallas was doing -- what her people were better suited to do than any other clan or nation -- was to drop on top of the cracked terrain that they had already claimed.

"This will be our best day," she promised.

When Broken was scared, colors looked richer. At that moment, Pallas was bluer than she had ever been, and her hair was as gold as the soft useless metal. He loved the woman and feared for her life. Which was the oddest piece of this experience. Afraid for Pallas, Broken neglected to think just how miserably terrified he was about himself.

"We die twice, but that's all," she promised.

Drop-sheaths waited. The full clan, minus Three Wings, was going to launch at that hilltop, exposed for the fall and easily slaughtered, should the Waywards decide on that tactic. But this was the least-awful plan. They were leaning on Till's shrewdness and his aeons of experience to keep messes from escalating. Except there was an army below, and armies always brought the chance for insubordination. Waywards were ill-disciplined by design. Some of those juggernauts were going to wake up. Once that thought took hold, Broken's body had to drag the frightened mind into his own drop-sheath. Some of the soldiers carried one or two of the severed heads. As charms to bring splendid fortune. But Pallas didn't, and Broken and Tyley didn't either. Why steal luck from the lower ranks? With his own head down and no weapon worse than a railgun riding beside him, Broken cleared his lungs with the one word, "Ready."

Everyone said, "Ready."

The ship counted down for no reason but tradition. They knew when they were going to launch, and it was.

Now?

Something small and vicious struck the thin, exceptionally frail hull.

Above the atmosphere, still far removed from any safe ground, a hundred sheaths and a hundred bodies were scattered along with the hypersonic wreckage, tumbling wildly for the moment it took AI pilots to conquer the mathematics, pulling the least lousy trajectories from infinite offerings.

Then the sheaths, knowing what was best, deftly killed everyone onboard.

Slug Insertions were simple and tough to defend against, and that was why they were beautiful. The major complication was that every supersonic touchdown temporarily killed the body, which was wickedly inconvenient, what with bones pulverized and organs turned to fluid. That's why it was smart to die as soon as you launched. That's why the soldier agreed to slide into her sheath, confident that the surrounding machinery would deftly shred everything but the bioceramic brain. Emulsified and numbed, her liquid form would be charged with power, allowing trillions of cells and ten quadrillion supportive appliances to swim into perfect locations, each possessed by some narrow task. Then the gelatin was flash-frozen, transformed into a highly refined, totipotent glass, that fancy carcass serving as armor to a mind that was now free to consider its plans and its terrors, but mostly just happy to dwell on the tiny crap that filled those long boring reaches of life between one slug insertion and the next.

Tyley loved this kind of fighting. Passionate love, and she didn't care that others were rather less eager than she was, or annoyed with her unblinking affection for controlled mayhem.

Nothing in life was better than mayhem.

Tyley wasn't vault-born, and she was younger than most of her clan. School and simple observation warned that she was only as smart as everyone else, and while adept in a fight, her skills were born more from spirit than any specific talent. Yet more than anyone else, Tyley relished a keen sense of her personal destiny. She knew what the future was bringing, and this wasn't simple premonition. Premonition was the residue of dream or pain-wrenched vision, while her foresight rose from a rare appreciation for the multiverse. The whole of Creation had made this girl a marvelous promise" Against phenomenal odds, and regardless what happened on this day or during the next million years, Tyley was going to become a dragon.

Sure, mention the truth and you sound ridiculous, insane. But what was standing in her way? Just one one-in-a-ten-trillion-event had to occur, and then a one-in-a-hundred-trillion event, and then a few thousand more unlikelies after that. But infinity was nothing less than boundless. The most ludicrous possibility remained possible, which was the same as guaranteed, and that's why the multiverse had no choice but give her everything she could want.

Dragons were born when Marrow was shoved against the sky. The last bits of life boiled and then the hyperfiber sky burned, pounding the world back into a harder denser version of itself -- a little ball of nonsense dripping with molten iron. The first dragon was bugs and the oily black trees that always returned, proving their role as the proverbial trigger. But triggers were mechanisms, and mechanisms could be fooled. That's why multiple dragons now returned from Nothingness. Till was as good as guaranteed. Miocene, a little less so. Washen and Mere were typical, and Washen's son too. Although not on this go around for poor Locke. Pamir and Aasleen? Common dragons pulled from the ranks of ex-captains and famous dragon children. And there were outliers, including aliens and unusual humans and even a few AIs. Making yourself into a dragon required nothing but brutal work and exceptional blessings, and this was just one Marrow, and the multiverse was stubbornly endless. Tyley learned that lesson as a child, sitting on a block of dirty iron, listening to the AI's lecture.

And those thoughts never stopped running through her, at least within some little wedge of her brain. The infinite had no choice but to be generous. And among the boundless gifts was a Marrow born with exactly one dragon.

Bugs and black trees. No inhabitants but stupid legs carrying stupid bodies. But what if a woman with focus and time could build a secret vault? Granted a million years of preparation, that ambitious creature would weave herself a spectacular tomb that would carry her into that ripe cycle. One chance in a trillion trillion quadrillion was the same as inevitable. A tall beautiful woman with parchment skin and glowing red hair would have to enjoy just a little more luck, emerging first into the new world, then spending the next million years maintaining her solitude while watching the sky pull close.

A million years to prepare the soul for one more certainty.

That was Tyley. That was the young woman who eagerly climbed inside the sheath, happy to have her body turned to froth and then glass.

Yes, the odds for dragonhood were calculable and ludicrous. Friends had warned her with statistics, strangers with insults, and being sane, she took both to heart. Yet today, against every expectation, one new dragon had appeared. This Elata wasn't a tenth as impressive as Tyley, yet she existed. And if that little blob of mortal tissue could swallow a klein, maybe the multiverse was more generous than anyone imagined.

That's what made this girl's mind sing ... even as her ship was shredded by an explosion, as her sheath tumbled until it found its aim ...

Perpetually ready, Tyley kept chasing the math to its magnificent end.

The Waywards hit sooner and far, far harder than expected.

Three Wings pulled the good from that ugliness. "Pin your anger on the others," he told the enemies below. "Ignore me until you're thoroughly screwed."

He wasn't trying a slug insertion. The lieutenant was still alive, his sheath draped in camouflage, and moving slow as a breeze, he skimmed low over a pure Marrow jungle, hunting for the best target, or any target at all. All he needed was a tidy bunker or shielded gun emplacement where Wayward nerves were strained. But one small surprise waylaid him. Nobody was defending this ground. One after another, potential targets proved to be illusions. Nothing but lying machines were relentlessly generating the look of Wayward encampments, and the stink of them, and Wayward sounds down to unique voices belting out songs about legendary terrors that nothing but a great fire could defeat.

Waywards certainly loved their music. And as much as Three Wings hated that nation of fanatics, they were wonderful vocalists.

No targets for the taking, his sheath set down and unloaded. Wayward-spiced skin and Wayward camouflage enhanced his disguise, but he also beheaded a slow hammerwing and ate three bites from the hot thorax, leaving his breath as believable as the rest of him. Then with the secret weapon riding on his back, he ran, barefoot and sprinting, aiming for the nearest ridge.

Scattered across the sky, Pallas' clan was trying to dive for the hill. A prize like that deserved a name. Dragon Hill was being shared on nexuses, but that was too easy, too lazy. "Three Wings' Mountain," he muttered. "Noble. Strong. The perfect title for a wonderful ballad."

He laughed and ran, and then topping the ridge, he heard genuine singing. Augmented ears found one young man standing inside a blind fitted inside an umbra tree, very nearly invisible and no doubt suffering from miserable boredom.

Three Wings stopped.

Shredded toes healed.

The nearby song ended after a flourish, and Three Wings saw his enemy's hiding place. Set in a random, unpredictable site, the blind was dressed in the best static camouflage. Otherwise there was no one lurking. And why so few soldiers? The most important piece of the world stood beyond the horizon. Till and his barbarians were focused on nothing else. Yet the Waywards' presence was intentionally thin, and that led to the obvious excuse: The single !eech could be building a beachhead for a full invasion. And what kinds of skills did Quest bring to bear? According to myth, her species could mimic any form, including bodies invented for a single occasion. They were geniuses at stealing faces and weapons and even a nation's infrastructure. Indeed, there was no skill that they couldn't master. Yet the myth didn't cast shadows until today. At most, the !eech were old nightmares, no more urgent or believable than the fabulous nonsense about stars burning inside a cold vacuum or humans being trivial to the invisible universe.

But today, one !eech was on the prowl. The gal was real enough to wear a name, and more ominous, her species might well have improved their talents since their last visit. So Till had made a very reasonable decision. He didn't send armies. He didn't deploy weapons. Don't give Quest any tool or weak mind that she could bend to suit any nefarious task.

Waywards were crafty-smart.

And Three Wings would never think otherwise.

"On the subject of monsters," he mouthed.

The secret weapon had to be uncloaked. Three Wings slowly, carefully eased off envelopes of metafabric. Then shadow-weave had to be cut away, exposing a second, more stubborn mesh of unfamiliar design. He and the knife developed a partnership while an offline nexus gave the official briefing. This weapon was discovered inside an early-generation vault, sleeping happy within a cesium bath, and Mere studied it until satisfied that it was long dead and buried by its killers, minus the brain and soul. But the immortal flesh should be robust enough. That's why Mere tried to splice in a neural package, but she failed. In the end, it was the Dragon of Machines who restored the corpse with assorted instincts, plus a fervent belief in the divine nature of the !eech.

Shadow-weave gave way to a buggy beast. In their native form, the !eech were usually built from five sections, but that was tradition and fashion more than nature. Quest was said to have three sections, like earthly insect, so the least-important two pieces had been punched out of the corpse before they embarked. Which would be no bother at all. Alien proteins and dense, intensely complicated nanogenetics were tied to the body's immortality, and central to this marvel were mechanisms that didn't just repair flesh. !eech flesh was a powerhouse that never stopped dreaming about inventing new flesh, and that's why this magic was swift and relentless, and that's why the man holding the prize couldn't help but tremble.

Three Wings flipped the bug on its back, delivering an injection that would jolt dead meat out of its latest hibernation.

What kind of existence would this be, changing shape and size with nothing but his own boundless will?

"I'll ask the girl when I catch her," he said.

The exoskeleton warmed, but nothing else changed.

Then in a tradition old as humanity, Three Wings gave the bug a quick, delicate poke.

The !eech vanished.

Instantly, without fuss, it passed from existence into invisibility. From this piece of space to somewhere else. Three Wings touched the empty, still warm ground, and laughing quietly, he stood. That very bored Wayward boy was singing a fresh song, something about the pretty girl whom he loved more than he loved life, the next verses describing the marriage to come and their next ten thousand centuries of joy.

It was critical that this fake !eech wasn't a great !eech. Three Wings wanted to panic a nation, but how could that happen if your bait remained hidden?

Except the corpse remained unnoticed. The hidden man paused his song, but only because he hadn't finished writing his frothy lyrics, needing a moment before offering up the final lines.

"A love we can eat, a love we can fly … love enough to power this world and a thousand more to come … "

Did Three Wings need to run up to the blind and kick that laggard?

No. A nervous sensor noted leaking heat, and a quiet Wayward alarm did everything else.

Here was a splendid opportunity to kneel and do nothing. Too bad Three Wings was no singer. But Waywards and their songs were in his thoughts. Why did they bury themselves inside an unending musical? Because by every other measure, their lives were wickedly hard. These were people who happily made clothes from their own immortal flesh, who fashioned tools from their own trusted bones, and who feasted on vermin every day. This was their life because they were so different and odd, and because a spectacularly odd life kept them bound together, singing in a chorus that proved, or at least pretended to prove, the unity that shamed every other nation.

And the best reason for song?

The Wayward dream was to fill Marrow with their splendid noise. In another million years, land and water might well be covered with these feral children, and standing on the summit of Three Wings' Mountain, when the hyperfiber was near enough to touch, the Waywards would celebrate with a chorus: Human voices by the billions reflecting off the hyperfiber sky. And with the echo, Marrow would shake. Would shiver. Would dance.

One clean, simple mission. That's what Mere promised. Kill your flesh and drop on the hill, and if your body healed soon enough, fight. Battle the Waywards until they made you into a carcass all over again. Unless there wasn't time enough to wield weapons, and the enemy painted that hilltop with your unhealed cells. Either route earned the same result. Two deaths but establishing a physical presence too. Invoking the Law. Nothing else mattered. A vault was trying to hide beneath the crust, and that vault was unique. Unless it wasn't a vault at all, which meant that the situation was more dangerous and maybe more blessed than anyone was ready to measure. But law and tradition didn't require explanations. Ground was ground, and Mere didn't have to remind Pallas that she and her people had first rights. Or for that matter, that every dragon among the present dragons respected rights and conventions, regardless how combustible situations might appear.

"You won't win the fight, but this isn't a fight," Mere had said. "This is custom, this is liturgy, and with that in mind, no juggernauts. Field munitions and knives only."

"Explain that to Till," Pallas had said.

An unusual moment, letting bitterness leak free.

Yet the little dragon anticipated the emotion, if not the sarcasm. "Oh, I've told him that you'll be lightly armed. And in the same spirit, I shared both your flight plan and battle orders too."

Pallas was silent.

"Every dance has obligatory motions," Mere concluded. Then came a smile and knowing wink, with the cryptic send-off, "But there's still considerable space between the steps."

Having no choice but to feel betrayed, Pallas cultivated anger until the anger got heavy. Then she focused on loading her people onboard a hypersonic coffin, but making certain they wore the best armor and the best personal shields. Lose the battle, yes. But nobody had to be wiped from existence.

Logistics had their own rituals, and in the midst of that work, something obvious occurred to Pallas. Bold, ridiculous, and perfect.

This was no job to delegate. Moments after launching, she slipped away from the others and set a shaped charge against the ship's interior hull. Waywards were waiting for a slug insertion, but she'd give them a dose of chaos too. Maybe the results would be worse. But then again, her people were marvels of inspiration, and what did it matter if they got scattered like seed?

Once everyone was tucked inside their sheath, Pallas gave the signal and the ship was shredded.

Pre-briefed, her sheath was ready for the blast. One hard roll and it righted itself, and then her body was liquified, cells stacked where needed and frozen hard before the boosters punched her along a clean trajectory. But the poor others had to deal with too many variables. Pallas' hope was for sheaths and soldiers to miss the target, ending up scattered, confused and usefully pissed. The public attack plan was shit, which happened to be the best way to protect the others. While their leader bore the responsibility of standing on the hilltop where this very bad day began.

Boosters surged and cut back, random jiggles confounding distant marksmen. Or nobody fired at her. She couldn't know either way. Then the sheath pivoted and obliterated most of its momentum. But only most. Hovering would introduce its own risks, and that's why the fuelless husk skipped across stone and hyperfiber and then back to the stone again, rolling to a graceless stop. Then the glass corpse was melted and a valve opened, spitting out the molten passenger, her armor and her guns, plus a magnificently legal declaration.

"This treasure belongs to me," the document claimed. With the addition of legal chatter and a brief synopsis of the last twenty million years of civil order.

Pallas would never wake. She accepted that likelihood. Wayward troops would leap out of bunkers and lava tubes, wearing armor instead of leather, helmets instead of braids, plus augmented boots and railguns and skills earned through drills and dreams. In war, every soldier wore the same garb, erasing most advantages. In war, you didn't leave children on top of strategic prize. Crack killers would gather around one helpless soul, and those holding juggernauts would fight for the honor of erasing her from existence. Pallas had considered a second bomb hiding inside her sheath. Just to make the situation a little more spectacular. But in the end, she decided that this gesture was ample. Let the Waywards focus on her, giving her clan the chance to hide and move, move and fight.

Her battle armor wrapped itself around the healing body.

What wasn't entirely pain turned into feverish joy.

Pallas ignored every sensation. For no reason, her left hand functioned before the right, and her left eye gave her just enough vision to bring a face into existence. A male face, and familiar.

Diamond.

The boy was kneeling over her. Which was preposterous, or reasonable. Maybe the precious vault below had spat out his twin.

Words. That's what the face was offering. Encouraging words, judging from what her scrambled auditories absorbed.

But this wasn't Diamond, was it?

The hair was black, which was wrong, and it was too long, and that wrong hair surrounded what looked like a grown face, and what sounded like man's voice turned from mutters into a warm, lovely presence.

She knew this voice.

Just as she knew the face, which didn't really resemble the enigma boy.

Till.

"Till," she managed.

Nobody else was kneeling beside her. The dragon's two hands were holding one of her battle gloves.

The vertigo worsened until the world stopped moving, and that was when Pallas' ears worked perfectly again.

"Just me," Till said.

Staring at the great, awful dragon, she managed to ask, "Where's your army?"

He laughed.

"Why?" he asked. "Do I look like I need any help?"

Inside a volcano's empty artery, cradling the machine stolen from an empty-head girl, Quest watched a world that was colorful and enormous, insistent and fascinatingly confusing. "Marrow." What the name meant was just another mystery. She didn't know how to ask for definitions, much less historic accounts. Human fingers inspired the view to shift, but she couldn't predict, much less direct, what she saw next and next and next. Sound worked better. Any human bark elicited reactions. Fresh images, other people's voices. Cities were common, human faces were common, yet much of the land was uninhabitable, twisted by fire or covered by deep drowning masses of water. And the gray ceiling was always above, smooth and tempting. That grayness had a palpable pull. Quest needed to reach the gray. She didn't know why that would be, but the instinct was urgent, maddening. And the tiny window cradled in her new hands was going to explain everything. If only she could just alone sit in this warm deep cavern, no one bothering her for another million days.

!eech.

That word always triggered the best imagery.

"!eech."

The human tongue clicked, and the entire mouth added, "eech," and then some new astonishment offered itself to human eyes.

A single !eech looked like Quest when she was simple -- the segmented shell and jointed legs and jointed arms, two or three or more crystalline eyes rising at domes from the head. But the creatures seemed happier to look nothing like her, to the point where it was a game deciding which organism inside the picture was her species. Her cousin. Perhaps her own mother.

A multitude of forms.

Giant, tiny.

And oftentimes, ridiculously plentiful.

Every scene was a spectacle of light and sharp noise. The !eech body could shift its nature faster than Quest had ever managed, generating mouths and rectums and every tissue between. This was beauty born of stark transmutative power. One !eech began as a human and became another human before turning into an animal with five legs. And then a few breaths later, she became the first human again. Massive physiological tricks were in play, but hidden beneath an easy, impossible grace. Quest thought of monkeys dancing across tiny tree limbs, mastering their balance despite the gyrations of wood and wind. Quest was never an expert monkey -- one embarrassing lesson learned too often. Yet not only did the !eech accomplish multiple forms, they did so with no visible effort, vanishing into monkey faces that couldn't look more appealing, more true.

In such a world, how could you tease the real from the fake?

The !eech were real and everything else was less than genuine. That idea lay buried in those moments when her new spine shifted against the rock floor, both hands holding tight to Marrow.

The most beautiful scenes showed war. There were compelling fires and blazes worse than any fire. Human cities turned to ash, while the deep smothering water boiled. Quest was a beetle watching great storms from the safest hollow inside the strongest tree. Death was given reign over the world, but this little !eech suffered only slight discomfort when all of that life was suddenly made dead.

In the midst of slaughter, she found the black-haired human again.

And this time, a name.

"Till."

A melodic shout from human mouths, and she repeated the name with her best singing voice.

"Till."

The man was standing at the center of a round plaza.

"Till."

More images in different locations, plus samples of motion and song and stomping feet. Till was singing or speaking, and unable to understand any of it, Quest repeated every word, every note, with perfect diction.

The imagery quit shifting. Standing at the edge of a great battle, Till and Quest watched the lovely !eech swarm across the landscape. Legs and arms were bigger than trees, and above those limbs, powerful bodies were covered with pieces of the gray ceiling. The !eech fired bolts of light, the nearby humans screaming as the air split with thunder, and Till remained on the highest, most exposed ground, watching what would never stop. This was the war's final battle. Humans were beaten. Once more, Till clicked his tongue and his mouth said, "eech," as he lifted a stubby weapon with a big barrel. The nearest !eech aimed at the hand, but transparent armor deflected the blast long enough for the human to take aim. Quest recognized Till's weapon. Today's children carried a similar gun, using it on the wounded Elata. But that machine produced a very gentle light compared to what Till unleashed. The imagery slowed and slowed and slowed as a furious drip of fire was released, the syrupy incandescence wrapping itself around Till's head, while his body stood for no reason but habit. And that was the moment when the gray ceiling vanished behind an onslaught of light. By then, time had collapsed until nothing seemed to happen. Till was a headless statue, his people as good as frozen, while the swiftest !eech had no chance to complete the next step before a new fire arrived, sweeping across the world: A stupefying brilliance that forced human eyes to blink.

Quest set the world down.

A few words learned, and one lesson. "I can be anything," she whispered, using the language she knew best. "And what do I want to be?"

The rock walls offered no opinion, and set against her chest, the world had fallen dark and silent.

Quest made herself into a human-sized !eech and then jumped back to human again. Once, twice, and then faster, but never fast enough. Fifty-three bounces for practice, and then she felt a vibration, both subtle and everywhere. Pressing both kinds of hands against the rock wall, Quest wondered if perhaps Marrow had its own voice and that was what she felt rippling through stone, trying to speak to no one but her.

Waywards were shouting, encryptions filling the air.

"They saw the !eech," Tyley said.

"Three Wings' girl," Broken hoped.

"But now they've lost her again. Whoever she is."

Lifting his head, Broken peered between the burly trunks of trees always known as iron-splitters.

"What do you see?" Tyley asked.

"One nervous platoon."

"First-league troops filling armor, standing behind more armor," she said. "Plus big railguns and a charged juggernaut."

Crouching together, half a kilometer apart, the two lieutenants were whispering across an encrypted channel. Broken was focused on a gem-woven bunker pretending to be rocks, plus the bright hot marker of one exposed soldier urinating. The lieutenants had already collected a dozen rebuilt soldiers, still scattered but very much organized. Any dash towards the hill had to take out that emplacement. Unless there were no troops, which was becoming a compelling possibility.

"We need to move," Tyley said.

Broken was closest to the Waywards. "First let's see if they want my head," he said.

Fear was doing its worst, but he wasn't crippled. What's more, dying a second time would earn a temporary peace, which was appealing. Broken crept forward and then stopped, spinning a coherent shadow out of volcanic dust and static. The black shape was wearing Broken's face, and it rose up and ran at the emplacement, carried by a convincing long-limbed stride. Nobody fired at the shadow or its builder. Nobody should be fooled by that simple trick. But the security nets gave his doppelganger too much consideration, which was a sure sign of AIs being in charge.

"The nest's a decoy," Broken said.

"And the rest of the platoon?"

He started to say, "Unreal."

And a gun snapped, nickel slugs aimed at his right hand. His reactive glove changed shape, deflecting the first three blows, but the hand was shattered with the fourth round and removed with the fifth.

Broken cursed.

Three of his people shot the attacker, destroying a preset gun. But that woke a genuine soldier hiding inside the false emplacement. Another supersonic chunk of nickel was aimed at Broken's nose, but his aegis chestplate reacted just in time, explosive flecks burrowing into the ground before igniting, a storm of lava grit and pebbles leaping up to absorb the thumb-sized enemy.

That's when terror took hold.

Broken was cornered, exposed. A stranger was trying to carve his brain from his body, or worse, and running away was a perfectly respectable tactic. If he had three minutes before the next shot. But three seconds would be a luxury. He released every possible camouflage. Shadows raced. Smoke pushed against the breeze. Flickers were thrown over the rocks, coordinating their flashes. And inside that overload of data, there was the possibility of revenge. Revenge was what coaxed him into a sprint. Brutally, magnificently pissed, he covered more ground faster than he had ever managed during his brief, wonderful life.

Five strides covered, and his chest-plate kicked up the ground again. But the next slug was more massive, better coached. Broken's transparent visor and the right half of his jaw were removed, and he remained upright for no good reason, blind in the right eye but seeing the universe with a clarity that would have been refreshing, on reflection. If Broken could have sat down instantly, carefully examining his state of mind.

Broken's field sensors spotted two hidden mines easily avoided, and then a third mine tore open the ground on his left.

Airborne, he felt powerful.

The illusion ended with him falling and rolling, grabbing his favorite little railgun in the wrong hand, in his left, giving it permission to aim and fire until he felt well enough to join in.

The gun couldn't find any target.

Somewhere in the world, Tyley was shouting orders.

Then a general alarm washed through every public channel. And with the cacophony, Till's voice.

"Target reacquired," shouted the dragon. "Ninety-one west, heading west … "

That's where Three Wings had dropped. The warrior had done his job.

Broken left his railgun with orders to defend him. On sprouted legs, the barrel aimed itself, and he was five strides away when the next slug destroyed his best weapon. But the enemy had exposed himself too. Smoke and running shadows surrounded a figure huddling between slabs of emerald. Armor always came in myriad flavors, and every kind of armor was good but a few were special. Hyperfiber was the best protection, and this Wayward was important enough to deserve a hyperfiber helmet covering the entire head. Cameras and other sensors created a bug-like face, multiple pathways leading into a mind that felt safe, buried as it was inside the most durable substance in the universe.

Broken threw what wasn't a bomb.

What wasn't a bomb transformed itself into gelatin, colorless and furiously sticky. Any greater distance and this would be futile. It was unlikely to succeed even at this range. But the device hit where it had to be, and covering the helmet in an instant, it shoved light and noise and even some awful odors into a mind that didn't want to believe that it was compromised. The Wayward saw Broken standing in the sky, a thousand-meter-tall figure with skin like night and the hair glowing blue-white, and he was bending over his foe, the house-sized thumb ready to crush the miserable bug.

Sneaking up on the distracted soldier was easy. Broken's left hand grabbed the backup railgun, shoving it into places where Waywards rarely bothered with hyperfiber armor. He shot away off the man's feet, and climbing on top, he used his weight and fury as well as the last shred of surprise, slapping down a second gelatin gob that spread across the helmet, firing white light and white noise into the blind, deaf Wayward.

Climbing off, Broken secured the man's arms, using his good hand and the exposed and very stubby fingers of his new right hand. And when that was finished, he sat on the prisoner's stomach.

Tyley and the others sprinted towards his position. And Till was everywhere else, telling his nation to watch the !eech but not to attack. Not yet.

"What are you doing?" Tyley asked.

What was Broken doing? He tried to explain, then remembered that his mouth was shot apart. On a nexus, he said, "Resting."

"No time. Pallas is up top."

"Already?"

"She dropped there," the lieutenant said. "She needs us, so go."

Broken stood once more. One little railgun left to fight with, and a bare hand too young to make a fist. Tyley and the others were close enough to be seen, and Broken ran too fast for breath to help. Stored energy carried him up the same ground they had climbed earlier today, but except for the pitch of the hill and the individual rocks, nothing was the same. A new forest was growing tall and thick, while Broken and his clan were as weak as could be. Far beyond the horizon, fleets of Wayward vehicles were launching. Till had held back his armies until now, and Broken told believe that the caution was because of them. If Pallas' weakest soldier could humiliate one of Till's finest fighters, then the entire Wayward nation should be terrified of what this clan could accomplish.

Broken's mouth was grown enough for a sloppy little laugh.

Tyley was ahead of him, lobbing float grenades that would hunt for trouble, sites marked by the detonations and her offering precise shots where needed.

Broken followed. This was what he normally did, trailing happily behind the others. Except that he wasn't terrified anymore. Time was scarce and he lacked the necessary wits, and while he didn't feel especially brave either, at least he found enough confidence that his healing mouth kept laughing.

Up ahead, his friend lost her balance and fell hard.

Tyley was shot.

Broken thought nothing else, even when he fell over.

He wasn't shot. Neither of them were. The ground had dropped beneath them. The hillside was trembling, a quake deciding to arrive now. Which wasn't possible. Fissures and the pressures running through Marrow were mapped every second. Every dragon had the tools. Cities and civilizations didn't survive long if they couldn't predict tectonic seizures weeks and years before they happened. And after finishing a series of healthy, very normal eruptions, the Blisters had entered a period of deep rest.

Yet here was Broken, rolling on his back, utterly helpless while the black ground rippled and rose and then fell sharply, gathering itself before lifting again.

Higher, faster.

When had Broken ever experienced such a massive quake?

Never.

This wasn't normal Marrow violence. This was something else, something new. Like a baby riding in his first ascending elevator, Broken was begin to appreciate how little he knew about so much. A vast odd unexplored realm had spat out a new dragon, and now for reasons of its own, the famous hill had decided that this was the moment when it should throw itself at the sky.

NINE

The simplest name was heavy. No creature carried a name unless she knew how to recognize distinct sounds or odors -- whatever label constituted the glorious Me. Recognition required neurons, and identity required pride, and pride had to be cultivated and then protected, which stole away even more of the mind's power. And as soon as one name was possible, then each of your blood relatives deserved distinct identities, and your entire species carried a worthy designation, as did competing species and edible species and the places that mattered and every critical instant in time. Soon the world was built from little sounds and little stinks, creating long histories and implications for the gray, unmeasured future, and names were perfect or they were wrong, and a portion of the day was spent wondering if you were worthy of your own great name.

This creature didn't bother with excesses.

This life, this existence, was wrapped around surviving the next moment and eating enough now now now and mating soon and leaving behind many tiny tough eggs that would increase the not-awful odds that her descendants would continue to rule this world.

"Hammerwing" wasn't her name. Not for herself or her species, and if she had ever heard "hammerwing," she didn't bother to notice and certainly wouldn't commit it to memory. That would be a thorough waste of a perfectly wonderful mind.

On this nameless unending and perpetually youthful world, she was a pinnacle predator. Any resemblance to the earthly dragonfly was superficial. Her carapace was far stronger than chitin, sapphire whiskers worked into silicas and tangles of complex, uncompromising organics that would hold their shape inside the hottest cookfire. Her six long wings were strong but malleable, abusing the air as they carried her wherever she wanted to be. Those faceted eyes saw the high violets and low reds, and unlike compound insect eyes, they revealed precise details. Lungs like bellows could pull oxygen from suffocated air, feeding a furious, hot-blooded metabolism, while complex, exceptionally ancient genetics hid trick upon trick, ready to meet any challenge in a landscape that was as furious and as nameless as she was.

The rock beneath her was shaking hard enough to split. This happened often and happened for one reason. Great quakes existed to force food out of its hiding places, lesser wings carrying bits of scared meat into her gaze. Because this was a time of wealth, she ate carefully, devouring the richest and rarest. And when her hunger was sated, which didn't take long, she caught one more favorite meal. Her mind knew the animal's flavor without the mouth tasting the prize, and because this was a delight best eaten alive, she tucked it beneath her powerful long body and flew fast through an atmosphere growing hotter and smokier by the moment.

In her endless, brief life, there had never been a quake this powerful. The ground roared and her wings roared, pushing her on a rising spiral. Yet even as she soared, the ground matched her pace. The oddest race had begun. Fissures opened beneath her, brilliant streaks of magma running quick while sounds larger than any voice threatened to shake her meal loose. Tossed across the blistering air, one way and then another, she screamed but never heard her own voice. Then the air was still hotter and suddenly much thinner, and she was falling.

That's when the living meal was dropped.

Just enough intellect lived inside her to grieve for what she would never eat. Nothing remained but to flail with her wings and steer higher, those spectacular eyes pointed at the gray sky.

Just for a moment, as the flames surged and the roaring ground surged, she imagined touching the sky.

Such a peculiar thought at end of this great life.

Life was often drawn from easy thoughts and stubborn thoughts, and for most souls, these were the sure routes to happiness.

But there were a few who could be tempted by seductive, dangerous ideas.

Aasleen's life began on a colony world -- a world that humans were aggressively terraforming. Tradition and strong gravity as well as the searing UV sunlight dictated black skin and black eyes, and physical strength, and every human colonist had an obligation to understand the machinery doing the bulk of the ambitious work. Many of those machines had rich minds. Some minds were happy to serve as companions to a smart young woman who preferred their company over human warmth and human complications. With her proclivities, Aasleen had little choice but to train as an engineer, and she had enough talent and luck to be handed the finest machine in the universe.

The Greatship.

Serving as an engineer on the Greatship brought a lot of joy, no doubt, but Aasleen remembered very little. Sipping at sleep, this dragon often dreamt that she was a lowly tech working with a balky stardrive. Dirty tritium and an unfamiliar reactor had to be dealt with, while the magnetic nozzles had been designed by the maliciously insane. This was no Greatship engine. That marvelous vehicle was the size and mass of Uranus, and despite being abandoned billions of years earlier, its moon-sized engines had been left in flawless condition. Humans happened to be first to land on the hull. Aasleen's species claimed the entire vessel as salvage, and she was one of the illustrious crew who steered the Greatship into the Milky Way, intending to take their prize on a long luxury cruise through the galaxy. And sometime during the next one hundred thousand years, after succeeding too well, Aasleen foolishly allowed herself to be seduced, joining the ranks of the captains, one exceptionally comfortable life suddenly replaced by another.

But what did Aasleen remember? Perched on immortality, ten thousand years were the same as one moment. She recalled serving as a captain, and there was hard data to support the comforting idea that she did well at her post. But only a few million disjointed memories survived, and she knew that full count because she'd made a thorough inventory. That was the nature of her mind. Accuracy was beauty. Precision was its own reward. Aasleen had even attempted to catalog those recollections while aligning them in their most likely sequence, building a scaffolding around the lost life, which brought up a lot of deep frustration that proved what she suspected at the outset: She didn't know shit about her own history.

"What was that, madam?"

"You heard me."

""Shit about my history,'" her colleague repeated, perfectly mimicking her voice.

"Exactly."

The workhouse was a kilometer-long building filled with lively machines. Some of the AIs had bodies, others were woven into the floor or ceiling, but the majority inhabited nodes beyond the hyperfiber walls. This was the hub of Aasleen's nation. Every dragon demanded control over her nation, but each had a bias for what "control" meant. Aasleen's biases were overlapping systems of light-speed data and quirky, intensely opinionated machinery. Most of her citizens needed sleep because sleep helped their brilliance, and most could wear faces because despite a deep ambivalence to organic bodies, their dragon enjoyed handsome faces and eyes looking back at her eyes, and every mouth revealed more than just sound when it spoke and when it remained silent.

At this particular moment, most of the resident mouths had forgotten how to speak, and the vast majority of eyes were baffled, watching a new mountain rising unexpectedly on the far side of Marrow.

The "what was that madam" colleague was an AI savant. Ancient beyond measure, he dressed in the facsimile of a human body, complete with a ragged white toga and sandals and the narrow, cartoonish face of a philosopher -- a visitor summoned from the age of mortal minds, when every idea pretended that it was being discovered for the first time.

"I don't understand my own history, which is a problem," she said. "Unless I'm mistaken and ignorance is a blessing."

"Ignorance should be a blessing," the savant replied. "Particularly when it frees the mind to follow fresh directions."

Savants were built to hunt down answers. The early models were asked to decipher the purpose or purposes of the Greatship, teasing out the hidden truths along with secrets nobody suspected could exist. And with their brilliance, they successfully imagined every wondrous event that had ever come to pass. Except not even the finest mind could yank the Inevitable from the Never. A million scenarios looked just as worthy as what was true, while billions of obvious and elegant and dangerously intriguing prophecies were embraced by the captains, each one of those mistakes believed until the moment when there weren't any captains anywhere onboard the Greatship.

This particular machine was somewhat newer than those savants. A neighboring dragon discovered the machine folded up inside a tiny vault. This was not a gift, and although Pamir asked for nothing, the dragon mentioned an ambitious, impossible timetable for building his nation's data infrastructure. Aasleen had no choice but offer aide in exchange for the prize. She had always cherished ancient and interesting companions, even when these poor entities were as damaged by the aeons as she was.

"You mutter quite a lot," the savant said.

"That sounds like a complaint."

Was it? Button-shaped eyes dipped, a skinny brass hand tugging at the optical cables that pretended to be a beard. "It is a complaint," he agreed. "Because sometimes, madam, listening to your self-absorbed monologues, I wonder about your sanity."

"Don't wonder," she advised. "My sanity is lost."

Other machines laughed at that.

But not the savant. Straightening a back not designed to be straight, he said, "This is a serious day. Why are we having this conversation today?"

"Serious, is it?"

Listing the reasons was unnecessary. A new dragon was in the world and every other dragon was scrambling. The first !eech to be seen in aeons was here too, and perhaps an invasion was underway. There was also the very unlikely son of Washen and Till. And what about the mysterious object that spat these strangers into Marrow? Every lucid prediction for the next million years had been rendered useless. Plus now, over just the last few minutes, a rude eruption was wrenching a landscape out of its natural position.

Yet the savant's dragon appeared utterly relaxed. Indeed, she insisted on smiling while making an odd statement.

"The past doesn't exist."

"What's that, madam?"

"And my past is particularly unreal," she added.

No word was remarkable, yet the two sentences generated multiple possibilities. He thought of all of them or nearly so. But which response would offer the most help?

Aasleen laughed softly, sweetly. "The future's endlessly fickle. A trillion events playing rough with each other, and that's when the next instant is realized. For the first time."

The savant listened, and he continued to watch what seemed to be the critical events. Waywards were chasing a decoy !eech, and because Aasleen built the decoy's mind, she was complicit in whatever happened next. Till had captured one of the strangers, or he had eight prisoners, depending on how the count was handled. Mere was launching her forces into a battle that had already turned violent, and she would lose, but she also had possession of five more strangers. And there was Miocene. The second most dangerous dragon had agreed to be Mere's ally, which made her Aasleen's ally. But Miocene demanded quite a lot in return, including possession of the Diamond boy. And if that wasn't enough to keep the mind busy, the massive eruption was growing in power and reach, contained signatures of phenomena that didn't belong and shouldn't be welcomed on the surface of this world.

"For the first time," Aasleen finished saying.

"But how can the past not exist?" he asked his dragon, irritated and happy to show it.

"Because nothing exists," she claimed.

Savants were always born creative, and that was still inside his nature. After a fashion. But his humor had been eroded along with his native joy, and nothing bothered the entity quite as much as unexpected thoughts delivered without the proper context. Which was what Aasleen enjoyed most about his companionship. Explaining your muddling doubts to others always made your muddle more useful.

"Multiple, nearly infinite pasts that bring us to Now," she said. "I was once a captain. Apparently. But now paint all the ways I might have traveled that career. A left turn instead of a right, a run instead of a flight. Ten thousand orders dispensed before breakfast, or I sleep past my usual minute. Countless scenarios coexist inside my brief, brief tenure as an officer. Yet each life leads to Now. I stand here and you stand there and both of us are destined to vanish when time yanks us to the next unfaithful moment."

Her companion said nothing.

And honestly, what would any good word accomplish?

Aasleen's face had the shape of an egg set on end, and her black eyes were closed, and he finally said, "Madam," as her eyes opened again.

"My mental health is just good enough," she promised. "What I'm doing here is confessing my personal model of the universe."

The savant absorbed words and intentions. "I do understand this particular theory," he insisted. "Though I can't agree with the implications."

"And thank you for your candor, but this is nothing but preamble. Do you know what I am thinking about most?"

"How could I, madam?"

"Those strange children that Mere found. They don't utterly fascinate me. Not when I first heard about them, not even when one of them seems to be a dragon and another is an !eech. Interesting, yes. They might be intriguing, yes. But they're not my responsibility today. Marrow is destroyed or survives. I have no role. Giant events transpiring in Wayward territory, and I'm as far from Till as possible. How can I influence events without further risking my nation, my machines?"

"Yes, madam. I respect our limitations."

"But this," she said, fingers poking at surveillance feeds from the far reaches of Marrow. "Something important waits underground. Miocene knows that much. She has more resources than I have, than Mere has. The alien signatures are enough to kindle her greed, and maybe even her curiosity. But I know what she can't know ... "

"'Can't know?'"

"And here's another confession. What hides under that hill is doing wonders to my mind. Because I do know this marvel. I recognize it. What we are seeing is a machine, a powerful squirming and very particular machine, and it's a wonder that could easily fill my days until the universe ends."

The savant compiled possible responses.

"How interesting," was a reasonable choice.

Aasleen closed her eyes again, her smile edging into a hard wince.

When she refused to elaborate, the savant asked one essential question. "And how do you know this marvel, madam?"

Bright eyes opened, the philosopher's face reflected in the blackness.

"Because I'm the one who likely buried it," she said.

Glass eyes blinked. "Likely?"

"Not that I recall the occasion, no."

"Then why do you think so?"

"Because there was an artifact. I knew an artifact with unusual, remarkable properties. When I was a captain, the artifact lay in storage inside the Greatship, waiting for me to find the proper means to study it. Then the !eech appeared, and I escaped to the smaller, softer Marrow. And of course I brought valuables."

"You brought this artifact?"

"Well, I can imagine myself bringing it here. And for safekeeping, I might have set it drifting in the iron ocean."

"You imagine and you might?" the savant asked.

"What I mean to say ... " Aasleen closed her eyes again. "I am a dragon. I am born everywhere and always, and while I don't recall bringing that one very odd machine here, my mirrors would have. Given time and the opportunity, every Aasleen should have tried to save it. Because this prize was that special, and possibly valuable, but most definitely fun."

"A machine that can do all of this?"

"No. Frankly, what I recall was quite small." With that, her hands spun circles, implying some insignificant volume. "Which is probably how it got lost in the first place."

Aasleen wasn't insane. The universe was racing into madness, and this savant had the only mind able to see it.

"I'm ordering an accelerated timetable," said Aasleen. "Now that I appreciate the stakes, I'm sending resources and bodies. Everything we can offer, as fast as possible."

This entire conversation deserved hard contemplation.

Then the savant said, "I'm scared."

Inside a long and crowded room that couldn't have been quieter, Aasleen laughed.

"And doesn't it feel splendid?" she called out.

The hill was surging, the countryside exploding, and those rivers of molten rock were nothing but harbingers for the white-hot iron sure to follow, plumes and fountains exploding half a kilometer tall.

Pallas had no hopes.

She had seen volcanoes born. Hundreds of craters, all reliably fun for a brave youngster, but not one of them was born under her feet. Or under Till's feet, which was what mattered. The dragon was standing when the tremors hit, and then he tumbled. But he found his legs again, and she managed to stand on her new feet. The basalts under them had shattered, but they were only skillet-hot. Facing one another, arms out, the two of them looked like acrobats balancing on frictionless wires. This was a party game and someone would fall first and it didn't matter who. Because this was a friendly contest, and nothing was at stake. Except of course everything was at stake. Bioceramic minds could withstand impacts and deep cold and common magma, but not plasma. And not the hottest iron either. If this was going to be the new mountain's crater, and if Till was consumed, then nothing but extraordinary luck would be able to yank him from the furnace before everyone else died.

Quite a lot was apparent, and then the ground shook harder and lifted faster, and Pallas fell first.

"I lose," she muttered.

Weeping.

The powerful, self-assured dragon remained on his feet. But only for another instant, then he collapsed with the same graceless inevitability. On his rump, he stared at the girl with what resembled bewildered amusement. Because for Till this was a game and a party, and he was immortal in too many ways, immune to the terrors that gave Pallas her fabulous panic.

"You have to survive," she shouted.

Her voice was lost in the roar of shattering stone.

She crawled to him, on hands and toes first, and then the ground accelerated upwards, and she was reduced to dragging herself on her bleeding stomach.

"Rescue," she cried out.

"Is coming," said Till. But it was brutal work just to lift one arm, pointing at the idea of salvation from the sky.

They were rising into the sky together. How could any aircraft find them and save him? Most of the Waywards were over the horizon, chasing the decoy. Very few were held back for new contingencies, and no help was coming, and Pallas looked at the world and inhaled another scorching breath, and suddenly every possibility but one was lost.

"My sheath," she shouted.

Till said, "What."

"Climb inside my drop-sheath."

The hyperfiber would protect him. Not forever, but long enough. Days, months. A few centuries, if need be. The Waywards would dig into the cooling iron, nothing spared until they rescued their leader, mummified but alive. And Pallas would have the distinction saving the world that she helped almost kill. Those ironies alone let her smile, repeating her very reasonable suggestion to a dragon that would certainly thank her, given the chance.

"Climb inside," she screamed. "And I'll seal it -- "

No.

The answer was delivered when Till shoved fingers into her mouth. Three fingers pressed down on her idiot tongue, and his bewildered joy was replaced with outrage and a very ugly laugh.

"You want to trap me," he shouted.

Why would he imagine that?

He said, "Bait. Is that what everything was? You want me caught and frozen hard and helpless."

An absolute untruth, right until the seamless logic struck Pallas. Till had to believe that this was a scheme. Because every scheme was possible. Because an elaborate plot was the explanation somewhere. Not on this particular Marrow, no. But elsewhere in the multiverse and too many times to count. This hill and the false dragon and a son that might be his, and then one unexpected eruption: Maybe the !eech marked the next invasion. Their greatest enemy had baited him into a trap. There was no worst scenario, and inside some portion of the multiverse, Till was being heroically paranoid and safer because of it. While in another portion, he and Marrow were doomed.

The ground's ascent had slowed. Not stopped, but the air was a little quieter, less agitated. Every stick and bug in the region was burning, and the smoky taste made Pallas cough, which was remarkable in itself. Immortal lungs rarely, rarely coughed. Then she stood and found Till on his feet, and knowing what was best, she threw herself back to the ground, groveling at his feet, begging him to please save himself.

"This isn't a trap," she promised.

With the air calm, the smoke could build. Suddenly nothing was visible but Till and the patch of ground under the two of them, and smiling at the silly child, the dragon asked, "What's your name?"

"Pallas," she said.

"One of my mother's favorites," said Till. Which gave him reason to laugh again, enjoying the added evidence of a crime. Yet there weren't any grudges. He didn't have the time. "My people are here," he said, reaching down for her. "So let me save you, Pallas."

She reached up, but the new hand hesitated.

Then as fast as possible, Pallas crawled away from him.

"No?" he asked.

"My people," she said. "They have to be rescued too."

Till was silent just long enough to ask his rescuers what was possible. Out from the smoke came a mechanical tentacle, and he gave her the sorry news. "Just me and you. The little pair of wings can't take anymore."

"But my clan's nearby," she said.

Till opened his mouth, to apologize or maybe to encourage this baby girl named by his hated mother. But the tentacle had more important work, grabbing his neck and his chest, and the dragon was gone so quickly that he must have been a hallucination from the start.

Pallas stood and ran to the drop-sheath. Should she climb inside?

"No," she decided.

Or she thought, "Yes," but then Tyley arrived. And Broken. With another two dozen of her people clambering after them.

So regardless of her decision, noble or otherwise, Pallas was left standing where she never wanted to be, riding the summit of a furious newborn volcano.

The dragon wanted to see herself.

She imagined a mirror and made the wish vivid inside her mind but nothing reflective was generated. So she tried again, using words this time, but with her old language, and again, nothing resembling a mirror appeared.

Diamond laughed at some part of this.

But King was the surprising comedian. "I left my looking glass beside my old bed."

Now the three of them laughed.

Nobody was happy.

Pamir had met them and then left them. There was a moment when another dragon was about to introduce herself, but Aasleen decided to wait until the world was saved or until everyone was dead. That's what her machine explained to Elata: A creepy mess of metal and glass, human-shaped and wrapped inside a sheet. The device looked real and sounded puzzled as well as shy, and before any questions could be asked, it evaporated. Elata explained the machine's apology to the boys, and now the three of them were walking across the ship's endless bridge.

Insistent instructions kept entering Elata's head, uninvited. These boys needed to be rebuilt. That's what the voices said, and that's what she told them, and King and Diamond were entitled to feel grim, even while making jokes and giggling. Plus the brothers were worried about Karlan and Seldom cooking inside their cocoons, and scared for their siblings, lost and suffering. Maybe dead. And everyone in the world had to be worried because of what was happening outdoors. Plenty of other immortals were watching the same window. The ground where Elata first appeared -- without clothes, without mirrors -- was being shoved upwards by powers that surprised the everyone. Mere's voice periodically came into every head, offering brave words. Yet the dragon was obviously shocked. And not only did the humans and aliens on the bridge keep talking about how all of this was wrong, but Elata caught news about the Waywards. This fabulous, uninvited spectacle had taken their dragon by surprise, and he might be lost in the middle of the mess.

Elata stopped.

"I want a mirror," she said with her new language.

The boys took more steps and then paused, glancing at each other before looking back at the new dragon.

Elata was holding a square panel of nothingness. What wasn't glass or polished metal rested in her fingers, weighing less than nothing. She had to restrain the new mirror to keep it from drifting away, and tipping her new possession, she made them look at their faces, at their own mournful eyes.

"I have a word for you," she said. "A word you should learn."

"Say it," Diamond said.

"Sky."

This new language was melodic and dense. Barely a note offered, yet both of them fumbled when trying to repeat the word.

"What is 'sky?'" King asked.

"Whatever is above the ground," she explained. "On Marrow, that means the air and winds and rain, and the emptiness above the atmosphere. Which isn't empty, since it's full of energies called 'buttresses.' And then comes the gray ceiling beyond everything."

Again they tried to say, "Sky."

She let go of her new mirror, watching it rise as if trying to escape. Then it evaporated, slipping back into the invisible realm where all little possessions waited to be needed.

"Our sky was below," King said.

Diamond was thinking, or he was in no mood to talk.

Elata walked between them. The voice from her nexus insisted that she bring the boys to the doctor two minutes ago.

"Minutes," she sang.

"What's that?" asked King.

"You'll know soon enough."

Dozens of floating windows showed the same spectacle. A mountain was rising like an animal, the world itself pushing itself towards the thin, upside-down sky.

She and the two boys went below, late by three minutes. A pair of cocoons were filled, two more built and waiting. A thousand eyes stared at her and the others, and she said, "Padrone, my savior."

"Elata, my pride and my purpose," he said.

She and the machine laughed.

One empty cocoon was twice as big as the other. King stood beside it, asking Elata, "What next?"

"What does he do?" she asked Padrone.

"Climb inside, or I shove him inside. Which does the harum-scarum prefer?"

She told King, "Crawl inside."

"If I must."

That cocoon was folding itself shut when Diamond touched Elata. He put every finger of his right hand on her shoulder, and she remembered when they last touched. Not only did she recall his arm sliding against her arm, but it was as if there were two Diamonds, each as real as the other, touching her in the same moment and the same way.

She laughed, and he laughed innocently with her.

Then again, Diamond tried to say, "Sky."

"Better," she lied.

"Is there another sky somewhere?"

"I don't know, and you have an appointment," Elata said. "Go in and come out again. If we survive. Then you can ask every question that you've ever wanted to ask."

And she kissed Diamond. On that silly little nose.

The last smile seemed happy, and with that, Diamond crawled inside a white container that was no more a cocoon than it was anything else normal. "Cocoon" was just another simple sound attached to a wonder that had no place in their old world.

Once Diamond vanished, Elata said, "Padrone. I have my own essential questions."

"And I'll offer worthy answers, I'm certain."

"If we die now. Which could happen, since the dragons are fighting and the iron is surging, or I don't know, maybe I'll get a strong urge to shoot myself in the head somehow."

"You will please not," he said.

"My question is," she said. "Will I return as a dragon? Just like Mere does, and Till, and the rest of them?"

"If you are genuine, yes, of course."

"Suppose I am."

"I can accept the premise."

"What happens when I return to Marrow?"

"You're interested in details," he said.

"Every possible detail, yes. Tell me. Unless you're too busy to bother."

"If you are a dragon, then knowing the mechanics is essential," he said. "Yes, I'll prepare you for every likely eventuality."

"Good," she said.

Padrone lectured, his voice swift and every word dense, and Elata listened and asked more questions when she was puzzled, or when she was a little scared, or she made up foolish questions to slow down a teacher who was able to continue for days and for years, without pause.

She expected to be bored, wich was what happened in every class she had ever endured. But this new brain was designed to thrive for a million years.

An hour of talk was one delicious moment.

Which led to the simple question: "Who would design a mind capable of boredom, or indifference, or any of those other flaws?"

Padrone paused. He was thinking, or preoccupied.

"Never mind," she said. "I know who."

"And that would be?"

"The same miserable, incompetent god that built the world that I came from. Obviously."

Pallas was standing beside her drop-sheath, healed and defiant, and there was just one conclusion: Alone, without anyone's help, she had conquered the mountain top. Tyley grabbed hold of that splendid idea and laughed about its ramifications and even went to the trouble of offering congratulations to their victorious leader. "We saw Till," she said through a nexus. "And then we saw the dragon fly away from you."

Facing each other wasted another moment.

Then Broken shouted.

Using his mouth. But the wrenching stone was screaming again, fumes and ash deadening every lesser noise, and Broken's voice was nearly lost. The white woman and blue woman turned, but in opposite directions. Where was Broken?

Tyley found him. The always fearful man looked furious, poised and utterly brave, and that despite carrying no weapon more potent than a newly grown fist. The fist was a prop. He swung his arm at nothing and cursed everything and then found the channel where Pallas and Tyley were accomplishing nothing worthwhile.

"We need a vault," he told them. "Any vault and climb inside."

Broken's fist was ready to smash basalt. Jabbing at the world, he revealed a beautiful focus.

Tyley fell in love with this new man.

And then she crushed him. "Do you see a vault? Can we walk to it? Get past the hatches and kick out its residents and do that in what? Thirty seconds … ?"

All true, but this Broken didn't need reason. "We've got to act and now and what do you propose?"

"Stand tall, and die with honor," she said.

Because nothing else was possible. A billion other Tyleys would have take up the mission of becoming the next great dragon.

Then Pallas said, "No."

Deep blue-water hands grabbed the lieutenants' faces, squeezing chins and bending their gazes to her, making certain that both paid strict attention to the voice on the nexus and the voice rising out of her throat. "Come with me," she said. "And bring everyone."

The call went out, and their people gathered. Twenty-seven bodies close together, and then the ground surged once more, everyone on their knees, on their backs. This was the worst acceleration yet. Tyley fully expected a geyser of iron, white and brilliant, reaching past the atmosphere before collapsing, slaughtering every dab of life for as far as the horizon. But the iron didn't arrive. Underground rock was being shattered down to hot gravel and sand and dust. Because there was no molten iron. Tyley found that idea and suddenly felt certain. An invisible something was emerging, big as a mountain or big as a world, and she was going to enjoy the most remarkable death, and what kind of epilogue would this bring to her legend?

And then the mountain's climb slowed abruptly, then came a dead stop.

In that sudden calm, Pallas led them across scalding gravel. The final climb ended with the hyperfiber trash, thin and round, and from the start, so obviously accidental. This was where the Elata dragon and her friends had first stood. But why would trash remain loyal to the highest ground? It shouldn't be here, yet here it was, and Tyley saw her leader's logic. The Elata dragon didn't just accidentally appear on old hyperfiber. No, there was purpose to the trash, and while nobody understood what that purpose might be, it was easy to become thrilled about a person's prospects when she leapt off the burning shifting miserable ground, feet on the good gray face of something that had already outlived Tyley …

The ground quit shaking and the smoke began to disperse, revealing a few last stragglers sprinting towards them.

There was no way to help anyone run faster, save for waving arms and shouting encouragements. Tyley was one of the castaways on a foundering raft, the sea was a towering wave of pulverized crust, and Tyley counted five soldiers swimming desperately for the only less-awful place left in the world.

None would reach the promise.

After a frantic long battle against gravity, the mountain decided that it was tired, that it was spent and done, and one catastrophe was instantly replaced by its equally dangerous sibling.

For as far as the bare eye could see, the land began its long collapse.

Fountains of molten rock surged out from underground reservoirs, accompanied by jets of unbreathable, rancid gas. The fierce lovely heat would readily to burn ordinary wood, but these black parasol trees refused to burn and refused to burn. Quest had never imagined any wood that wouldn't steal a flame and make it her own. Yet this place was ridiculously different, and she decided that this forest would continue to grow, happy beneath masses of syrupy orange paste. So perhaps melted ground was the same as rain at home, and this was the sweet drenching that came before flowers and fruits. A fetching idea, but then the heat grew just a little worse, and that caused flashes of light and one titanic **woosh**. Some critical temperature had been achieved and every woody cell ignited, and it seemed to happen everywhere and inside the same instant. The landscape exploded, and the subsequent blast flung the girl higher into the scalding winds.

Invisibility was lost.

And the world whirled around her. That was the sensation. Quest was a solid, unmoving point, and this Marrow was a giant ball revolving her magnificence, and she almost convinced herself that if she could give any little push, she would kick away one world and find it replaced by another.

A fiction. An illusion. Yet wondrous to imagine.

Quest rebuilt her camouflage, improved the fresh wings, and then streaked off along a random line. The ground was rising like a cloud, and the cloud was very quick. Silent, terrified animals jammed the air around her. Nothing squeaked or whistled, even when eaten whole. Every creature spent its full power doing what Quest was doing, but not as swiftly. Doubling her mass was easy, and she doubled herself again, and the country below her burned itself sterile, the air choked with coarse black soot and rock dust and those terrific roars that on their own could have shattered stone.

Once she was strong and invisible, Quest soared high above the landscape. Brilliant air was a treat, and she built eyes to look everywhere and then tore them apart again. Because every eye had to absorb light, and absorption was a signal. A weakness. Then she made herself as bright and empty as the cold high atmosphere, and the world seemed far below but never small. She and Marrow were linked, and there was no escape.

"You."

A voice had found her. Despite endless caution, she was seen, and she had heard enough to know what was said, even if the voice wasn't using a true language at all.

"You," meant her.

"Me," she answered. In her mind, then as a word.

"Me," the voice echoed.

This could be the same voice Diamond had heard and King had heard. Watching the last normal morning -- one dead world in the past -- her brothers heard a mysterious presence. The voice had promised that this would be a great day. Which it was and wasn't, and just the possibility that the same voice found Quest was terrifying and quite a lot more.

She wished she had heard nothing, or she was insane. Either answer was better than a disembodied god whispering lies to another vulnerable child.

"Me," the voice repeated.

This time, the word offered a clear direction.

"Come to me," it added.

No god was talking. On the surface of her true mind, tinier than a single bacterium, was a feature that didn't belong to her mind at all. But it had come to life, revealing powers that she never imagined for herself.

"Come to me."

This was the same as her voice, in its anguish and hope. Here was the secretive route through which one !eech could beg attention and help from others. It was impossible to imagine humans sensitive enough to notice such a soft, perfect cry. Quest noticed only because she was so high and gliding, struggling to be watchful in more ways than she had ever been before.

"Come to me," the voice begged, and tipping her wings, Quest began a steep dive along the line described by another !eech.

She was following the decoy, which she couldn't realize, and she probably wouldn't have changed actions if she suspected it. She was chasing something familiar, crossing back into the smoke and then flying beneath it, low enough to find a !eech odor mixed with a human's foulness. Then a human laugh ambushed her, and Quest followed that joy to the end. Even as the ground rippled, and with the wildfire approaching, a gray-colored boy was squatting happy on hot rock, taking so much pleasure from removing the head of an enemy soldier.

Quest remembered one of those two faces. This was the gray boy who had carried a heavy pack covered with living lost heads, and he was the same boy who stabbed Diamond in the heart.

Three Wings didn't notice the newcomer. He was focused on nothing but the Wayward's stubborn neck. Then the living !eech appeared before him. "Quest." He said her name once, then again. "Quest." She stood over him, a giant built from ad libbed muscle and translucent wings. Her beauty was a shock, and so was that glorious smile, and Three Wings started to say her name one last time, but her thunderous voice interrupted, singing words pulled from the window now hiding beside her various hearts.

"Marrow," she said.

"Till," she said.

And then, with perfect diction, "!eech."

"Shit, you are," he agreed.

She sliced Three Wing's head off his body and then she spent a moment waiting for doubts. But doubts never came, and she swallowed Three Wings' head and the second head beside it.

For the next few hours, as the disaster spread and panic reigned, Quest consumed quite a few Wayward skulls. She might have kept hunting, claiming hundreds more, but their collective mass was a burden leaving her barely able to fly. She was tired and there was still no trace of night rising or falling. No kind of darkness was emerging from any portion of Marrow. Yet Quest continued to fly and hide, finding a little Wayward city that she approached without being noticed, and beside what looked like a popular road, she vomited up thirty-one heads, repeating the same few words to each of their outraged faces.

"You are all I could save," she said.

In the only language that she trusted -- the monkey barks of mortal humans.

The machine reached inside the dark cocoon, and using a doctor's self-assured voice, explained what was best for the patient, and most importantly, defined the patient's duties towards his wondrous master. Diamond was ordered to do nothing.

"Nothing at all and that begins now," said Padrone. "Be still and be quiet, particularly inside your mind."

Except the patient insisted on posing reasonable questions. "But what are you going to do with me? How will this change me? And is any of this less than necessary?"

A language built today delivered words and authority and what sounded like answers. Diamond's body had to be dehydrated while increasing its latent power. That was a very important trick. Overtopping museum repair systems with new genetics and fierce new routines. Cysts applied to the mind, of course, which would streamline a much-needed education. And the original skull had to be reinforced with the highest available grade of hyperfiber, which was a feature few other organisms deserved. Those were portions of what the doctor explained before repeating, "Be still and be quiet."

Diamond's circumstances felt more confusing than ever. "And you're sure that's all possible?"

"Quite a lot more is possible," the doctor insisted.

"But a gift might go wrong."

"I don't allow failures."

"You never make mistakes?"

Confidence arrived with a prickly tone. "Failure is the ultimate disease, and in so many ways, I am immune."

Except failure wasn't a disease. Nor was it a condition or curse. Failure was the great blessing.

Only defeat revealed what mattered most, and how worthwhile was any opinion fed a diet of infinite success?

The insight surprised Diamond, and that's when he finally fell silent, listening to the thoughts roiling inside his uneducated mind.

"Very good," said Padrone.

The blackness turned cold, strong frigid fingers engulfing his body.

"I'm preparing to suffocate you, Diamond. Then I'll ease you inside a rigorously structured coma. Time will cease. Loud thoughts and quiet thoughts will cease. And you'll wake after what seems like a moment. Except much more than a moment has to pass. Several days at a minimum. But you'll wake completely, feeling rather the same as you feel now. Except faster to heal, improved in memory and cognitive skills, with a cursory knowledge about local language and great history and why you might be worth all of this trouble."

"Thank you," said Diamond.

No one answered, but the invisible hand did what was promised, pushing the last breath out of that inadequate body.

Diamond tried to repeat his thanks, only his voice was gone. The coma must have begun. Unless it hadn't. Because thoughts kept coming. One and then a thousand more. Each idea felt familiar -- some notion that he already knew quite well. Diamond pictured himself inside the cocoon, helpless in every fashion. He didn't believe motion was possible, except his hands managed to lift up, and he was reaching for the cocoon's inner wall, curious to know how it felt. But his fingers found nothingness. Fingers passed through what should have been rigid and stubborn. Because this was an illusion, obviously, and as a second test, he touched his bare chest and then pushed deeper, fingers curling around the slowly churning heart that looked human ... why?

That was the next question to ask. Why did immortal, machine-infused bodies pretend so hard to be animals with wet hearts and blood?

"Thank you," someone said.

Diamond said it. His mouth had finally delivered its words.

Padrone gave no answer.

But a distant voice offered a single word that felt like a familiar short happy name. Someone was calling to someone. That was why Diamond sat up on the table, one hand and then the other feeling the smile on his mouth.

Again, he said, "Thank you."

It had to be his voice that spoke before, and he was convinced that the other person was calling to him.

Diamond moved his legs, and a room appeared. He had been returned to his childhood bedroom, which was so sensible. Padrone was wrong. The boy might be bathed in a coma, but he was dreaming nonetheless. The dream needed him off the bed, but jumping free, he discovered a long fall to a strange floor made of pink rock. The rock was worn smooth by many feet. That was a detail that he understood with a glance. Taking one step and another two, he paused, waiting for more explanations to find him. But insights weren't offered. So he continued walking until the new voice returned, repeating that happy little name, and Diamond realized that he was a real boy again, and his mother wanted him.

Fast as he could, he ran through the familiar, unknown home.

She was waiting where she should be, kneeling because she wanted her face as close to his face as possible. The rug beneath her knees was very familiar. Woven from the silk of an alien creature, it was slick under his bare feet and smelled like a bubbly bath, and it was cold and warm and soft and never soft. This rug was what people walked across inside every good dream, and that's why a powerful and very good woman spent too much, purchasing what its owners would have given her for nothing, out of love.

Washen smiled at him.

The boy was wearing his best smile.

"So you came out of hiding," she said to him.

He had, yes. He knew exactly what she meant, and he was thrilled to agree with her. "I slipped out from the hiding place, Mother."

"And you brought everyone?"

"Of course."

"Name them."

He didn't know the names that burst from his mouth, but there were three of them, just three, and one of them was the Eight.

The boy had never felt so wonderful.

But Washen held a rather different opinion. With her pretty mouth narrowing, she asked, "But what about the other one?"

"There is another?" he asked.

She said nothing.

He asked, "Did I leave someone behind?"

She didn't explain. Perhaps she thought the answer was obvious, or maybe there wasn't time to spare. A hand that he already knew touched his face and not softly. The ageless palm was pushing against his cheek as she asked, "So how long have you been hiding?"

"I don't know," he said.

"Try to count the years."

"I will."

She waited.

"No," he confessed. "I keep losing count."

Then her face changed.

His mother was scared, and she was never scared. Washen's hand abandoned him, and her voice grew distant, even with her face so near. And from a distant land, she said, "Everything is wrong. Everything is lost. Unless you … alone … unless you can find some other way … "

TEN

The woman was an expert at death. She had watched death and sometimes participated in its peculiarities, and she even temporarily died a few times, by surprise or by plan. Yet that long narrow and exceptionally stubborn body would deftly heal itself, or subordinates saved her mind and titrated a marvelous new body around her. For a thousand centuries, she was the invincible First Chair, and no one dared challenge her authority or test her minimal patience. Save for the Master Captain, of course. But then the Master failed at her sworn duties, and the First Chair won a mutiny that was soon followed by a messy second mutiny, and in midst of chaos, the largest possible demise found this woman -- the kind of death that should have carried the soul into nonexistence.

"Who murdered me," she muttered, too quietly to be heard by others.

"Don't forget who," was her response.

Always.

Every other piece of the past could be lost. Millions of years were free to strip away victory and failure. But not the murderer's name. Not that face or the hot blood behind the face. Her son. Her lovely Till. His hand and his madness had tried to kill the Great Ship, but she fought him, with fists and words, and everything that she remembered would claim that she had won that battle. But then Till turned to her, enraged and focused and steady and murderous, one hand hold a fully-charged Wayward plasma gun …

… and then ...

Nothingness.

Pure true and endless.

She pictured the murder and how she expected to remain murdered, which explained her considerable surprise to find herself inside a hospital room, filling a hard bed meant for no one but her.

A stranger offered his name.

Then he named her.

"Miocene," said the unknown man.

He was a doctor, perhaps, and what might be his patient managed a shallow breath, then said, "No."

"Your aren't Miocene?"

"No, because that woman died."

The man was standing beside the bed, saying nothing.

She shared a piece of her past.

The slightest nod was offered.

She shared more, including the menacing appearance of a plasma gun.

No reaction.

"The plasma vaporized," she began, familiar fingers touching what felt like her face. "Vaporized my mind," she meant to say, but didn't. The rejuvenated mind dragged those fingers across her unclothed body, proving that everything was whole and healthy, wet in normal places and scared everywhere.

"Plasma is wicked news," the man agreed.

Her hands returned to her head, squeezing the hard scalp that was stripped of its thick black hair. A quick, inadequate inventory of memories didn't find gaps, and then she finally asked, "Where am I wrong?"

But having posed the question, one answer offered itself.

"The gun malfunctioned," she said.

Her companion gave no response.

"Or Till missed me," she said.

"Perhaps your son had doubts," said the man. "Or he let his hand flinch."

"No." She repeated that important word several times. "No, the weapon failed in its sworn duties."

She paused.

He waited.

"Except why didn't he finish the job later?"

Her companion let her speak, but something in his nod and the tight smile told her quite a lot.

Miocene was excellent at reading faces.

"You don't know what happened to me," she said.

"Perhaps I don't," he agreed.

"But there is an explanation."

And he said, "We can only hope so."

Once more, she pulled her hands across her face, breathing between her fingers. Then crossing her arms on her new belly, she said, "Time."

Silence.

"Has passed. Too much time, and nobody knows what happened to me."

A small nod.

"My name is Miocene."

A larger nod, and he took a shallow breath.

"You don't know," she stated. "You found my mind. In a bottle, in a drawer. Buried in the ground, maybe. You didn't know whose brain you had, but you ran the rekindle operations and laid down flesh. Because you were curious, you were bored. Because you were ordered to. And then my face appeared."

He didn't exhale.

"Infinity is inventive."

He didn't exhale.

"And the Creation found the means to save one Miocene," she said.

The tiny breath escaped slowly, and as the man began to sit, a gray stool sprouted from the gray floor.

Everything about this room was gray, including him.

"Aeons have passed." She said the words and sat up on her hard gray bed, one hand stroking the slick face of the wall beside her. That particular grayness was cool and extraordinarily strong. Not the best grade, no. But the first millimeter was as strong as a hundred meters of steel or granite. The Great Ship was built on this miracle, and she was hoping that this room, whatever its purpose, was woven into that ancient, precious machine.

"Hyperfiber," she said.

"What about it?"

"Strong strong strong on its own. But it also steals strength from adjacent worlds. Worlds too close to touch or see. When I push, another trillion mirror worlds fight my power with their hyperfiber."

"That is the principle," he said.

"One Miocene pushing against the Creation," she said.

The doctor sighed.

Or he wasn't a doctor. That assumption was obvious, but attitudes were as easy to wear as clothes. What if she was a prisoner and he was her jailer? That possibility deserved respect. Though frankly, doctors and wardens were very similar creatures, both holding ultimate power over the weak.

"I nearly died," she repeated. "But chance saved me."

No nod. Not this time.

"Chance," was a good word. She repeated it several times. But then with a sturdy voice, she said, "Or maybe it wasn't just luck. Maybe the multiverse is exceptionally fond of Miocene, and so here I am."

A deep breath was necessary. Then he said, "No. That is no answer, no."

The calm doctor voice was gone. And it was unlikely that a warden would push so much passion into his response. But that's what the stranger gave her, a dose of outrage undiluted by the pretense of manners.

Miocene preferred this voice.

"Explain that to the dead," she said.

"The Creation doesn't care about you." He jumped to his feet. Literally, a leap and then standing on the gray hyperfiber floor, his hands swept through the air. "I cares about none of us, no. We are impurities. We are flaws. And every day, the universe dies."

"'The universe dies,'" she repeated, her voice flat and skeptical.

He stared at her contemptuously.

"What does that mean?"

"Don't you know?" He sounded disappointed, or perhaps betrayed.

"I'm an ignorant soul," she agreed.

And she waited.

A few deep breaths, and then he told a considerable story. Not just about the mortal universe but also about one everlasting world. This new fable was exceptionally intricate, invoking a cycle of utter destruction followed by rebirth of the chosen few. Dubbed "dragons" by the fools who dispense inadequate names. All in all, the man was describing a multiverse ruled by very brutal means, but with at least a thin skin of hope remaining. Which made his fable exactly like the most of the successful religions inside the universe that she remembered.

He stopped talking and sat again, and nothing was said.

Then he stood all over again. "Miocene," he said, and his hands dropped. "Can you believe me, Miocene?"

Belief had no value. Learning everything about her immediate, very narrow reality was what mattered. And in that spirit, she asked, "How much time has passed?"

The man offered hard numbers but zero evidence.

"And are we still riding inside the Great Ship?"

He let those words come and go.

"Maybe you have a different designation," she allowed. "'The Great Ship' isn't the finest name, I would think."

"A million options would be better," he agreed.

She said nothing.

He kept quiet.

Then she said, "Dragons."

Just slightly, his body tensed.

"You're waiting for me to ask, "So who are these great dragons?'"

The gray face was stiff, eyes tiny now.

"But I already know who," she promised.

Then the man nodded, a faint little grin offering itself.

"And I know where this leads us," she said.

"Yes? Where's that?"

She jumped off the bed. Prison wall, hospital wall. Distinctions didn't matter. What was important was to grab one of those gray hands and kick the man's feet out from under him, then push the hand hard against the gray hyperfiber.

"Feel this," she said. "That pressure, that enormous fabulous strength. That is a trillion trillion Miocenes back from the dead, and all of us shoving as One … "

Astonishments.

This day kept offering astonishments -- common principles finding startling ways to misbehave.

Think of the rock that the boy keeps beside his bed at night. A pretty rock. A lucky rock. The modest souvenir from some childhood adventure. Whatever its tiny fame, the boy knows that rock perfectly. The feel of it and its mass and what it does to his emotions as he reaches through the darkness of a windowless bed chamber, fingers anticipating what they will find and there it is and just the smallest touch is enough to reassure this sleepless fellow that he can rest easy. The universe is built on enduring principles, and the most critical principle is that no one else will ever know this lump as thoroughly as he knows it, particularly during this one lonely night.

Till's rock was Marrow. That's how well he knew the world, or at least that's what he always believed. Till was Marrow's most likely living resident, and thinking back and back and back, the dragon couldn't recall any moment when this landscape was any less familiar than as his own voice and his own skin.

One unimpeachable rule was that Waywards built intricate maps and models, capturing landscapes that never stopped warping their shape. Catastrophic tremors and idle thumps of hammers were valuable tools, shockwaves diving through the crust and into the dirty iron ocean below. And if the natural shocks weren't enough, set off a tritium charge. The world had to be as close to transparent as possible. Faults mapped to the millimeter, pressures interpolated to the kilopascal, and not one mineral that didn't give up every secret. That's why he knew where the next ten quakes would come, and why volcanoes were named years before their birth. Marrow's tectonics were as obvious as tomorrow's rainfall or the outcome of a one-sided battle, and that grand expertise allowed even more important work.

Vaults. The vaults were the main reason to look inside Marrow. Big vaults and little blisters tried to hide, and there were many ways to remain invisible. But not when they rose close to the crust. And absolutely not when the artificial body was massive enough and stubborn enough to push hard against a ceiling of fresh basalt.

What began the day as a small hill was being shoved into the sky, and the surrounding landscape was gamely riding along. Till watched from the calm of the stratosphere, while distant Wayward labs deployed neutrino knives, cutting through the new mountain and through the world before reaching linked sensor arrays. Vault armor and shadow matter should have twisted those knives, yet nothing was found. Other tools hunted for high-gain stealths, but powerful camouflage demanded reactors that had their own signatures, and those were absent here. Even more remarkable, no similar event was waiting to be found inside any library. Yet despite the relentless mystery, Till's astonishment remained under control. That's because AI specialists and the most creative few humans in Till's science corp had already managed an explanation, or at least what passed for the foundation around a useful, panic-free theory.

Speaking through his most secure nexus, a voice quietly said, "Hyperfiber."

"Past high-grade," he guessed.

"Living in the theoretical realm." This was the daughter who stood near Till on the Great Round, who first warned him about the hill and the troubles to come. She was exactly where she began the nightmare, standing inside a command post and standing inside his ear, and her job was to simplify a river of speculative noise. "It wears some impressive names -- "

"Ultimate," he said.

"I prefer 'terminal hyperfiber,'" she said.

"We build it sometimes. Inside end-of-a-cycle labs, when there's extra resources, and never more than little spheres of the crazy business."

"This isn't a little sphere," she said.

"So it seems."

Hyperfiber was not a single substance. It was a continuum of radical cheats using baryonic atoms riding inside quasicrystal formations, first bolstered with enhanced bonds and then aligned with identical hyperfibers living in alternate universes. Strength came from sharing the loads. Even the sloppiest grades were strong, but the Waywards could already synthesize the medium grades, while the finest hyperfiber built the sky: A hollow sphere superior to everything else. Except, of course, for the ultimate, the terminal.

"Sky-grade hyperfiber nestled inside a quark-gluon bath," she reported. "Then compressed. On all sides, and with perfect symmetry. That's how we make those tiny samples."

Which Till knew. But it helped his personal urgency, hearing his daughter's excitement with this very new knowledge.

"Crushed to the brink of total collapse," she said. "Compressed until it's a speck of matter on the edge of becoming a black hole. Except that speck won't grow any smaller. Terminal hyperfiber rests at an inflexible, invincible point, and it has odd properties, and most important, it has mammoth capacities to store information. And if it was only difficult to build, we would build it. But as you say, Father. Only when we're rich and done with the other work can we afford to make any of the magic stuff."

So that's what this had to be -- a unique vault carved from unlikely ingredients -- and the dragon's mind immediately considered suspects and methods and the most obvious goals. Which brought him back to the new dragon and that eight-headed guest inside his jail, and to the !eech still flying wild somewhere beneath him. As amazing as this day was, there were still explanations for every part of the saga.

Then the new mountain began its collapse.

But no, that couldn't be strange or even unexpected. Any miracle machine capable of pushing hundreds of square kilometers of crust was capable of being fickle. That kind of vast urgency might simply grow bored and dive deep again. Maybe the rising ground was preparation for this phase. That's why the land beneath him was shattering and retreating, some of those wounds leaking white iron and boiling rock. Of course the dragon instantly ordered every free hand to save those in the most danger. It was a tiny gesture, instructing his generals to pick up Mere's people along with their own. Tiny because the invaders were few among several thousand scattered Waywards. But with those orders, Till reminded the world that the !eech was somewhere and she was powerful and her name was Quest and this magnificent chaos was the perfect cover for any kind of escape.

His daughter was still happily lecturing about the highest physics.

Till listened, but only with a splinter of his attentions.

The collapse accelerated, and another one of his splinters noticed the Pallas girl. That noble child had stayed behind to die with her clan, and the dragon focused tools and eyes on what used to be a mountain peak. There. The blue girl was visible, and her soldiers were huddling around her. Babies, all of them. Not more than two or three centuries old, which was nothing. A shame they were doomed. On knees and on bellies, they had nothing to hold but each other. That little disk of hyperfiber had already plunged far below the surrounding land. Avalanches were coming. No doubt at all. Masses of pulverized rock would fill this gaping new hole, and bioceramic brains might survive the impacts and pressure, but only if the molten iron didn't feel as cruel as usual.

A god watching little ones die: As awful and inevitable as could be, that was Till.

Yet when the next instant arrived, Pallas and her people surprised him.

They were gone.

Vanished.

How?

Later, armed with data and considerable cleverness, leading authorities would decide that the same force that brought a new dragon and an old enemy into the world had been unleashed again, but in reverse. Which was precisely what Till assumed as he realized that the hyperfiber disk was empty. A stubborn believer in his own intuitions, he was flying above his subjects and above his foes, feeling a little dizzy about all of these novelties. Yet still, given a few moments and a couple deep breaths, nothing would feel too perplexing.

That surety survived for another full minute.

It was a terrible minute. Thousands of Waywards, including Till's finest warriors, were trapped on the shattered ground. Not enough of his ships were in position to help, and being loyal soldiers, many of them resisted any aid, desperate to keep up the hunt for the !eech. There was one moment when Till intended to rescind the pursuit order. He even devised the wording that would best shake the hunters out of their blindness. But that was when one more surprise arrived, small next to the eruptions, yet totally unexpected.

Miocene.

Camouflage-draped hyperfiber ships struck the upper atmosphere, making the bright sky brighter, and a voice led the way, singing to her son, "I'm here to fight for a hill. But you had to steal the hill away, didn't you?"

Against every expectation, Till did not hate his mother.

Because hatred was simple, and what Till felt was never simple. Miocene deserved far worse than antipathy or chronic mistrust. She was a vindictive creature unashamed by her nature. She was manipulative and emotionless yet somehow shrill at every turn. Reliably mean, creatively petty, and with a fabulously long memory tied to events still scratched raw long after every other past moment was lost. Miocene wasn't just another enemy. No, she was a season onto herself. She was a force of nature. Not just Till's nemesis, but she was also his purpose. Alone, mother and son were just two more dragons and two more gods. But together, facing one another across a public nexus channel, Till became the soul of Marrow, and the universe was depending on his strength and hard-earned wisdom.

And here, now, a remarkable day's greatest astonishment began.

"I'm here to fight for a hill," Miocene began.

The chaos had let her forces to steal this close. But surprise and a few impressive aircraft wouldn't win any war begun today.

"But you had to steal the hill away, didn't you?"

So many possible responses. What would her son do?

"Give aid," he said. He ordered. On a public channel, with a voice that wasn't begging or weak. "According to the Laws we subscribe to, every citizen in mortal danger demands your help."

"Well, I suppose I should," Miocene began.

Her voice was instantaneous. The dragon had to be flying with her soldiers, and any counterattack would be supremely dangerous.

"But you do need to thank me," she added.

Till guessed his mother's likely demands and how he should respond. There was no time for negotiations, which was why he settled on the bland promise, "You'll earn everyone's gratitude."

Yet Miocene wasn't impressed.

"No," she said.

"No?"

"I want a son's appreciation," she said. "That's why you need to thank me. Thank me now, this moment, and I have to believe you."

"And if not?"

With easy malice, she promised, "I will sterilize the world from horizon to horizon."

And here was the day's greatest astonishment:

A tight little but very believable voice came out of Till, and he said, "Thank you for your help, Mother. Thank you so, so much."

Marrow would never count time with earthly increments. The human scourge had survived for four full cycles, and from the world's point of view, nothing else needed to be measured. But former captains and officers and all the Waywards believed in years, and that's why they used a system born on a lost world. Their best count claimed that four million, six hundred and nineteen thousand years had been crossed, and inside that magnificent calendar were the many little pulses where the world grew some and then turned dark, and then shrank a little and went dark again. And with a mastery of time as well as a genius for engineering, these two competing civilizations were able to build vaults and bury themselves as well as key resources, diving just deep enough to survive the next Burning.

At the end of the fourth full cycle, Marrow's atmosphere became a toxic brew of liquid-dense gas and slow, blast-furnace winds. There wasn't one good pond left in the world. High peaks were flattened against the hyperfiber sky, while the surrounding crust was pushing ever higher. As it was, Washen remained on the surface longer than she should have. But the risk seemed small and worthwhile. Being first from her vault meant having the advantage, and quite a lot of good might happen. If her people grabbed enough land and momentum, they might be able to control Till and his Waywards, and the next long cycle might be the last. Unite most of this world and then leap up to the Greatship. That was every ex-captain's plan. Reclaim everything what wasn't Marrow, and Miocene's son became a smaller problem, and in another million years, what looked like peace might be built between here and there.

But plans rarely obey the reality. Despite diving underground late and trying to keep herself shallow, the iron pulled Washen's vault deep and kept her there until the next cycle was well underway.

She woke to find Mere's hands holding hers, and a face that would have looked small on a child was smiling at her, after some fashion. But quite a lot came with the expression, and the grip was too light, and the first sound made by her officer was a heavy, worried sigh.

"What's wrong?" Washen asked.

Mere let the hands fall and then she rose, one more sigh necessary before she said, "We have to hurry, madam. I'll explain on the way."

That was a lie. Mere could speak to any creature on any topic, and in multiple languages, yet she didn't share more than a few words during their brief, rapid flight. The landscape of black rock and steam was expected, and the now-distant ceiling of hyperfiber, but where were the outposts and open vaults and armed teams making surveys and doing research? Washen asked questions according to their importance, and when no answers were offered, she repeated her questions just to make noise. Their aircraft had been pulled from a Wayward vault, and it was being flown to exhaustion: Two more intriguing details that didn't deserve explanation. Their destination? A rough hillside with a boiling spring at its base. Other tiny aircraft were parked on the hill's crest, but Mere set down near the shoreline. Hundreds of familiar faces were watching. Including Till. Handsome and confident, the Wayward's leader stood before everyone, smiling at the latecomers, waving with one arm and then the other, not only calling to them by name but with friendly words strewn into the general blather.

Aasleen was already present. And Locke, relieved to see his mother yet nervous enough to tremble. Other ex-captains were mixed among the important Waywards -- some but not all directly related to Till. The site might have been chosen for the abundance of basaltic blocks that made for natural seats, with a basalt stage down front. Or it was selected for no reason at all. Washen didn't ask. The question didn't occur to her. So much had to be considered as she strode into the midst of a compliant if uneasy audience. The simplest explanation? Somehow Till had gained every advantage, winning the world, and sitting his best among Washen's finest was just another show of the total merger that had happened while she drifted inside the iron, ignorant and utterly useless.

"I'll lead the rebellion," Washen promised herself.

Her son waved to her. But no, Locke pointed to an empty block near the front. Plainly, that hard chair was reserved for her.

Washen was to sit beside a familiar man.

Who was also Till.

She looked at the sitting Till and looked at the standing twin. Then she stared at the man beside her, and he laughed as if embarrassed and dipped his head, becoming the shiest man in existence.

"I don't know you," she said to the shy Till.

"But you do," he muttered.

She stared at the rock where she was meant to sit.

"That other one," her companion began.

"What is he?"

"A dragon, he claims."

"What the shit does that mean?"

That was when the bold, confident Till jumped from the stage and stepped forwards, one hand placed on Washen's shoulder and then the other hand too, pushing until she was off her feet.

Surviving on Marrow for more than four million years. That was just a piece of what Washen had accomplished. And before that were those brief thousand centuries living in the glorious chaos of the Greatship. And what was most remarkable about that magnificent life was how inside even the most normal day, without warning, Washen so often found herself ambushed by surprise.

The aircraft was a madhouse of sponge-iron and diamond, and it was a slow ship, a clumsy graceless weakling kept aloft by large pockets of vacuum, with engines just strong enough to bring it to its destination at a stately subsonic velocity. Except that destination was lost now. A gigantic hole had eaten away the hilltop, and the hole was still growing. Hundreds of square kilometers had already fallen, and the surrounding countryside acted ready to join the general collapse. Unless new magma was tapped and a ring of fresh volcanoes rose up. The data were conflicting and fickle and very peculiar. A mysterious object was just beneath the crust, or nothing was. But eyes streamlined with experience and biases could gaze down at the mayhem, and the attached voice could declare, with authority, "I don't know what to do. So we stay aloft, keep back from the edge, and wait for the hole to decide how big it wants to be."

They were minimally armed and completely exposed. But there were also two dragons onboard, and the Waywards wouldn't launch anything worse than insults against Mere's floating city.

Mere mentioned that to her companion.

Elata was standing next to a diamond pane infused with data streams, and the girl was making a game of touching the warm surface, generating holographic shapes jammed with information.

"Pretty," said Elata.

The ancient dragon sent greetings to Till.

No one answered.

"Those little ships down there," Elata began.

"Wayward."

"And the big gray machines?"

"Miocene and her soldiers."

"They aren't fighting each other. Or are they?"

"You're watching a war," Mere said. "Till and his mother are battling for the honor of rescuing every survivor."

The girl laughed at that. A pleasant laugh, all in all.

Elata asked, "What about Pallas?"

"Missing. And her lieutenants are missing too. But most of her clan has been recovered."

"Alive?"

"Most of them. But crushed and burnt, and they'll need new mouths before they can thank their saviors."

Elata poked the diamond pane, smiling at the curlicues that sprang into existence. This was the sort of youngster who would always smile sweetly, walking like an innocent through any crowded room, causally bending everyone's emotions. Mere couldn't shake that impression. Yes, Elata might be spectacularly young. Her timetable claimed was that she wasn't even twenty years-old, and maybe younger. Yet she was already entering adulthood. Fast weak sloppy biology. This was what happened in dangerous worlds where mutations were essential and sex was the clumsy best way to find success. An impressive story existed inside that body. Brown flesh implied strong sunlight. Those golden teeth would enjoy any meal, animal and vegetable. Diurnal eyes. Big shoulders and long strong arms for easy climbing. And that substantial nose could be a signpost for spectacular health or her great beauty, or the nose meant nothing. Evolutionary history wandered like a river, and quite a lot about her might signal nothing but chance. Yet this was a human frame, and it was a peculiar frame that Mere had no experience with, human only in the most archaic sense of the term. Which, once again, was exceptional. Elata and these archaic brothers talked about trees rooted in the sky and a sun below and flying aliens somewhere between the two. And where could such a world hide? That was a spectacular, temporarily unanswerable question. But their home was certainly not below them. Not in any physical sense, certainly not visible using all of the tools onboard this airborne city that was fabricated just today.

"I can't believe how fast my thoughts are," said the new dragon. "Padrone gave me a huge brain full of lightning bolts."

An intriguing way to phrase it.

"But of course I can believe it," Elata added. "Because this mind's always ready to tie itself into new shapes. Whatever I need."

Finally, a Wayward nexus answered Mere's long-ago greeting.

"Little Mere?" One of the multitudinous daughters appeared inside a mind's eye. Almost as pretty as her father and plainly relishing this moment of symbolic importance, she said, "The Waywards' master is quite busy now. With rescue efforts and so much more. But he wanted me to deliver a message to you."

"Pallas?"

"Missing still, we are sorry. But one of her lieutenants has been recovered. I don't know the circumstances, but I'm certain that he will be returned to you, along with the others we have found. Only first, please, show us the consideration of backing that monstrous machine past your own border again. Please."

"As soon as you back away too. Of course."

"Of course."

Civility and Mere's flying city: Two great machines held aloft by ancient mathematics and bottled vacuum.

The link was severed exactly when both sides expected that to happen.

Nothing had been accomplished, which was the point.

Another few moments were invested in small tasks and the unexpected pleasure of watching a little girl playing with lights.

"How deep is that hole?" Elata asked.

"Nine kilometers below the old summit. So far. But the collapse doesn't seem ready to finish."

"I keep expecting avalanches on those steep sides."

"So do I. But it's wiser, I'm learning, to ignore my expectations."

Again, that pleasant girlish laugh, followed by a few pushes at spinning cobalt pyramids. Then the new dragon said, "Oh, and by the way, I think I know where we came from."

"Which is?"

"A dream." The long, apish fingers gestured at a cavity that kept reaching deep inside the world, and a voice that couldn't sound more certain said, "We came from a dream. There's a bigger, better mind underground, and its lightning bolts invented us, and here we are."

"Your world was a dream?"

The smile shifted, revealing pure joy.

"Was and still is," Elata said. "And now that dreaming mind is dreaming about you too, and about Marrow, and I don't know how much more. But you've been very nice to us, and I thought you deserved to be warned."

Never had so much ingenuity and energy been used to build shovels. Fancy, never-before shovels with a single purpose, and that was to dig one very deep, very simple hole.

The most exceptionally deep hole, truth told.

The finest hyperfiber had to be pierced. Not ten meters of the miracle. Not ten kilometers. No, there were thousands upon thousands of gray kilometers, and not only that, the shaft had to be wide enough to bring bodies and pride and equipment and greed through. This was a species of excavation never imagined, never attempted. But what made the best shovel? Shaped gamma-thumpers and micro black holes were possible, but those were clumsy tools that with any bad luck would turn tragically wrong. The least-awful answer involved hot narrow beams of pulsating plasma, and that's why the fiercest torches ever wielded by humanity were built, and that's how a hidden world was eventually revealed -- named Marrow, in honor of the iron-rich black goo inside the original human bone.

In secret, Miocene had assembled her team from the best captains. Washen was a favorite, Aasleen was the reigning engineer, and among the ranks was an ambitious fellow named Diu. An unmapped world was waiting at the Ship's core, and it was the duty and honor of the captains to study this unexpected mystery.

Pamir wasn't part of that team.

He should have been. Pamir had served as a captain, and any honest measuring stick placed him among the exceptional captains. But not because he was gifted about following orders or giving orders. No, Pamir had a talent. A unique genius. But how to describe that quality? Modern human bodies: They were built on archaic idiosyncrises. Four-chambered hearts, five fingered hands, and something rather like the ancestral black marrow inside the bone. And in the same fashion, every living body wanted to eat, and the gut had to digest whatever went down the mouth, leading to wastes, which resulted in another blackness that wasn't all that different from its namesake.

Shit.

In any group, in practically any circumstance, Pamir was first to smell the shit.

Miocene and her captains were ambitious souls, and each of them was smarter than Pamir and prettier than him and far more accomplished. Yet they always found what they wanted to find inside any tightly-folded intricacy. Pamir's particular genius was getting the first whiff of bullshit, and just as important, his blunt caustic and screw-everyone attitude allowed him to report what he thought about everything. Careful words were a charity, and he wasn't a charitable creature. Parsing the truth into digestible bits … well, yes, that was a game that he could play. If necessary. If there was time to waste, and if his audience wasn't populated with idiots who would never accept what they needed to know, particularly when the truth didn't conform to their spectacularly narrow interests.

If Pamir had been included in Miocene's mission, shit would have been smelled early and given its proper name, and millions of years of history would have been bent out of all recognition.

But Pamir wasn't a captain anymore. When his ex-colleagues went down to Marrow, he wasn't even Pamir. He was a civilian with a borrowed face and a forgettable name -- a criminal hunted by every ship officer. And all those great captains gladly crawled down that idiot hole. Which was when Marrow turned off the lights and killed every unshielded machine, and the captains found themselves marooned.

Complications and coincidences, and ignorance too. Those were the ingredients for every history.

From nothing, the marooned captains built a vibrant new civilization, and for reasons of love and utility, they had children. Who had their own children and grandchildren, and the Waywards began. And after more tangled events, Miocene and her son led the Waywards into the sky and up the long shaft and took the Great Ship for themselves. But it could be argued that the key moment was when Pamir found Washen. Found her dead and gave her a new body, and she made Pamir into a captain all over again, and the two of them reclaimed that enormous and improperly mapped complication of ancient machinery and forgotten purpose called the Great Ship.

Oh, if Pamir had ever walked on Marrow, he wouldn't have been fooled.

At least that's what he told himself. A hundred years into the mission, he would have recognized Diu as the true enemy. Originally a very rich passenger, Diu had all kinds of imagination and arrogance. Diu was first to notice hints of this new world. A micro black hole, electrically charged and guided like a surgical tool. That's what he likely used to dig a much narrower hole. And finding Marrow was just another beginning. Sensors and AIs and patience and a transport designed to leap to the volcanic world and then back again. That's what Diu used, studying the world's odd rhythms and its potential. Then this singular man climbed back to the Great Ship again, patching the tiny shaft before throwing himself into a captain's career, then subverting every security system in reach.

The tenacious force that invented the mission and sent the captains into a trickster's hell. That was Diu. He lived openly with Washen, and they had a son. Locke. But he was also the father of Miocene's only child, and If Pamir he been there, he would have smelled some or all of the scheme, and everybody would have heard his wisdom.

Unless he smelled nothing or nobody listened to him.

"No," he warned himself. Every day, with a brusque voice, he said, "I would have been as blind stupid and trapped as everyone else."

But if he had gone to Marrow, Washen would have been at his side. And united, they would have beaten Miocene and Diu and the rest of the Waywards too. That was the likely scenario. Not because Pamir wanted it to be true, but because later, when it was the two of them, that was exactly what happened.

Diu was dead.

Till tried to kill the Great Ship, and failed. And then Miocene was dead, most accounts making her son into her murderer.

Then Washen became the Master Captain, and on her explicit orders, the shaft to Marrow was plugged.

But not permanently so.

The Wayward war had shoved the Great Ship on a happenstance course, carrying them into the body of an alien infesting an interstellar cloud. The polypond engulfed the Ship with water and fusion fire and anguish and its own bullshit. But they survived that hazard. No, the worst troubles began when the !eech arrived, or when they came out of hiding. The !eech were the strangest damned aliens ever spawned from matter and thought, and surrounded by chaos, they found the perfect moment to take control. The Great Ship began to accelerate; nobody understood how. Then Washen and her son and Aasleen and the others escaped the only way they could, wrenching open the old hole and climbing down and then closing the hole above them. They planned to jump into a sanctuary or into death, but Pamir preferred to stay above, acquiring new faces and forgettable lives while leading the resistance against the unbeatable foe.

Ages passed and too much happened and very little changed. But sometimes the !eech felt especially strong, and since patched hyperfiber was never as tough as the original, they opened up the shaft again, launching full-scale invasions of Marrow.

About those wars, Pamir knew very little. What he assumed was that the Waywards or Washen or some hybrid force delivered enough punishment that the Ship's rulers had to retreat and close the hole behind them. Then more aeons would pass while the !eech dealt with their embarrassment. But they proved just as stubborn and tenacious as the captains, and they always made ready for the next assault.

One part of the future was assured: The !eech were going to keep scrambling down the same damned hole.

Pamir couldn't allow that to happen.

A rebellion succeeded, at least for a little while. Very good souls were sacrificed on critical missions, and billions more were murdered for no purpose at all. But in the end, a two-time captain and eternal troublemaker had the resources to find his way back to a world of iron and secrets.

Marrow proved smaller than expected. Half of its face was molten, while black vegetation covered the colder regions. Inside a shielded craft, Pamir rode through the bright buttresses and into a hot, water-drenched atmosphere. Complicated, idiot insects greeted him. Inky foliage grew fast and cracked open the ground, umbra trees and rot growing up from the holes. There was no obvious sign of Waywards, or Washen, or any trace of human civilization. Marrow's defenders were hiding. Maybe. After all, Pamir might be the !eech in disguise, and letting the first scout walk about the place, growing wonderfully foolish, was probably a useful trick.

Overhead, an army of ten thousand was finishing its work. Harum-scarums and humans as well as other species weren't just refilling the hole. This time, the high-grade hyperfiber was being seeded with mines and weapons that were much, much worse. Alien tech pulled from lockers and museums would make it difficult if not impossible for anyone to follow after them. This uncharitable man had given Marrow a great gift, and despite his basic nature, Pamir kept hoping someone would notice and thank him for what he was doing.

"Washen," he said.

By various means, for days and weeks.

Then just as he was ready to give up, Washen answered.

The voice led Pamir to a vault tucked inside an empty lava tube. He didn't know what a vault was, but assuming this was a bunker or a jail, he spoke to Washen for most of a day while fighting the sealed hatch. That nose for shit had quit working. Had gone awol. He spoke to her voice, and her voice answered exactly as he expected. But so much time had passed. Too many lives lived, far beyond any useful count, and of course this woman was nothing and everything besides that long forsaken lover.

"Eleven million years and change," he admitted. "I would have come sooner, but I was busy."

Pamir was always a clever mechanic. Yet the hatch refused to open.

Then he stood back, telling the faceless voice, "I miss that bedroom with the olivine floor."

That's when she opened the hatch. Or that series of words triggered the mechanism. Either way, the freshest air in the world came out with a woosh, and emerging with it was a convincing illusion of Washen.

"Where's my friend?" he asked the holo.

"Not here, not this time," she said.

"What does that mean?"

She didn't answer. Not then, and not for several more days. There was too much else to talk about. A world that was just moments younger than the universe had to be described. Marrow was always growing and always being consumed by flames. The first dragon was busily crawling and flying, always making spores and splitting the stone and iron underfoot. But there were other dragons now. Till and Washen, although not in this particular incarnation. With Mere and Aasleen and several others deserving their chance. And Miocene's name was mentioned, which was another ridiculous detail inside this ridiculous noise. But then Pamir learned how each dragon was born inside its own history, and none were spawned from exactly the same past. Which was entirely reasonable, since the exceptionally unlikely was what made them so fiercely inevitable.

Senseless news, all of it, and delivered with a voice that Pamir had never forgotten, with the face that he loved a little and respected quite a lot.

Eleven million years without seeing one another, and he wasn't seeing her now.

"How soon will your friends arrive?" she asked.

What could the bottled personality see, glancing at the sky?

"Another six weeks, everyone comes down," he said.

"Build your civilization fast," she said. She warned. "Vaults are swimming underground. Wake some of those people and let them help, but make your civilization your own, as spectacular and sturdy as possible. And in another million years, build your own vaults. Sink all of your people underground, but you stay above. Just you. And when the only surface life is a little puddle of bacteria and a little puddle that's you … you die with this Marrow and maybe you come again with the next Marrow, and maybe for the next thousand after that … "

"Yeah, well, what if I don't want to?" Pamir asked.

His companion laughed at his question, or she laughed to be polite. Either way, her joyous voice said, "Believe whatever you want. Freedom includes being lazy or denying my reasons. You can even convince yourself that I'm a liar and turn away from all of my advice. But this is what will happen: Three times in a million, Pamir. Do everything I ask, just three times in a million, and then you and I will stand on this ground again. Together."

"I need better eyes," she said.

Her ship was as high above the atmosphere as deemed safe, skimming through the buttresses' EM basement.

"On top of the phenomena," she said to a cabin jammed with minds. "Mere's perspective. She has the best array. Show her that I want docking space. Show her now."

Adept at deciphering her master's wishes, the pilot bent the fusion plumes, the teardrop hull plunging out of the vacuum. Thin air screamed and burned, but instead of braking, the pilot accelerated. Railgun slugs didn't reach these velocities. The flight lasted deep into the troposphere, unleashing a sonic boom that shook the shattered countryside even more. Then at the last moment, deceleration. Engines capable of sending explorers to far stars were wasted on this little show. But how else could an engineer boast about her skills?

These gee forces would liquefy flesh.

Very little flesh was onboard.

Aasleen was in war-mode. The comfortable, water-immersed body had been chiseled loose and thrown away, replaced with machinery that only looked and felt and sounded like her old form. She was protected even better than usual, but because this might be war with the !eech, her mind was enmeshed in clever boobytraps. The impact did nothing but crush legs meant to be crushed, while the bioceramic mind sitting inside her chest enjoyed the sight of a mighty shock wave pushing ahead, racing across fifty kilometers of empty air before slapping hard against Mere's floating city.

The mind laughed, but not the face.

She hailed Mere, lying when she said, "I am sorry."

"I accept your apology," the little dragon lied, in turn.

A berth was offered, scanned. Found wanting. No specific security problem was waiting for them, but this was a day without precedence, and the usual cautions should be overlapped with every paranoia too.

Aasleen complained.

Mere complied.

The visitor claimed a neighboring berth, selected at random. Accompanied by a squad of mechanical soldiers and her ancient AI savant, Aasleen entered a facility already being made into a home. Scented air. Ruddy alien light. Plus potted alien jungles and potted alien ponds lining the broad hallway.

The AI asked the obvious. "Why these?"

"Mere always uses her tenure to cultivate aliens," Aasleen began. "I guarantee there's a story behind this blue foliage. We'll probably hear that story during our run to the observation room."

But ten steps into the journey, Aasleen's soldiers told her to pause. Insisted, actually. Then a brass hand took her by the shoulder, and the savant sounded a little scared when it shouted, "Miss, you don't belong with us you need to move away."

A young girl was standing in the hallway. She was wearing simple white clothes, bare feet, and a face that no one knew until today.

"Elata," said Aasleen.

The new dragon smiled. "You might be Aasleen."

"I am, and you're here to welcome me?"

"Not at all." That response ended with a quick laugh.

Aasleen didn't know children, human or otherwise. But something about this arboreal animal struck her as odd, and that was without considering that she was a dragon too.

"No," Elata continued. "I just thought you'd want to meet someone. Before anything else happens."

"I want to meet you."

"Not me, no." Again, the laugh. "So Diamond goes to Miocene. That's the decision, right?"

"Has it been decided?"

"While Till gets Quest. Sure. Wings ripped out of her back and her body stuck inside a tight bottle."

A new mind was humming inside that child, playing its games.

This was fun, watching Elata's shifting expressions.

"Mere gets me," the girl said.

"Does she?"

"Or am I wrong? The other dragons are adopting us, or dividing us, or whatever this process is called."

The savant interrupted, declaring, "No decisions have been made."

Elata glanced at the machine, then stared at the dragon. "Pamir gets King. Because Pamir rather likes harum-scarums."

All reasonable conjectures.

"I don't know about the Eight," said the girl. "Or Karlan. But if you're in the mood to grab someone, I know who you should have."

"You're talking about the boy named Seldom."

"Who's waking up now. So come meet him."

The world below them was being transformed, and some wondrous great machine was revealing itself or lying about itself. What else could matter today?

"All right then," said Aasleen.

"Should you?" asked the doubting savant.

Aasleen silently ordered her guards to watch for good news and bad, but there was no special danger here.

She obeyed Elata.

And just like that, every plan shifted. Every future was remade. Down the tamed avenues of dark blue vegetation, two dragons walked together.

"I think this is the best way," Elata said whenever she made a wrong turn. Which was intentionally, probably because she wanted to keep close to Aasleen, gathering up … impressions? A sense of comfort? What?

"I like being strong," the girl said.

"I'm glad you are strong," Aasleen answered.

"No, you're glad that I didn't exist before today. But since I'm real and alive, we have no choice but work for the best outcome. Don't we?"

"I suppose we do."

The hospital was a large, mostly empty room. Surgical limbs had been dismantled. Two cocoons balanced on tabletops. Diamond and the King boy needed more days of work before they emerged. But mortals were simple jelly easily retooled. Two examples of rebuilt jelly were sitting on padded chairs, clothed at the waist while gazing at new bodies that only looked exactly like the old bodies.

Karlan was the big one. Looking up, he laughed at Aasleen. "That's the blackest skin I've ever seen," he said.

"Yes, it's hard to improve on," she said.

Then the little fellow looked up, shy and then less so.

"I asked to learn," he began.

"Wonderful," said Aasleen.

"Yes, wonderful," said the savant.

Then Seldom shouted and leaped from the chair while slapping his hands to the sides of his head. Dancing. He suddenly threw his knees high and danced in place. And with a voice that might be happy or might be outraged, he said, "I wanted to know, and he taught me. The surgeon. He let me see everything. Do you know what the universe is? Do you?"

"I assume I do."

"And I do too. Including a profound sense of how much time has passed."

Beautiful bottled libraries had been fed into this resculpted mind. Reasonable or not, that's the truth that would have to be faced.

"What interval are you talking about?" asked Aasleen.

"Since you and the other human dragons came down here. How long you've been trapped. And the universe above us ... vast, ancient, lost."

"Estimates," she warned.

"How long is long?" Elata asked.

"Three or four at least," said Seldom. "And maybe five ... "

"Five what?" the girl needed to know.

"Billion years. These dragons have been trapped here that long."

Those numbers earned a pause. They deserved silence, but not puzzlement. Everyone in the room fully understood what one year was, and what the number "billion" meant, and someone needed to speak next. Who would?

Karlan stood and walked up to the AI, staring into the glass button eyes. But he was speaking to Aasleen, asking, "Is that right, black lady? Five billion years stuck inside this hell, and you still can't escape?

"That sounds ridiculously weak, if you want to know how you seem to me, an idiot newcomer ... "

"Every day has its end."

A mother's voice brought that bit of sound, using an extinct language that would feel rough in the mouth when Elata spoke it again. If she ever bothered to speak it again. A cliche meant to give comfort, except it brought nothing to the daughter beyond the truth that what was good was just as doomed as what was bad, and there were going to be too many days where a clever observant but bittersweet girl was either going to wish for better or want to die before the awful returned.

The machine guards took the lead and Karlan kept close to them, smiling while he talked. That bully voice had been changed, becoming larger, a little more majestic. He was chatting with the closest machine, smiling when he asked, "How strong are you? How quick, how dangerous?" The subject made him buoyant and silly. "Compared to me, I mean. How much better are you in a fight?"

The machine paused. Glassy black eyes changed shape, and what wasn't exactly a hand became the barrel of a gun. "A little bit better," said a very human voice.

The two soldiers shared the next laugh.

Elata wanted to stay with Aasleen, but she also wanted to keep close to Seldom. The boy had jumped out of the oven as an immortal, and as he hoped, he came out understanding quite a lot about whatever waited past the sky. "Sky." A fabulous word, sung with a bird's lightness. Making Elata wonder if that's what the birds back home were always singing about. They remembered the sky. From before, from wherever. Sweet dancing voices reminded one another about the wonders of an atmosphere rising overhead, and skies without a sun, and the meaning of wings that could carry the soul so far.

She laughed, and Seldom asked why.

A nexus lay between them. No conscious decision was made. Just the two of them sharing words, not thoughts. Because no mind could be read, and no soul was transparent to any other.

She stopped laughing. With the nexus, she asked, "Is it scary, what you know?"

"Yes," Seldom said.

"How is it scary?"

"That's difficult to explain." Time was crossed, and five steps, and then he knew. "It's like scaffolding, what I know."

"I don't understand."

"This model inside my head," he said, touching the new brain. "Science, mathematics … it's the scaffolding that the construction workers used when they built the universe. The universe we can't see from here. What I know about are the boards and rope and the broken carpenters' saws and lost hammers and the monkeys who are still hanging around, remembering the lunches they stole from the carpenters. The universe stands outside the scaffolding, and I can see a lot of that too. But the house that they were building … "

His voice dropped away.

"The house they made," she said. "It's finished now, right?"

"No. The house never is done. It was built tiny but has always been growing larger, and I can't see past a certain point."

"What point?"

He said, "The speed of light matters."

"Light has a speed?"

"Yes."

"It's quick, I hope."

"Not quick enough. Not inside the full universe, no."

"And that's what scares you?"

"No." Then he said nothing.

"So what does?"

The boy bent close, talking with his mouth, whispering into Elata's ear. "The house has a flaw. At any time, for any little reason, the flaw comes out and the universe collapses and dies."

"Well, shit," she said.

"Yeah."

"And where is this mistake?"

"Below us, right below us. And I didn't say that it was a mistake. By the way."

Another pause for thought. Elata's contemplations, and Seldom's. Up ahead, Aasleen was telling to her robot friend about the blue plants growing inside the big bowls. How they came from a world named Absolute Never, and Mere claimed to have brought them home from her travels. Which was five billion years ago, it seemed. While behind Elata, Karlan was telling the fighting machine about how he was hero in his old world, and a famous killer of monsters.

"This day," Elata began.

"What about this day?" Seldom asked.

"I'll tell you," she promised. "Soon."

The observation room had once again shifted its position inside the airship and grown larger. Aasleen passed through a sequence of doors, flanked by her guards and by Karlan. Karlan had claimed that position, uninvited and undisputed. Mere stood the middle of that vast round room, watching a dome of light and color and noise and numbers. Pamir must have just arrived. Aliens surrounded him. Resembling King, most of them. Except bigger and quieter and even more fierce. Words and ideas flashed between the other dragons. Elata sensed as much, but she heard nothing. At first she felt excluded and a little angry, but then very fortunate. No one paid attention to Elata, while she could let the sight of them pour into her glorious new skull.

"'This day,'" Seldom repeated.

"Will never end," she said.

"But it does," he said, the same as the original Seldom would have. "Marrow has a very strict cycle of long, long days and brief nights."

Washen was nearby. Nobody said so, but Elata felt it. Each of these gods glanced at the same piece of the wall before a door formed, and in strode the tallest, most beautiful woman. Shit, she did look a little like Diamond, didn't she?

More nexus greetings.

Motions of hands, ritual songs of shared purpose.

Then Mere said a name and another name, and Miocene was suddenly drawn with light, and Till arrived through the same ethereal tricks. Even when they weren't real, mother and son refused to stand near one another.

Elata watched everything.

"In another few thousand years, this day comes to an end." The infinitely clever boy insisted on telling his story. "That's the day cycle on Marrow, ridiculous as it seems. And after another million years, or so, the sky beats the world back again. That's when everybody hides or dies. Except for dragons like you. You get to live past every night and every fire."

"But that's not what I'm talking about," she said.

"Well, that's the truth," he insisted.

Elata pushed two fingertips between lips as warm as her lips, saying, "No. You have zero sense about what I'm thinking."

The boy couldn't help himself. He kissed her fingers.

She laughed at that.

"Salty still," he reported. Then, "What are you thinking, Elata?"

"This is just one day. All of this, always. Marrow is the same day repeated forever, and their endless life is our life now, and nobody gets to escape, and this is the finest day that anyone can ever live.

"That's what fills up my head, Seldom.

"And also, that I've always kind of, sort of loved you."

"You love Diamond," he said.

"Do I?" A big laugh. Another touch, the kissed fingers on happy wet lips. "All that knowing, the entire universe twisting inside you, Seldom, and you still don't what's real. Do you?"

ELEVEN

A language of beautiful song had been made recognizable and less beautiful.

One after another, the people inside the room would say his name. Not everyone spoke just to him, but when they did, Diamond heard the special, simple tone used with the sleeping and the dead.

"Can you hear me? This is so-and-so, Diamond. Padrone says that you should be awake. We all want you to wake up, Diamond. Why not open your eyes? Everyone is here, Diamond. Join us, will you?"

Except not everyone was where they should be.

Nexuses inside the rebuilt head had been opened up, sample conversations leaping across the world. Strangers were using his name, discussing how Till and Washen shared a son, and Miocene had a grandson, and that odd boy brought this new dragon into their world, or Elata brought Diamond. The full truth wasn't known. The best explanations were patiently waiting for experts standing tall in the future. No, today was reserved for sitting quietly with family, with good friends and your best enemies, thanking Pallas and Mere and Padrone for everyone's continued survival.

It would be easy, closing off some or all of those nexuses. But that would show the world Diamond was conscious, which he didn't want. Eyes and mind had to remain closed, letting him stay with darkness and stillness and his oldest thoughts.

A familiar voice offered two names.

"Diamond," she said. "I'm Washen. The old lady who somehow happens to be your mother."

This woman had the same voice as the other Washen.

Then a man said, "And I'm Till, your father. Who would very much like to hear your thoughts, son."

Diamond was dead on a soft bed, and he was also walking through a strange home, conversing with the dead woman whom he loved.

Till said, "Padrone."

"Yes, sir."

"I think you've broken my son somehow."

"And I know you are wrong, sir."

"Regardless." Till's voice retreated and grew bigger. "The Waywards have first claim to this ground and the child is my blood, and give him up to me. My specialists are superior to all of yours."

Mere said, "No."

The other dragons said, "Never."

With the language of trees, Elata said, "Diamond."

Seldom did nothing but make sad little noises.

"He's faking," Karlan said. "This is an act."

"Diamond," Elata repeated, but in the new language. "You've been finished for five of their days. And it's been ten days since we came to Marrow."

"Just put him in a drawer and leave him," said the dragon named Miocene. "Or wait for him to mummify. My attentions are fixed on the Pallas Arcanum."

What a very odd name. But Diamond didn't react. His true mother was putting a hand on his shoulder, and once again, she gave her baby tastes of advice too diluted by time to make sense.

Diamond needed to remain here, not there.

"There" was full of hurried purpose. Jangling energies and habit. But simple words mattered more, and comforting touches, and his mother was bending low to say another special word worn thin and beautiful by the ages.

Then Mere came close and said, "Maybe so."

Who was she agreeing with?

"We meet again tomorrow," Aasleen said.

"Insights?" Pamir asked. "About what your brother's going through?"

"No, sir," said King.

A different Aasleen was visiting Mother's home. And a different Pamir. The three of them were watching Diamond, and the child started to ask an urgent question. His mouth moved, and his voice fought to find its shape. But then an armored hand took him by the chin, and King said, "They're gone. It's just you and me."

Diamond sat up.

And **there** became **here**.

Eyes closed, Seldom saw the universe.

And with eyes opened, even just a little, the universe remained everywhere and overwhelming. One idle thought about clouds drifting in space caused hydrogen to collide with hydrogen, massive disks of cold gas turning hot in the center. Fusion was a special fire, and some of the new worlds were roasted while others thrived. Seldom saw the galaxy as numbers and principles that kept building living worlds. He didn't wish this and couldn't stop himself. Now every living world needed a respectable name, and his new mind wove a long history into each example. These were simple, simple tellings of what was possible, yet each felt genuine and the boy felt guilty about creating them and then letting them die, because every world had to die and he had a tough but insignificant mind with very little time and a thousand more worlds to shepherd across what was possible.

The Pallas Arcanum. That problem was more real and urgently more important than any galaxy full of dream worlds.

Seldom was standing between his brother and Elata.

Furious days had seen six nations claim ground around the collapse zone. This was a calculated tactic balancing promise and danger, and allowing for the frictions between certain dragons. Nobody knew what the Arcanum was capable of, no one dared deny its importance. Increasingly sophisticated sensors and competing armies of AI wizards projected layers of data. Seldom's minimal skills understood nothing, but that seemed equally true for everyone else. The Arcanum insisted on looking like a hole, just a hole, and its bottom was still a shard of misplaced hyperfiber, and the ancient dragons didn't bother to hide their puzzlement or their growing frustrations.

Elata was listening to the other dragons, watching them in the same ways Elata had always watched people, missing very little.

Then everyone suddenly fell silent together, and Elata winked at Seldom.

What did they know?

King had remained behind with Diamond. But now the alien walked into the room, following after his tiny human brother.

Seldom didn't have Elata's gift for people and their emotions, and he was rather glad for that, since he had so much else to do. But something had happened between King and Diamond. Or maybe the same thing happened to both of them. Because they were different than before. King had come out of the cocoon quiet and thoughtful, yes. But the change was more obvious now. While Diamond walked like a man who knew what he wanted ...

Like a man, yes.

"If one-tenth of my brain can invent worlds," Seldom wondered, "what would Diamond accomplish with ten days alone?"

The man stopped walking, and just like that, he was boy again.

Elata hugged him, kissed him.

Seldom hugged himself and then Diamond and then himself again.

And Karlan put on his biggest, most dangerous smile.

Mere was the only dragon truly with them. The others were holos rendered at lightspeed. Which was this fast and this slow, and with only ten days inside a new life, the complicated magic was being pressed flat and made normal.

Mere greeted Diamond with his name and watchfulness.

The boy smiled. To her and everyone, he said, "Thank you for everything you've done."

"You're quite welcome," Mere said.

One naked foot lifted up, that high arch very sensible on this world. But not Seldom's foot, which was flat and ugly and sporting useless long toes.

Diamond looked at his mother. His smile stayed the same, which was only friendly and only thankful and warm just to a very careful point. Then he looked at each of the other dragons, ending with his father.

That's when the boy smiled, charming and sweet as can be when he said, "You're still hunting for our sister."

"The !eech," Till began.

"You won't find Quest," Diamond said. "Unless it's accidental, and that would be ugly. Especially if you're wrong and she is our true dragon, and someone kills her, and everyone dies."

Till nodded, and at lightspeed, said nothing.

"So I'll catch her for you," said Diamond.

"Well," his father said, "that would be appreciated."

And then the boy turned into an adult again. The way he stood, the way he sounded. The same voice, but he was speaking forcefully to the gods, telling them, "But when I do this, it's for everyone good and not for you. And then, I promise, you will owe me so much more than some grateful little song."

Quest began every breath certain that the next scan would notice her stolen machines, or maybe one of her honest cells had escaped, or most likely, a Wayward child would try to incinerate her latest body just for the joy of it. This new life was woven from many ingredients, but mostly impermanence, and every next mistake promised disaster. That's why Quest needed to build her most invisible form and then make a long, secretive journey. After all, Marrow was vast. Stolen field gloves and lost nexuses kept teaching her about this bizarre world. Oceans. She was falling in love with the idea of oceans. All that raw young seafloor and a million deep-water volcanic vents, and an alien that nobody understood could find food and perpetual night in places like that, and maybe a measure of peace too.

Yet for now, Quest stayed where she was and how she was. She was pretending to be a harum-scarum-style animal, like the beast she once ate and spat out again. Sitting in her tidy nest, pretending to sleep, she was beginning another breath when Diamond called to her.

"I can't see you, sister," the broadcast began.

Every nexus was speaking. First in the old language, then the new. Across the Wayward nation and everywhere else too, public and private screens were being used. And if that wasn't impressive enough, the dragons were throwing images of Diamond into the stratosphere, that forever-human face gazing down at the !eech and everyone else too.

"I can't see you but I want to see you, sister. Because as long as every nervous gun is watching for you, the world is too dangerous.

"I want to see you because my father promises that you won't be abused and your quarters will never, ever be boring. Though you will have to live inside a facility built for you, you alone, which is to keep Marrow happy and you safe.

"But more than anything, I want to see you because I miss you and trust you. I do and I do, little sister. So much work is waiting, and we don't know what the work is, and I'm afraid that we'll die before we finish. But you know that already. All of us know that we are important. Four infants tucked inside the corona and hidden inside that other world, and I know you're hungry to know why."

The spiny little animal rose from its nest, watching her brother smile down at the world.

The most powerful trick in existence.

Honesty.

"Show yourself to me, Quest. Please now. Please."

The long blue-forested street was lined with doors, each door different from its neighbors. The door Karlan wanted was covered with faces. Pallas. Tyley. Broken. He remembered those names and guessed that the other faces had also been lost inside the Arcanum. A good man might wrench open up a nexus at this point, learning polite details about each missing soldier. Empathy was effective with some people. But he was the Karlan that he had always been, and he was a soldier with a mission, a warrior with purpose. What he wanted was on the other side of this slab of white wood and lost souls.

Karlan shouted a name, and nothing happened. Then he reached for the door, both fists ready to pound, and the door vanished. Vanished because it wasn't real to begin with. Just an image thrown up by these silly magic tricks.

Fresh clothes and a fresh body stood before him, bone and flesh titrated around a mind that had survived battles and quakes and being eaten whole by his world's sworn enemy. Gray skin, black hair, plus a passion for heads or pictures of heads that needed to be left hanging on public display.

"Remember me?" asked Karlan.

Three Wings hit him with a furious stare.

Karlan liked the boy straight away.

"Why are you here?" the boy asked.

"Well, there's something I have to offer you, and because you're going to do me a small favor first."

"What's the favor?"

"I want you to chop off my head."

A blink was coming. Karlan saw the surprise, but then it was gone. No blink. "All right," said Three Wings, backing away from the non-door.

The apartment felt small and comfortable. A strange man was watching them from inside the far wall, and Karlan looked at the face and then Three Wings, making a guess and getting it right.

"My father," the soldier said.

"Dead, is he?"

"Yes."

A nod seemed like plenty.

Three Wings walked into a different room. At a glance, Karlan recognized what had to be an arms locker, tall and long and filled with shelves. Those gray hands were pushing aside guns and bombs, hunting for the best knife.

Karlan laughed. "Are you going to ask why I want this?"

"No."

"I'm going to tell you anyway." He knew that if he sat, a chair would grow. So he sat and got comfortable, smiling when the soldier came out carrying a long white blade made from his own femur. "It's great, what's been done to me. The strength, the speed. Twelve days inside this new body, and I can't tell you how many times I've cut into myself. Just to watch the gash fill in pretty and vanish again."

Three Wings stood in front of him, moving the knife between his hands.

"Anyway, I keep thinking about how heads are trophies on Marrow and nothing bad comes out of it. Except for embarrassment, I guess. But since nobody else wants to do this for me, and I don't seem to have the coordination ... "

"You have restricted reflexes," Three Wings said.

"Like the safety on a gun, yeah. Because I might be the real dragon, and I might be suicidal like Elata used to be. They don't want me able to burn the world back to a cinder. Which removing my own skull wouldn't do, or so I've been told."

"You're no dragon," said the gray boy.

"Yeah, but I was special. In my old world, I was strong and fierce, and a little bit famous too. All of which I miss." A shrug, and the chair held him close when he sat back. "Here, I'm ordinary. And that's not the natural order of things. Know what I mean?"

Three Wings decided to sit.

Leaning forwards on his new chair, he asked Karlan, "So what are you here to offer me? After I do this little favor for you."

"Pallas and the others. Do you want to help find them?"

Now the eyes blinked.

"Of course I do," said Three Wings.

"Well, I'm delivering the official invitation," Karlan said. "There's a meeting to discuss a lot of business, and it starts in … well, I think we're going be a little late to the show … "

"Who's meeting?"

"The dragons. My crew. With Diamond in charge, of course."

"The boy?"

"Yeah, that kid you so thoroughly gutted at the very beginning." That was worth a long, loud laugh. "You heard how Diamond coaxed that !eech monster to come out of hiding. And being the smart hero, he's using his temporary fame to make a few demands."

"He wants to rescue Pallas and the others?"

"No, that plan's already decided. Till and Mere and your other little gods have taken a vote, or whatever they do. I'm just here to tell you that my buddy, the kid whose heart you sliced up, will make certain that you're part of the team that goes first into that Arcanum pit. Back to my old world, or somewhere else. And if there's answers, they'll bite you first."

The knife was held by the left hand, pointed down and kept still.

"Also," said Karlan, "this meeting will be your best chance to thank the evil !eech for saving your life. She'll be nothing but a picture on the wall, true. Sitting inside her prison cell. Which sounds bigger and nicer than this little shack of yours, by the way."

That earned a reaction.

"She is not evil," said the mind that had been carried inside the !eech's stomach. "Or she is evil but adept at acting otherwise."

Karlan nodded and said, "Two choices, is it?"

"There is no difference." Three Wings said. "Between acting good and being good. Is it all that important which you are?"

"I never cared either way," Karlan said.

The knife got itself lifted higher. "Two, three, four slices. Pressure more than pain, and then your anaerobic metabolisms kick in."

"Neat."

"And then I'll put your head back down on your shoulders. Two, three, four seconds. Then the healing grabs hold, vessels marrying up and the nerves retying themselves, which takes another thirty seconds."

Three Wings stood and walked behind Karlan.

But when the knife came for the throat, Karlan put up a hand, razor-bone slicing through fingers while he laughed, saying, "Wait now. Just wait. I don't think you understand what I'm asking for."

Feet set, King defended the hallway.

A show of respect, regarding the other as his foe.

The dragon walked alone. Short pants and a heavy jacket, antimatter beside the heart and nothing on the broad feet. One glance up with no break in his gait, and then he grunted, "Drop your spines and run away, little boy."

King was half again larger than he had ever been and powerful in ways that he still hadn't measured. Yet what mattered was feeling certain about his nature. He belonged to The-Clan-of-Many-Clans, and cowering before his superior was a thrill, scales and spines flattening agreeable, and then as the dragon passed, that bald, misshapen head gave a nod, coaxing the happy child to follow.

Saying nothing, they walked together as far as King could bear, which was only two abbreviated strides. "I saw your twin," he confessed. "When I was inside my coma, inside the cocoon, he visited me for a little while."

The dragon kept walking. "So was my twin unpleasant?"

"More than most humans, he was."

A rough cackle. "Sounds like me."

Joy made King laugh and laugh.

Eventually Pamir said, "So tell me what we talked about."

"I don't know."

The pace slowed.

"I can't remember words. But what I feel is … I have a clear impression ... about where we were … "

Pamir stopped and turned, first looking into King's belly and chest and then finally staring up at his face. "Where was that?"

"Past the sky. Inside your Greatship, maybe."

That deserved a careful nod and prolonged, thoughtful silence.

In the dream, Pamir was the giant looming over one tiny baby. Aiming for truth, King said, "I was barely hatched, probably not old enough to understand language. But I heard a river roaring and animals talking and the trees were shaking and talking too. And your twin never stopped talking. To me. He was teaching me or warning me, or maybe he was filling me with noises that I was supposed to remember long enough to share with wise others."

"Well, that sounds like a weak shit plan."

King laughed, helpless not to love this human.

"Anything else happen?"

"You cut off your own hand."

"Did I?"

"With a steel saw."

"Which hand pissed me off?"

"The right."

"Huh."

"Then you put the garbage hand into my hands. This is what I remember best. While I held the wrist, you pulled down each of your dead fingers. One finger, and you said one word. The second finger, and another word. The third, and a much longer word. And then the fourth, which was me. You told me my name, and that's something else that I have forgotten, or I never understood."

"Intriguing," Pamir said.

"And then the thumb. It was important to push your dead thumb into my face, and yell. The loudest sound in a very loud world, and that's all it is. Sound."

"And then?"

"I woke up."

Pamir waited.

"But Diamond and I … we think we know what you were telling me … "

"And I know what you want to say next."

King fell silent.

Standing on his toes, reaching as high as he could, Pamir set both of his thumbs against King's face, each blocking a different mouth. "We listen to you. Everything you say, King, and every word Diamond utters. Even in your old language, which we translated days ago. So consider this a polite warning. If you need secrets, you'll have to be more clever than you have been so far."

The thumbs tasted the same as before.

"And by the same token, if you ever need my help, King, for any reason, all you need to do is talk to the wind."

Till served as their escort, but as a spirit only. Light and false noise dragged a shadow as they made the long walk from the landing bay, and because the hallway was endless, and because Divers couldn't help herself, she asked Till why he was anywhere but here. An important meeting was about to begin. The Eight were invited, and everyone else who emerged from the Arcanum, plus the old dragons too. And why wasn't the most important creature in this world striding into the midst of his foes? Wouldn't the brave god take control of the moment, forcing others to tremble with respect if not undiluted fear?

Till stopped walking.

Real or not, his gaze felt genuine and the voice was toxic. "You're Divers. Am I right?"

"Absolutely."

"Well, I prefer Kai. Let Kai do your talking."

That was why Kai was given the mouth.

"Except I have nothing worth saying," he admitted.

"And now you know why I like you."

The walk ended with a gray doorway, shut and sealed.

"The gathering has been delayed," Till said. "But you need to go inside and wait for the rest of us."

And then, the greatest dragon dissolved.

Kai had the mouth and control of the entire body. This had never happened, not in thousands of days of life, and he didn't waste his chance. When the hyperfiber door lifted out of the way, he took the Eight inside a room they already knew. Light came from everywhere and nowhere. The ceiling was a dome and the gray floor was round, that windowless wall making a circle, and in the floor's center was a fire pit or a tidy hole or maybe a gateway to still another awful world.

Diamond was using the pit as a chair, his feet resting where the flames would play.

Seven voices suggested obvious questions.

"Are we going back to the Creation?" Kai asked. "Is that what this means?"

Diamond seemed the same as always. He knew how to smile when he wished, and laugh, and both of those reactions faded into something more serious. "Sit," was his advice. "And no, this is just a model of that other room. Mere built it to help the work. Nobody understands anything, but this might be a good starting place."

The Eight remained on their feet.

"No, sit," Diamond repeated. Then he jumped up, staring the long face and bright golden canines.

Kai laid them down on the hard gray floor.

"The dragons know what you are," the boy said. "At least they've seen parts of you before. Kai? You are the direct descendant of a creature called a polypond. Your ancestor was the sky, and he rained down on the starship called the Greatship, and then you and your living ocean rode the Greatship when it fled the galaxy."

Words, not a life story. But these words promised more to come, and Kai was sick with joy.

"And Divers? You are one profoundly modified human once called a remora. Remoras were famous for living on the starship's hull, surrounded by vacuum and radiation, remaking their bodies and selves in spectacular ways."

Divers stole the mouth to repeat, "Remora."

"But your people weren't riding the hull when the polypond attacked. When Mere left the Greatship, the remoras were refugees. The easy guess is that your ancestors went home again, up into that living ocean, and those same skills could have been a treasure."

"Treasure," she repeated.

Then Kai retook the mouth. "The other Six?"

"Unknown. Memories are thin, and libraries old enough to help are rare. But the half-believed records and best recollections hold nothing about Tritian or the other siblings. Which might mean that the six came to you later, and nobody dares to guess how."

Kai kept his mouth shut.

But to the others, he said, "I am the ocean in my dreams."

Happy and miserable in the same moment.

Silent now, Diamond walked once around the fire pit, one foot after the other riding the sharp lip.

Then he glanced at his empty hands.

And with a quiet dark voice, he said, "We are old. We got buried in a belly for too long, and damaged because of it. I don't remember enough. King's certain about less than I am. Quest might hold answers, but Till refuses to give enhancements like my brother and I have enjoyed. Which leaves you. The Eight. Though you'll remember even less than King. And why do I know that? Because you're more damaged than anyone. A single entity with eight minds, and you should be a wonder. A powerhouse roaring with ideas and focus. But no, you act like a mortal child who gets hit in the head with a hammer. The brain's damaged beyond repair, and your world never stops spinning, and the rest of your days will be spent being stupid and impulsive and wrong and then right and then wrong again. Because you don't recognize what is smart and best."

Every toe curled over the edge, and for no reason whatsoever, the boy jumped over the hole.

"Divers, I despise you. And I'm so scared of you. And knowing nothing about the rest of you makes everything worse. I can't trust what you might be or you might become. I need a partner willing to do what is necessary."

Again, he jumped back across the hole.

Across the unknown.

"But today, and maybe for one time only, I have power. I did these little gods a favor and handed Quest to them, and she's safe enough, I hope, and we're all well enough for the time being. So my next need is to give the Eight what they've missed for so long.

"Order.

"Discipline.

"A voice that can't be ignored."

With that, the doorway behind them opened again, and a gray boy walked inside. Something was in his hand. What was he carrying? Then that odd something smiled at the Eight, and without air or lungs, what seemed to be a face mouthed the words, "My children."

Karlan was grinning.

"A splendid monster about to be born," he said without sound.

Kai hearing every word as a thunderous scream ...

AFTERWORD

And what happens next?

I have predictions. As the author and as someone deeply invested in this saga, I have quite a collection of imagery still to be used, and plot points and plot twists that startle me, and basic questions that need to be answered, and maybe I already know those answers. Or maybe, getting into the hard work of many pages and added details, I'll think of something else entirely. Something better, I can hope. We can hope.

This is an elaborate undertaking. In some ways, the Greatship is guaranteed to be the impossible undertaking. Billions of years laced within the infinite multiverse, coupled with a hyperabundance of characters and species and shifting ideas … well, I won't pretend that I can make a dent in the full story. Just the biography of a single dragon would be a ridiculous goal. A madman's dream. What I think I can achieve is a dramatic resolution that satisfies me as well as a healthy portion of my readers. That endpoint has already been written. Inside my skull only, but still, it is my goal. Everything else that I write has to serve that seminal moment.

Three novels are in the works. The first follows up on events in THE DRAGONS OF MARROW. Which stands to reason. I have this delicate balance of dragons and children, and there is a mysterious hole that needs to be investigated, and something waits to be discovered. Something unexpected, yet in the same breath, entirely reasonable.

DRAGONS is around 80,000 words. Its sequel might come in half again larger, or bigger. It depends on how I cobble together what has to happen -- elegance playing with my patience and endurance.

The next novel takes place on the Greatship proper, and at this point, I'm planning that almost every event happens inside the same modest room. Which sounds rather limited, doesn't it? Not at all. I picked the best room for this sort of fun. And it will probably be the longest and most complicated of these coming novels.

The last book is the gorgeous fierce relentless and traumatic capstone. About its details, I know nothing. Nearly. But that's why it will be fun to write.

My best guess is that I will publish books every 3 years. Or maybe in less time. But hopefully no slower than that.

I'm not a dragon, that I know of. And I'll be 62 in a few months.

The clock is humming away.

Printed in Great Britain
by Amazon

48283025R00236